Running
with the
Werewolf

by

LAURIE LONDON

CHAPTER ONE

Daphne

I perched on the armrest of my garage sale sofa, chewed on a hangnail and wondered if I would die today.

"Pull yourself together, Ms. Dupree."

Easy for him to say. His boss didn't want him dead, his co-worker was still alive, and he wasn't about to lie to federal agents.

Amazing what could happen to a girl in a single afternoon.

Agent Mulder gave me a stern look over his black horn-rimmed glasses, while Agent Scully checked her notes. Not their real names, of course, but given the amount of stress I was under, I couldn't remember what they'd told me when they showed their badges. This was just easier.

Scully cleared her throat and consulted her notes. "So, you learned the test results for a drug your company is developing weren't good? And you believe that Mr. Griffin is covering this up?"

I knew it for a fact. Although I wouldn't call it *my* company.

I'd only been working as a lab tech at Griffin Pharmaceuticals in Atlanta for a few months.

I nodded. "Let's just say that for men using Staminax, an erection lasting more than four hours would be the least of their concerns."

Mulder grimaced and took a step back as if he were about to be kicked in the balls. Scully didn't have the same visceral reaction. She was as stoic and unaffected as...well, the real Agent Scully.

Being a lab technician wasn't my dream job by any stretch of the imagination, but I liked being around test tubes, raw ingredients, measuring scales...and having a good medical plan.

Problem was, the CEO was this smarmy whiz-kid who treated his female employees as if they were dying to blow him. A few days ago, he'd called me into his office, promptly hit on me and told me how hot I was. When he leaned back in his executive leather chair and put his hand on his belt, I *noped* the heck out of there.

In my haste to leave, I'd inadvertently grabbed a few things I shouldn't have.

I rubbed my eyes, still watery from the news that Deanne was dead. She was more than just my supervisor at the lab. Newly divorced, with a popular beauty channel on YouTube and a fondness for teriyaki, she was my friend too. Her car had been found at the bottom of a steep ravine, her latest Ulta haul and teriyaki takeout strewn everywhere.

Agent Scully continued. "Let me get this straight. You gave everything you discovered to your supervisor, and she planned to address the issue with Mr. Griffin."

I opened my mouth to say, *No, not everything. There's a really strange book I accidentally picked up too.* But when I tried to tell this to the agents, no sound came out of my mouth.

Okay, that was weird. I tried again.

Still nothing.

The words hung on the tip of my tongue, but I literally could not say them. Shaking my head, I tried to loosen whatever brain fart I was having, but I couldn't make any sort of sound that resembled the English language. Just a series of *uhhhs* and *ggggs*. I sounded like a total nutter.

And then, without warning, I vomited.

Horrified, I ran to the kitchen and rinsed out my mouth. Then I grabbed a towel, some cleaning spray and a carpet scrubby thing. My cat barfs up hairballs on occasion, so fortunately, I kept these items close at hand.

As I cleaned up my mess—thankfully, it was a fairly small amount—I could feel Scully and Mulder staring at me. No doubt trying to decide if this chick was sick, on drugs or just plain weird.

Sick? I felt fine a minute ago.

Drugs? No.

Weird? Debatable.

"Are you okay, Ms. Dupree?" Agent Scully asked, clearly as perplexed by my antics as I was.

Since both agents were still waiting for an answer to Scully's original question, I knew I had to tell them *something*. And since the opposite of *no* was *yes*, I blurted that out instead. And wouldn't you know it? That worked. My temporary brain-to-mouth blockage was gone, along with the urge to toss my cookies again.

"I'm…uh…just rattled about Deanne, that's all," I said with my wobbly, newfound voice. "Yes, I…I gave her everything."

I hadn't planned to lie to Scully and Mulder. I wanted to share what I knew, which included telling them about the ancient-looking book with its strange markings and elaborate metal clasp that I'd found under the manila folders in Pharma-Douche's office. How I hadn't realized I'd grabbed it was beyond me. The thing was fairly heavy.

I shot a wary glance at my messenger bag, still on the floor near the front door. I could've sworn I'd handed the book to Deanne along with the files. But when I got home after work last night and dug around for my house keys, there it was, still nestled inside my bag.

"The accident investigators say her brake lines were cut," Scully said. "Her car crash was a deliberate act."

I put my head in my hands. This was all my fault. If I hadn't gone to Deanne with what I'd discovered about Staminax, she'd still be alive right now, and I wouldn't have just lied to federal agents.

But I couldn't just sit around and let Pharma-Douche hide those test results. Men everywhere—well, those wanting longer-lasting erections—would be in a world of hurt.

Mulder frowned, his expression growing sterner. "Which means her accident was no accident."

Yeah, um, okay. I got that already. Which was part of why I was freaking out right now.

My phone buzzed. I grabbed it, thankful for the distraction. Although I hoped it wasn't one of those mega-long bricks of texts that my mother was famous for sending at the most inopportune times—my world has not been the same since she learned how to dictate her texts. Mom was on a cruise with her friends, so it was likely to be about how irritated she was with Carol's loud snoring, Marielle's complaints about her bunions, or how the prime rib at the all-you-can-eat buffet was entirely too fatty.

I looked at the screen, and my heart nearly stopped.

"What is it?" Agents Scully and Mulder said in unison.

I turned my phone around so they could see for themselves. It was a photo from an anonymous sender. A poorly punctuated Wicked Witch meme, to be exact. In large block script it said, *I'll get u my Pretty and yur Little Dog to.*"

Since I'm the kind of person who can't share a meme with a spelling mistake, I found this cringe-worthy on several levels.

I had a cat, however, not a dog. Speaking of which, I could really use a snuggle, but George was more chicken than cat around strangers and was probably hiding under my bed right now.

"Is there somewhere else you can stay?" Scully asked, her voice tinged with concern. "With a friend or a relative, maybe."

I looked around my sparsely furnished apartment. The threadbare sofa. The cluttered shelf filled with all my favorite books that I couldn't bear to part with. The three boxes of supplies for my online apothecary store that I kept under my cute dining room table, which, by the way, I'd rescued from the side of the road and painted.

I hadn't been here long, having moved here from Chicago when I was hired at Griffin, so I hadn't formed a huge attachment to the place yet.

But it was *mine*. And only mine. After the messy breakup with my fiancé, I wanted nothing around me that used to be "ours." I'd closed that chapter of my life and didn't plan to reread it.

In fact, I'd just gotten permission from my landlord to paint the living room from institutional gray to dove gray and had a few samples taped to the wall.

Then my gaze fell on the flimsy front door. It didn't have a deadbolt or a chain. Just a push-button lock on the handle. Easily kick-in-able.

Mulder's eyes were monstrously huge behind his glasses as he looked down his nose at me. "This is serious stuff, kid."

Irritation bubbled inside me. Number one, I was a full-grown woman, thank you very much. And number two, had I *said* it wasn't serious?

"Mr. Griffin is a man of means," he continued, enunciating each word as if he were talking to a child. "Which means he's got the means to do some serious harm. You know, the money to pay bad people to do bad things on his behalf. Just like he did to your supervisor. You don't want the same thing to happen to you. Do you, Ms. Dupree?"

I gritted my teeth at his mansplaining, my patience running as thin as nonfat milk.

"For how long?" I asked, expecting them to say for a couple of days at the most. Just until they arrested Mr. Griffin.

Scully shrugged. "Depends. A few weeks maybe—or months. Cases like this are complicated and can take time to put together."

Months? I jumped to my feet, unable to contain my shock. "You've got to be kidding me."

Mulder folded his arms. "We're federal agents, Ms. Dupree. We don't kid."

"Isn't there a safe house or somewhere I can stay until you arrest Pharma D— Mr. Griffin?"

Scully's expression was apologetic. "Sorry. Government cutbacks."

I paced around my pint-sized living room. Staying at my mother's wasn't an option. She lived in a retirement community that didn't allow underage houseguests for more than a night or two. My father wasn't in the picture—I hadn't seen him in years. The wound from his desertion still stung, so I didn't like to think about him much. As for my brother? I couldn't exactly couch surf at his place. He was stationed overseas. My two good girlfriends were out of the question too. One had a new baby; the other was traveling with her new boyfriend.

Where in the world was I going to go? Sure, I could stay at a hotel for a few days, but with my tight budget, I couldn't afford weeks or months.

By the time I came up with an idea, I had gotten pretty dizzy. It wasn't a perfect solution, but it would have to do for now.

CHAPTER TWO

Travis

I wasn't sure who I wanted to kill first: the lawyer sitting across from me or the half-brother I'd just met. If my father were still alive, he'd have been at the top of my list.

"This can't be legit." I shoved the papers away, scattering my father's last will and testament across the top of the mahogany table. "Darkaway Ranch has been in the family for generations. *Our* family," I said, indicating my sister Jada and me. Our three younger siblings weren't present, but I meant them as well. "Not some shirttail relative." I pointed a finger at Merrick, who just sat there, scowling like a brainless idiot.

"I'm sorry, Travis, but it's true," the pack lawyer said. "Your father was very specific about his wishes. It's stipulated that upon his death, if his eldest-born son doesn't have a mate by the next White Wolf Moon, his next eldest son—provided he was mated—would inherit the property. As the Alpha, his word is pack law."

I growled. Even from the grave, my father was an arrogant, manipulative asshole who tried to control everything.

A friend of mine who worked with me on the set of *Secret Shadows*, the supernatural soap opera I starred in, would say it wasn't good to think ill of the dead—ghosts often had anger-management issues—but I didn't give a fuck. My father and I had stopped being cordial long ago. Death wasn't going to change that.

Reaching into my pocket, I pulled out the signet ring and slipped it on my left pinkie. For decades, it had sat on Franklin Monroe's finger as the leader of the Darkaway Island Pack. Now, it was mine. I held up my fist for them to see and gave it a righteous shake. "*I'm* the rightful Alpha, and I say Jada gets the ranch."

The lawyer shook his head. "I'm afraid it doesn't work that way."

I glared at the little weasel. If I were in my wolf form, the fur on my back would be raised, and I'd be baring some fang. "Are you suggesting we fight to see who becomes the pack leader?"

The lawyer gave a nervous laugh. "Of course not. Those old ways are long gone."

I shot a glance at Merrick, a guy whose muscles were a whole lot bigger than his brains despite the fact that he wore studious-looking glasses.

You want a piece of me?

Although we weren't packmates and couldn't read each other's thoughts, he got my drift. He squirmed in his chair, his gaze not meeting mine.

Next to Merrick was his bony, angular wife, whose name I'd forgotten. Her facial lines indicated she did more frowning than smiling. I wanted to grab them by the scruff of their necks and toss them out the window. Or better yet, shift and tear them to pieces.

Jada poked me in the ribs, sensing my rising anger. "Cool it, little bro," she whispered. "Just think how I feel."

Irritated, I reached into her thoughts, packmate to

8

packmate. *What do you mean, how you feel? I'm trying to save the ranch for you.*

She flashed me a sharp look. *Think about it, you stupid lunkhead.*

It took me a moment until it dawned on me, and I instantly felt like a jackass.

Our father's will had completely skipped the fact that Jada was his first-born. An intelligent, competent daughter who was already mated. To a great guy. Jada had been capably running our family's dude ranch for several years now. She was the one who had made it successful and profitable, something our father had never been able to achieve.

Under her watch, the place had become extremely popular with the supernatural creatures who vacationed on the island. A number of magazines and travel blogs had written about Darkaway Ranch. Nestled like a "gem" at the base of Mystic Mountain, it "promised an authentic cowboy experience for monsters of all types." It had even made the cover of *Paranormal Paradise.*

The keyword being she was his *daughter*...not his son.

"Heaven's Moon," I muttered. "Sorry, Jada."

If the will was legit and legal, which it appeared to be, my sister would lose everything she'd worked tirelessly for. I, on the other hand, would simply fly my private plane back to Vancouver to the set of *Secret Shadows* and be just fine. I never wanted to be Alpha anyway. Jada was the real loser in all of this. All because I wasn't mated—and our father's ridiculous, archaic demands, of course.

Now that I thought about it from her point of view, how could she remain so calm? I flexed my fists under this big-ass table, wanting to punch something.

"And what if that son is illegitimate?" I spat to the lawyer with as much contempt as possible. "What does pack law say about that?"

Not that I didn't believe our father had cheated on our mother when they were married—he'd done that a lot, which was one of the reasons I hated him—I just didn't know he had an entire second family holed up on the mainland, complete with a trophy wife, two kids and a minivan. That explained the missed birthdays, the unexpected business trips, the sudden absences. I was glad Mom told him to go fuck himself last year. Not in those exact terms—she didn't use words like that—but she was very active in the senior dating scene now and was currently visiting her new gentleman-friend on the East Coast, a retired college administrator.

"All that matters is blood, Travis," Merrick's wife said with a syrupy smile. "Surely, you know that."

Merrick shot his wife a dark glance but said nothing. Except for a few grunts here and there, the dude literally had not said one word. Maybe he was mute.

When Jada and I left the office a short time later, we took the stairs instead of waiting for the elevator with my Neanderthal half-brother and his wife. What able-bodied wolf takes an elevator in a two-story building anyway?

Once outside, the warm ocean breeze ruffled my hair as I slipped on my sunglasses. Sure, the weather here was great, but that didn't make me any less angry. We were two blocks from the beach, and everyone you saw was either going to the beach or coming from it. They all looked happy as fuck. Which made me even madder. I couldn't wait to leave.

My sister hooked her arm in mine. "Want to grab a coffee?"

Not waiting for an answer, she started to pull me in the direction of Unholy Grounds, a popular coffee shop on the island owned by two nuns.

Honestly, how could she be so chipper at a time like this while all I wanted was to shift and attack someone? Unfortunately, I was about to find out.

"I'd rather have a beer," I told her. "Ten of them."

"No problem," she said, her wolf-green eyes sparkling.

We turned and headed in the opposite direction down Nightshade Avenue.

Dazed and numb, I wasn't sure I was fully comprehending the ramifications my father's will would have on our family. Except for my sister Ruby, who lived on the mainland, Jada, Rhylan and Reece all lived here and worked on the ranch. Where would they go if we lost it? What would they do? Nothing about this was fair or right.

My jaw clenched so tight it ached, and a low growl threatened in the back of my throat. Just thinking about it made me hate our father even more, which was really saying something.

After signing autographs for an exuberant group of teenage fox-shifters who'd changed into their human forms as soon as they recognized me, Jada and I turned onto Hemlock Street. The neon sign for the Oasis blinked cheerfully up ahead. The dive bar had a wide variety of local beers on tap and played live music on Friday and Saturday nights. I wondered if they still hosted a not-quite-legal fight club in the basement.

I was going to walk right past the place—Jada didn't do crusty dive bars—but, to my surprise, she opened the door and pulled me inside. The smell of spilled beer and grilled onions assailed my nostrils. I tried prodding her thoughts to get a sense of what she was up to, but she wouldn't let me in. Glaring at her back, I followed her to a quiet booth.

One thing was certain. My sister was up to no good. And I was pretty sure I wasn't going to like it.

In true Jada fashion, she pulled a wet wipe from her purse and proceeded to sanitize the table, including the edges and both vinyl bench seats. Then the bartender came over, and we placed our order.

"Okay, what's going on?" I asked her, my BS meter on full throttle.

"What are you talking about?" She looked at me all innocent-like, but I wasn't born yesterday.

It ticked me off I couldn't read her as well as she could read me. I should've suggested a run in the woods rather than coming here. As packmates in our wolf forms, she'd have had a much harder time shielding her thoughts from me.

"Stop messing around," I snapped. "You've either done something I'm not going to like, or you're planning to do something I'm not going to like. Which is it?"

She rolled her eyes. "So negative. What happened to my adventurous little brother? The guy who will try anything?"

That was so unfair.

"Gee, I've never lost my family home before," I said in a mocking tone, twisting a finger into one of my dimples. "I wonder how new and adventurous that will feel."

She flicked a hand at me dismissively. "Don't be a grumpy asshole, Travis."

The bartender returned with our drinks, trying to cover up a smile and pretend he didn't just hear that.

I rubbed my temples, feeling the start of a headache forming. "I can't believe you're not as concerned about losing the ranch as I am."

"Nothing happens until the White Wolf Moon," she reminded me, taking a sip of her mineral water, "so calm down."

"*Calm down?*" It was never a good idea to tell an upset person to calm down. They were likely to fly into a rage. Or in my case, rip out a few throats. "Do I need to remind you that the next White Wolf Moon isn't far away?"

"Three full moons from now." She sounded entirely too chipper.

I took a long pull of my beer and wiped my mouth with the back of my hand. "Like I said, not far away."

Jada reached across the table and patted my forearm as if I

were a small child. "But you've forgotten the most important part of the will."

I pulled away and folded my arms, not liking where this conversation was heading. I knew exactly what she was getting at. "The part about me being mated?"

She nodded, and I bit back a curse. Jada hated when I swore. Her husband's family was churchy, and some of that had rubbed off on her.

"You seriously think I'll be mated by then?" Had my sister taken crazy pills and fallen off the deep end?

"Matthew and I fell in love on our first date and knew we were destined to be together. So yes, it's totally possible."

If I didn't know better, I'd think she believed in the whole werewolf/fated mates nonsense. I grabbed a napkin and proceeded to shred it. So, my sister was banking our family's entire future on me finding someone at the drop of a hat and falling instantly in love just because she had? I'd say those were pretty crappy odds.

I guzzled the rest of my beer and motioned for the bartender to bring over another. "Let me remind you that I've dated a lot of women and haven't run into 'the one' yet. Don't you read the supernatural tabloids?" Being in this business made me pretty jaded when it came to love. So many people weren't into me for me—they liked the bright lights and celebrity status of being with me.

"Oh, Travis," she said with a hint of a smile. "Sometimes the broken-hearted just need a little help in the love department."

She clearly *had* been reading the tabloids. The engagement and break-up between me and my sexy co-star Pamela Pinkly had been completely fabricated by the network. Fans ate it up, they said, claiming an off-screen romance validated the on-screen one. Unbeknownst to fans, however, was that Pamela was already in a very serious relationship. With a woman.

Just once, I'd like to date someone who didn't want something from me.

My inner wolf simmered just beneath the surface. "What makes you think I'll be mated by the next White Wolf Moon? In case you hadn't noticed, I'm not currently going out with anyone, and I prefer it that way."

"If you'll shut that pie hole of yours long enough to listen, I'll tell you."

By the time our one-sided conversation came to an end, I'd finished my burger, downed two more beers, shredded a few more napkins, and added another person to the list of people I wanted to kill.

My sister.

CHAPTER THREE

Daphne

I stood on the rain-soaked deck of the ferry, the Washington State coastline now far behind me. The fog bank ahead was like a solid wall of concrete rising from the gray water. It did not say 'tropical vacation' to me. Not a good sign when all you brought were sundresses, sandals, and a borrowed tankini.

Holding back my hair so it wouldn't whip into my face, I sighed heavily and shivered. What kind of person believed they won an actual vacation on the internet?

I'll tell you what kind. A gullible, desperate one.

Although my friend Bettina wouldn't have cared that I had planned to hide out in her apartment back in Atlanta, it hadn't stopped me from feeling a little guilty about it when I got there a few days ago. She'd asked me to water her plants while she and her boyfriend backpacked around Europe, not crash on her couch indefinitely.

But as soon as George and I arrived, her elderly neighbor had knocked on the door and handed me a parchment paper

15

envelope with really pretty calligraphy. Mrs. Baker had found it on the doorstep addressed to me, and she didn't want to leave it lying around.

At first, I thought it was a special delivery from Pharma-Douche. You know, like a thin bomb or some anthrax. But the woman had assured me it arrived just after my last plant-watering visit—long before my life was in danger.

I'd skimmed the cover letter and groaned, then Mrs. Baker demanded to know what it said.

"It's one of those scammy sweepstakes," I'd told her. "Says I've won a singles trip to paradise. What a crock of baloney."

"To where?"

"Darkaway Island, where the monsters come to play," I'd said, reading the promotional material then shoving it back inside. "It sure doesn't sound tropical to me. Sounds like Halloween Town for cosplayers."

To my surprise, Mrs. Baker had snatched the envelope from me, put on her readers, and rifled through the papers herself. "Darkaway Island," she'd said rather dreamily.

I was surprised she'd heard of it and asked if it was a real place.

"Of course, it is," she'd replied. "My second husband and I spent our honeymoon there. The beaches are quite lovely. And at the higher elevations, there's snow. You can sunbathe and snow ski on the same day."

I still didn't buy it. I wasn't a senior citizen who easily fell for that kind of bullshit.

Mrs. Baker had lifted an eyebrow, as if she knew what I was thinking. "It says you entered an online contest and answered a bunch of questions."

"I didn't enter any contest." But the moment I'd said it, something niggled at the back of my mind.

"You don't remember filling out a questionnaire asking about monsters?"

And then it hit me like a pallet of bricks.

Unfortunately, I happened to have an unhealthy addiction to online personality quizzes. You know the kind I'm talking about. *Who's Your Celebrity Twin?* (Emmy Rossum). *How Badass Are You?* (7 on a scale from 1 to 10). *What's The Likelihood You'd Survive A Zombie Apocalypse?* (83% because I wasn't willing to double-tap my mom.) They were like sugar. Impossible to resist and fun while you were doing them, but once the high was over, it was over.

On my last plant-watering visit to Bettina's apartment, I'd stumbled upon the quiz in question. Her wi-fi was much faster than mine, so I liked using her computer to check my email and social media. It was literally impossible not to click on *Who Is Your Monster Dream Date.* I mean, who wouldn't want to find out they're compatible with Beast and get their own library? It was every reader girl's dream.

When I'd finished the lengthy quiz, and submitted the results, a flashy pop-up filled the screen saying I'd won a four-week, all-expenses-paid singles trip to paradise for me and my cat. Yeah, right. Then I promptly forgot about it.

But Mrs. Baker had called the hotel, and they supposedly confirmed everything.

Now, as I stared out from the ferry deck at the cold, gray water studded with white caps, I didn't care what Mrs. Baker said about the island. She was a sweet old lady but probably a little Alzheimerish.

Three teenage girls with matching cat-eye contacts were taking selfies near the rail. Arms around each other, they struck various poses—smiling, goofy, model-serious—while the tall girl on the end held a selfie stick. Not far from them was an adorable elderly man and woman who reminded me of Rose and Jack in their later years, if Jack had lived. (I used to write non-canon Titanic fanfic where Jack had climbed onto the door with Rose and lived. It was plenty big enough.) An androgynous goth couple in black stood arm in arm near the bow, gazing toward our destination, their coats billowing around their ankles. Now that would make the perfect promotional meme, I thought. *Dreaming of Darkaway.*

Just then, the door to the ferry's passenger area opened with a bang, and I turned to see a small child running onto the deck. Coat unzipped and flapping, he beelined straight for the bow. Except that he wasn't actually wearing a coat, I realized, but a wizard robe. Wait. It didn't have sleeves. A superhero cape? A vampire? Underneath, he wore red shorts, a matching t-shirt and a pair of Velcro sandals. It made me cold just looking at him.

Not seeing an adult with him, I caught the boy right before he reached the rail. "Whoa, there, little dude. Where are you going?"

"I wanna see. I wanna see!" he cried, trying to squirm out of my grasp.

"It's too foggy," I said. "There's nothing *to* see."

I was about to ask him where his mom or dad was when a harried-looking young woman carrying an infant like a football dashed through the mist towards us.

"Thank you so much," she said breathlessly. "I was inside, changing the baby's diaper, and when I looked up, Austin was gone."

"No problem." I'd once nannied for a family with a boy who bolted the moment you turned your back, so I could relate.

The woman shifted the baby to her other hip and took the boy's hand. "Austin, don't ever run away from Mama like that. I didn't know where you were."

He stuck out his lower lip. "But I wanna see the mom-sters."

"I know you do, honey, but they're not out yet." She winked at me over the boy's head.

Austin squatted in front of George's carrier and started to

stick his fingers inside, but I caught him just in time. "Careful, sweetie. He might bite."

"Is this your son?" the boy asked.

His mother laughed. "He's just a regular cat, honey." Then to me she said in a low voice, "He thinks every animal coming to Darkaway is a—" The sudden sound of the ferry's horn made me jump and drowned out her words. "Thanks again for catching my little monster," she said, not skipping a beat as she smiled gratefully and turned to go. "Hey, why don't you stop by Midnight Garage and Nails on Nightshade Avenue for a mani/pedi. My treat."

"Midnight *Garage* and Nails?" I wasn't sure I'd heard her correctly. In fact, nothing this woman said was making much sense to me.

She nodded. "My husband works on cars, and I do nails."

Well, that was a combination I hadn't heard before. I shoved my hands into my pockets, not wanting her to see that I was a nail-biter. "Um, thanks."

She hesitated and looked at me a little more closely, but not in a harsh, judgmental way. "Is this your first time on Darkaway?" she asked with a friendly inquisitiveness.

"Well, I entered this contest and—"

"Oh my gosh, you're one of the contestants!" Excitement sparkled in her caramel-colored eyes. "I read about it in the Daily Epitaph. The whole town's talking about it."

I hurried to correct her. "No, no. I won a contest, but I wouldn't call myself a contestant."

"You *have* to stop by the Garage," she gushed. "I know it doesn't look like it now, but I'm really good with hair and makeup. I'm Portia, by the way."

But before I could ask her what in the world she was talking about, her little guy took off again.

"Ack!" Tucking football baby back under her arm, she chased

after Austin. "I'm serious," she called to me over her shoulder. "I'd love to help." Then she disappeared into the fog.

Help? With what?

I touched my hair self-consciously. Normally I wore my dark hair pulled back in a tidy bun for work, so I hadn't bothered to have it cut in a while. Did I look that pathetic? Was I in desperate need of a beauty intervention?

That made me think about Deanne's YouTube channel, where she uploaded a new beauty video each week. Another wave of sadness threatened to engulf me, but I shoved it away before it could take hold. I couldn't think about what had happened to my boss. Or what would happen if Pharma-Douche found me. I was here to have fun and relax, and let Scully and Mulder do their jobs.

Portia said the whole town was talking about a promotional gimmick by the resort. What had I gotten myself into?

Just then the ferry sounded its horn again, and I nearly jumped out of my skin. Three long, mournful blasts that said we were a big-ass ship and would run over anything that didn't get out of our way.

Visibility was so poor now that I could barely see George's carrier at my feet. Mist swirled in front of my face, and when I inhaled, I tasted a little cinnamon on the back of my tongue. We were sailing through that heavy fog bank now.

I glanced around. Where were all the others who'd been out on the deck with me a few minutes ago? Were they still out here somewhere, but the thick fog was making it impossible to see them? They probably had more sense than me and had gone back inside already.

I grabbed George's carrier and my suitcase, then stumbled blindly toward the doors. Almost immediately, I bashed my shin against something metallic and said a filthy curse under my breath. It really hurt.

Someone in the fog chuckled. "Looks like you've got your

hands full," a very masculine voice said. "Let me help you, darlin'."

My cheeks burned with embarrassment. It wasn't my habit to use such vile language out loud like that. Just in my head. "I'm good, thanks."

"Watch out for the—" A strong hand gripped my elbow, jerking me to the right, and I gave a little yelp. George hissed inside his carrier, ticked at being jostled. The man practically frog-marched me through the fog—a little presumptuous, but I went with it anyway, letting him guide me this way and that. Better than bashing my other shin, I supposed.

Unfortunately, I couldn't make out what he looked like. I could tell that he was tall and muscular, though, with broad shoulders. And he smelled good. Fresh and cedar-ish with earthy top notes.

"Is the fog always this thick?" I asked.

"It's part of the island's charm," he said from behind.

I wouldn't exactly call it charming, but maybe that was what locals told themselves so it didn't seem quite so oppressive.

"Here we are." His shoulder brushed mine as he reached out and grabbed a door handle I was just now seeing. I got another faint whiff of his cologne. "After you."

A wall of warmth hit me as the door opened, and I sighed with relief. I should've come inside earlier.

Stepping into the passenger area, I tugged hard on my rolling suitcase to get it over the threshold, remembering how it had gotten stuck on the way out.

Before I could turn to thank my tall, mysterious, incredible-smelling escort, the three girls with the cat-eye contacts shrieked in unison and jostled past me, converging like hungry vultures on fresh roadkill. And they weren't the only ones. Others quickly joined the stampede. Although I held tight to George's carrier, I lost the grip on my suitcase handle, and it toppled over. As I bent to retrieve it, I came very close to getting impaled when a woman's high heel brushed my hand.

Straightening back up, I saw that the man was now surrounded by what appeared to be adoring fans. Was he someone famous? He had to be. No wonder he struck me as slightly pushy. He was used to being fawned over and barking orders to his people.

I wish I had "people." I'd tell them to take my things and fetch me something to eat.

As I backed away from the crowd, I tried to get a better look to see if I recognized him, but all I caught were glimpses of dark hair and the flash of a movie-star smile.

I wandered around for a few minutes, looking for a window seat, and finally found one at the other end of the ferry. Although, honestly, what was the point? There was nothing to see through the windows except that impossibly thick, gray fog. I sure hoped the ferry captain was experienced and knew what he was doing. A boat could get lost out here. Was there such a thing as a Bermuda Triangle in the Pacific Ocean?

Two nuns were seated in the next booth over and appeared to be having a fairly heated argument. Although I'd never heard nuns arguing before, and I was dying to know why, I thought it would be rude to eavesdrop.

I put on my headphones and ate the yogurt I'd bought from a vending machine, saving the last bite for George. As he licked the plastic spoon, I told him what a good kitty he was. I was glad to see he hadn't lost his appetite.

When he was done, I propped my feet on the top of his carrier, zoned out to some classic rock, and worked on the crossword puzzle I'd started on the plane. Besides online quizzes, which I was no longer doing—thank you very much—I loved crosswords. But not the New York Times one. Ugh. Way too hard.

As I worked on the puzzle, I decided I was going to make the most of my time on the island, despite being snookered into thinking it was going to be a tropical vacation. By the time it was over and I went back home, hopefully Scully and Mulder will have wrapped up the case against Pharma-Douche, and I could go back to my regular life. But would I even have a job if the company's CEO was in jail? Whatever. I'd worry about that later.

I'd be perfectly fine here, as long as it wasn't one of those freaky, hedonistic resorts where people ran around naked looking to hook up. Based on the few interactions I'd had with other passengers, I didn't see any evidence of that.

I glanced at the nuns, who were no longer arguing. One was holding open a tin of mints as the other plucked out several. A peace offering, perhaps.

I was deep in thought, listening to an old Van Halen song and trying to come up with a nine-letter word for *lycanthrope weakness*, when I was suddenly blinded by brilliant sunlight streaming through the windows.

"Whoa!" My hands shot up to shield my eyes, and I was pretty sure I just drew on my face with my pen. I ripped off my headphones and heard cheering and clapping erupting around me. Out of every window, all I could see were brilliant blue skies and ocean. What had happened to the fog? The weather looked downright balmy.

"Here you go." A harried-looking ferry worker handed me a pair of free sunglasses that said *Darkaway Island* on the temples.

"Uh, thanks." I turned to ask the Sisters in the adjacent booth what the deal was with the weather, but they were gone.

"Welcome to Darkaway Island," said a voice over the loudspeaker. "Where monsters come to play." A few more cheers and wolf-whistles erupted around me.

All this hullabaloo over the island's theme reminded me of a small town we'd driven through when I was a kid and my parents were still married. My dad had this thing about wanting to visit all the contiguous states by car. We'd visited three before my parents divorced, but I don't think the car trips were related. The town had been decked out like a Bavarian village, which seemed quaint at the time, but I learned later it was just a marketing decision by city planners to attract tourists.

"We'll be docking in a few minutes," the voice continued. "On behalf of the entire crew, we truly hope you enjoy your time on Darkaway."

As soon as he signed off, a Bob Marley song began playing over the speakers. It was an island-ish song about not worrying, which was perfect. I planned to do a lot of non-worrying these next few weeks. I didn't know all the words, but I found myself humming along anyway.

I caught a glimpse of the view from the front-facing windows and gasped. A lush green island rose like a jewel in the middle of the ocean, with palm trees waving in the ocean breeze and tall cliffs soaring behind white sandy beaches. A halo of fluffy clouds hovered over the tip of a craggy mountain.

And above everything stretched that brilliant azure sky.

Maybe Mrs. Baker wasn't Alzheimerish after all.

We sailed toward the ferry dock under a huge black arch that said *Welcome to Darkaway*. The ride had taken only a few hours, which seemed impossible from a geography perspective, but who was I to argue with what I could see with my own two eyes? Maybe there were rain shadows and pockets of tropicality that I didn't know about. I was, however, pretty thrilled to be here, far from the danger back home.

I hurriedly lugged George's carrier and my rolling suitcase up the stairs with a *thunk, thunk, thunk*. The ferry engines reversed momentarily, followed by a gentle jolt as we docked. Once outside, fragrant island air warmed my sun-starved skin, and I took a deep breath. So many strange and wonderful scents.

Guess this vacation wasn't going to be a bust after all.

I got in line with the rest of the passengers leaving on foot, trying not to bump George's carrier against anyone or anything. We shuffled over a narrow gangplank with safety rails that connected the ferry to the dock, then down a ramp and finally stepped onto the island. With all the cars streaming off the ferry just a few feet away and people jostling me left and right, I needed to watch my step.

Several dark shadows passed overhead. I glanced up to see what kind of birds would cast such large shadows and was instantly blinded once again by the bright sun. Blinking a few times to get rid of the black spots dancing in my vision, I realized I should've put on the sunglasses the attendant gave me when I had a chance.

Music was coming from the opposite corner of the intersection. If I had a free hand, I'd have shaded my eyes to get a better look. But from what I could see, two street musicians in monster costumes were playing a fiddle and a ukulele in front of a candy store. It took me a moment to recognize The Monster Mash, and I chuckled.

Nice detail, Darkaway Island. Very nice.

Beyond them and to the right was a Ferris wheel and a boardwalk with lots of interesting-looking shops. To the left was a grand hotel on the beach with dozens of the most beautiful kites I'd ever seen.

My breath caught in my throat. Could that be where I was staying? I couldn't wait to check in, change into my tankini, and go down to the beach. I would order a cocktail with an umbrella in it and catch some serious rays. Or maybe I'd visit the shops first. I hoped the candy store sold saltwater taffy; a bag or two was definitely in my future. But there was no need to do it all today. I was here for a month—four glorious weeks—and I'd have plenty of time to explore.

Hearing a commotion behind me, I glanced over my

shoulder and instantly froze. The good island vibes I'd been feeling were replaced by sheer terror.

The crowd parted, and three dogs the size of Jon Snow's dire wolf were charging down the sidewalk. Growling. Teeth bared. Heading straight for George and me.

I scrambled wildly to get out of their way, then screamed as I tripped on the curb and fell into traffic. The screeching sound of car brakes filled the air, and for the second time in less than a week, I wondered if I would die.

CHAPTER FOUR

Travis

O ver the years, I've killed a few people. Not a huge number, but when you're a werewolf, death happens.

Most of them were scum of the earth bad. The kind you wouldn't want to run into in a dark alley. Killing was a side effect of our nature, unfortunately. Animal instincts were harder to control as a wolf. But it only happened during a full moon with my own teeth and claws. Not in the middle of the day. With a vehicle.

Heaven's Moon!

I slammed on the brakes of my rental car and jumped out. The woman I'd helped in the fog was sprawled on the pavement just inches from my front bumper. But thankfully, not dead.

With my heightened wolf senses, I didn't smell blood, though I did notice how soft her hands were as I reached down and pulled her up. "You okay, darlin'?" Her suitcase sat on the road next to her, the pet carrier on its side. Her cat seemed fine too, but angry as all get out, given the hissing.

"I...I think so." She blinked a few times, looking a bit dazed as I brushed tiny bits of gravel from her hair and the back of her denim jacket.

She was beautiful, though not in the traditional, heavily made-up sense that I was used to seeing on photoshoots or the set of *Secret Shadows*, but in a healthy, real woman sort of way. She wore flip-flops and a loose-fitting blue dress that was oddly flattering. A tangle of dark curls fell past her shoulders, messy from the windswept ferry. She had expressive brown eyes, a heart-shaped face smattered with freckles, and a red pen mark on her cheek.

"Where did they go?" she asked, eyes wide.

I looked around at the gathering crowd. "Where did *who* go?"

"Those huge dogs," she whispered. "They were about to attack me."

Blood coursed through my veins like a flash flood. *The Crutchfield brothers.* I'd seen those hooligans bounding down the ferry ramp in their wolf forms a moment ago, shoving people aside.

"Those selfish jackasses are gone," I told her. "They have no regard for anyone but themselves. I can assure you, not everyone on the island is like them."

"Well, that's a relief to know," she said breathlessly, smoothing her dress with shaky hands. "Would you mind handing me the cat carrier behind you?"

As I turned to grab it, someone in the crowd shouted. *"Look out!"*

My head snapped up, and I saw a minivan with two nuns in the front seat plowing into the back of my car. The sounds of screeching tires and twisting metal filled the air. Instinctively, I pushed the woman off the roadway, but I didn't have time to get myself or the cat out of the way. So, I did the only thing I could do. Using the strength of my wolf, I pushed as hard as I could against the grill of my car to stop the forward momentum.

And it would've worked too. But then my outrageously

expensive cowboy boots with their smooth leather soles slipped on the pavement.

There was a crack. And a sharp stab of pain—a lot of it. Then the road rose up to meet me.

"Oh goodness, Travis!" Sister Elenor rushed from the van, her hands flapping around her head like two bony birds. She, along with Sister Mary Francis, had taught me in Sunday school when I was a pup. "I was distracted by the kites and didn't see that you had stopped." She patted my cheeks briskly. It wasn't at all comforting. "Are you okay, honey? Where does it hurt?"

"It's nothing, ma'am." Trying to ignore the piercing pain in my leg, I got to my feet, grabbed the pet carrier and hobbled over to the woman from the ferry. She seemed equal parts grateful and horrified.

"You got hurt," she choked. "Trying to save us."

I started to tell her I was totally fine, hardly worse for the wear. Then she stretched on her tiptoes, and for a second, I thought she was going to give me a peck on the cheek. But instead, she held my face in her hands and planted a big old kiss on my mouth.

"How in the world did you do that?" she asked, her sweet breath warm against my lips as she pulled away. "If I hadn't seen it myself, I'd never have believed it. You saved George's life. And mine."

My inner wolf flared to life again, and I nearly growled. Instead, I touched my mouth, tasting the remnants of her cherry lip balm. I could've kissed her a little longer, to be honest. "I almost killed you. It was the least I could do."

"Well, you didn't." She took a half step back, seemed to collect herself, then thrust her hand out and gave mine a firm shake. It was the kind of handshake that said, *Forget about that hot, impulsive kiss just now. This is what I want you to remember about me.* "Thank you very much for saving George and me. I'm...uh...Daphne, by the way."

She looked at me expectantly, her long-lashed eyes the kind a man could get lost in. It took me a moment to realize she was waiting for me to introduce myself as well. Like she truly didn't know who I was. I can't tell you how refreshing it was not to be recognized, especially here on the island where I grew up. "Nice to meet you, Daphne-By-The-Way. I'm Travis."

She laughed softly, letting go of my hand as she wiggled her fingers inside the cat carrier. "George says thanks too."

I bent down, trying not to put too much weight on my knee, and peered inside. The black and white cat hissed and took a swipe at me, almost scratching my cheek. *Little asshole.* I jerked away just in time, wrenching my knee even further.

"George!" Daphne chided, looking aghast. "I'm so sorry, Travis. He can be pretty ill-tempered."

"Must not like dogs," I grumbled.

"Hates them. With a passion."

Sister Mary-Francis, who'd been directing traffic around the fender bender, clapped her hands like a schoolteacher. "All right, you two lovebirds. Let's go."

Daphne held up a hand in protest. "But we're not—well, I was... It was just—"

"You can kiss all you want at the hospital," Sister Elenor told her. "I'll get someone to move your car, Travis."

"*Hospital?* I don't need to go to the hospital." Then it occurred to me. "Unless Daphne—"

She shook her head vehemently. "No, no. I'm perfectly fine. Just a little dusty from the road."

It was then that I heard the siren. I looked up to see the flashing lights of an emergency vehicle barreling down the hill toward the ferry dock. "Heaven's Moon! Who called an ambulance?"

I glanced around at the growing crowd. Most of them had phones in their hands.

I gave a rueful wave to them. So much for anonymity.

CHAPTER FIVE

Daphne

Despite my protests, one of the Sisters shoved me into the back of the ambulance with Travis. "Up you go, dear."

The other took my suitcase and George. "We'll meet you there," she said, giving me a finger wave.

"Careful with my cat," I called out as the EMT was closing the door. "He can be a really—" The door shut with a bang. "— naughty kitty."

I had no choice but to take a seat on the bench next to Travis.

The man was distractingly handsome with his tousled dark hair, chiseled features and a muscular, well-proportioned body. I couldn't believe the Sisters thought we were *together* together. Okay, so I'd kissed him. I mentally slapped a hand to my forehead while trying to stay outwardly calm. Ugh. What *was* I even thinking? I was thankful, yes, but a simple handshake would have been sufficient.

"Sorry 'bout that," he said. "The Sisters can be pushy sometimes, but they mean well."

31

"As long as they don't try to take George out of his carrier. He'll scratch the hell out of them. The *heck* out of them," I corrected since they were nuns.

A dimple formed on Travis's cheek. "Trust me. They've dealt with worse. They taught me in Sunday school."

I laughed, appreciating the levity after almost getting killed, then cast a wary glance at his leg. "Does it hurt a lot?"

He shook his head, a muscle ticking in his jaw. "All of this is just an overreaction, but that's what you get on Darkaway. People nosing into your business, thinking they know what's best for you."

"Doesn't seem like an overreaction to me. You got hurt and could've been killed." Had he really braced his hands on the hood of his car, thinking he could stop it?

"Nonsense," he said, rolling his eyes like it was no big deal.

His gaze swept over me as if he were seeing me for the first time. Acutely aware of our close proximity, I felt the little hairs on my arms prickle. I hoped I didn't look as disheveled as I felt after a day of traveling and being windswept on the ferry deck. Then I remembered Portia's offer to fix my appearance and realized I probably did. Oh well. I wasn't here to impress anyone. Although damn, why did he have to be so incredibly hot?

"You've...uh...got a pen mark there," he said, pointing to my face.

Of course, I do. I licked my thumb and rubbed my cheek. "Here?"

"A little higher."

I followed his direction. "Here?"

His brows drew together. "You got it. Most of it, that is."

The ambulance lurched forward, and the paramedic, a short man with rather pointy ears, squatted down in front of Travis. "Got yerself into a wee pickle, aye, Mr. Monroe?"

"It appears so." Travis gave me a little side-smile that turned the butterflies in my stomach into jumping beans. "Call me Travis, though. Mr. Monroe is—was—my father."

The EMT reached for the storage bins to the right of the bench and rummaged through the drawers. "I was sorry to hear of your old man's passing. The whole town was. The memorial service was very moving."

"Don't be sorry," Travis clipped out. "But I appreciate the sentiment." The way he said this made me think he didn't care much for his dad. Had his father been a deadbeat dad like mine? I wondered.

The ambulance felt like it was moving at a snail's pace. Or a slow-motion ocean liner making a turn. Maybe they sped only when someone's life was on the line. When we went over a bump, I had to grab a nearby handle to keep from bouncing clear off the seat. I looked back to see that Travis's cowboy boot had been removed and one muscular leg was bare all the way past his knee. I glanced around to see what the pixie-ish EMT had used to cut Travis's jeans but saw nothing. The guy must be fast and efficient—he'd already put it away.

"So ye were driving, aye?" the man asked, carefully attaching a brace to Travis's knee. "I thought ye flew yer float plane back to the island whenever ye visit. At least, that's what the Daily Epitaph says."

Travis pointed a thumb over his shoulder. "I did, but it's being serviced on the mainland right now. Haven't been able to find a place up in British Columbia that I like as well as the one near Seattle. Figured that since I'm staying on the island until after the White Wolf Moon, it was as good a time as any for its annual maintenance."

The EMT perked up. "Ye'll be here for Monsterval? That's fantastic, mate!"

Travis frowned. "Festival of the Monster falls on the same weekend as the White Wolf Moon?"

The EMT nodded. "Yes. It's going to be a huge event this

year. The missus is on the organizing committee. She'll be thrilled that Darkaway Island's favorite son will be home for the festivities."

Favorite son? As in, small-town boy goes out into the world and gets famous? That would explain him getting mobbed on the ferry. And all those cell phones recording him after the accident. It really irked me that I didn't recognize who he was. I hated not knowing something that everyone else did.

I pulled out my phone and turned the screen slightly away from Travis so he wouldn't see that I was searching his name. Bummer. I didn't have any cell service.

When we arrived at the hospital, I stopped in the waiting area and tried to tell them I didn't belong here, but the place was bustling with activity and no one would listen. An orderly pushed Travis in a wheelchair through the double doors of the emergency room, and I was ushered along with him.

"Is that his fiancée?" I heard someone whisper as we passed the nurses' station.

"I didn't know he was engaged," said someone else.

"It's all over the tabloids, silly."

"I don't read that trash," the second person remarked.

So, I'd impulsively kissed a guy who was engaged. *Great.* Inwardly cringing, I sent out a sincere apology into the ether to his fiancée. I'm not the kind of girl who preys on taken men. Trust me. That's a job for wedding singers.

Once inside the exam room, the orderly helped Travis get onto the bed.

This was getting even more awkward. Here was a man I hardly knew getting ready to be examined by a health care professional. I definitely needed to get out of here. "I should probably just—"

The door opened, and a tall, blond man in scrubs strolled in.

"They told me you were on your way in," he said, giving Travis a fist-bump. So, these guys were friends too. Sheesh...did everyone on the island know everyone else? "You don't look too worse for the wear. Sorry I couldn't be at the old man's memorial service—I was in emergency surgery all day."

"No problem, Carlisle. You didn't miss much."

"Still, I wish I could've been there," the doctor said, adjusting his stethoscope. "For you, Ruby, and the rest of the family. Your father may have been a major asshat, but he was the step-asshat I never had."

Ruby? That must be his fiancée.

The doctor held out his hand to me. Though his smile was warm, his skin was unexpectedly cold. "I'm Alexander, an old friend of Travis."

Hadn't Travis just called him Carlisle? Maybe that was his last name. I glanced at the hospital badge clipped to his lab coat and frowned. It said Dr. Lesauvage.

Noticing my confusion, Travis chuckled. "Have you seen the Twilight movies? They were a big hit on the island when they came out, weren't they, Doc?"

The movies? *Humph.* The movies wouldn't have existed if it hadn't been for the books.

The doctor shrugged and washed his hands at the tiny sink in the corner. "It started as a joke. The nickname stuck."

A joke? I scrutinized him again. Handsome, blond, and a doctor. Okay, I got it. The island sure took this monster stuff to the Nth degree. Well, I could play along too.

Smirking, I covered my neck with a hand. "I hope you've fed recently, Dr. Cullen."

The doctor winked. "I'm a vegetarian, remember?"

I laughed. Good one.

He turned his attention back to his patient, and I took it as my cue to go. I didn't want to see any needles or hear any groans of pain—much less see this guy naked. Well...at least not in a hospital and under these circumstances.

Girl, no. He's engaged. Remember? And you're not a skanky wedding singer.

"Guess it's time for me to skedaddle. Let you have a little privacy. Thank you for—"

Travis shot a hand out and grabbed mine, pulling me closer to his bedside. If I'd been wearing heels, I probably would've lost my balance. "Stay here, Daphne. Please."

This took me completely by surprise, as did the electric tingle running up my arm. His fingers were long, the short nails neatly trimmed, not bitten like mine. And unlike the doctor, his touch was surprisingly warm.

I looked into his handsome yet worried face. Did blood and needles always freak him out? Maybe he was in a more fragile state than normal because of his father's recent death. What if his father had died in a car accident and the almost-accident with me had traumatized him further?

I couldn't tell him no. He...needed me. I owed him that much. "Um...okay."

"There won't be any blood, if that's what you're worried about." The doctor pulled an overhead light and shone it on Travis's swollen knee.

I felt so guilty that George and I were the cause of this. And those stupid dogs. The island ought to have stricter leash laws.

"It should heal quickly on its own," Travis proclaimed in a low, gruff tone. "I'm not sure what all the damn fuss is about."

The doctor removed the brace that the EMT had put on and prodded the joint, manipulating it this way and that. "You really wrenched this thing. The full moon was...what? Last week?"

Travis groaned, squeezing my hand tighter. "You bloodsuckers are all the same. Couldn't care less about the moon or what phase it's in, but I'll bet you know exactly what time the sun sets tonight."

Alexander chuckled without looking up. "Point taken."

Another monster reference? I gave them a courtesy laugh.

"For your information," said Travis, "Full moon was two nights ago. A blue moon, to be exact."

Once in a blue moon. I couldn't remember what that even meant. A full moon that appeared blue because of atmospheric conditions? A moon that was closer to the earth than normal? All I knew was that they were special enough to have a name. And what was the White Wolf Moon that Travis had mentioned earlier? The opposite of a Harvest Moon? I'd try to remember to add these to my list of things to google when I got to my hotel.

"With your wolf blood," Alexander said, "you'll heal fast, but given the extent of the damage, it may not heal correctly on its own. And that would not be good, my friend. Plus, the moon's strength is waning. It's a good thing you came in—we'll need to do x-rays and an MRI. See if anything is broken or torn and get things set and aligned if necessary."

I gulped and blinked a few times. Did he just say...*wolf blood?*

"At least give me something for the pain first."

"I'm not a complete monster, Travis." Alexander gave me another wink, then stuck his head out of the door and barked some orders.

The back of my neck prickled with heat. What was it about the island and all these monster references? I looked at the two men. They seemed like such normal, intelligent, good-looking guys. It had to be a series of inside jokes among old friends. Although all of this was bordering on weird. *Too* weird.

A nurse with salt and pepper hair and a dragon tattoo on her neck entered the exam room. She handed the doctor a small tray with a vial and syringe. I'd have taken a step backward and moved away to give them some room to treat their patient, but Travis was still holding onto my hand pretty tight. I grabbed a nearby folding chair and sat down to face him at the head of the bed. If I had to stay here, I sure as hell didn't want to see him getting poked.

"You're going to feel a slight pinch," the doctor told him.

Sure enough, Travis winced. "Shouldn't take too long for it to kick in. Don't be surprised if it makes you feel groggy and a bit loopy." He dropped the used needle into a red receptacle mounted to the wall and held the door open for the nurse with the dragon tattoo. "I'll be back in a few minutes to give that a chance to work."

"I really don't want to be here," Travis admitted to me after they had left. "And I *detest* needles, so I appreciate you staying."

"No problemo." I wanted to ask him about the wolf blood comment, but it sounded so stupid. I had to have misheard the doctor. Travis would no doubt look at me and wonder if *I* were the one on drugs.

However, I couldn't help but notice that under these bright, overhead lights, his eyes did look a bit more golden yellow than brown.

"Where are you from, Daphne?" he asked in that slight drawl of his. "Where do you hang your hat?"

I smiled at his charming turn of phrase. "In the suburbs outside Atlanta, but I'm originally from Michigan." I wasn't about to tell him I didn't exactly have a safe place to hang my hat at the current moment—that would inevitably lead to a whole host of questions I didn't want to answer. Or *couldn't*, I thought, remembering that disastrous, vomit-y interview with Mulder and Scully. "What about you?"

He lifted an eyebrow as if he found my question amusing. "Born and raised here, actually. But I split my time between Vancouver and L.A."

I was confused. "But your accent..."

He chuckled. "That's what hours of voice coaching will do to you. I have a hard time getting rid of it when I'm not on set."

Ahhh. Of course. The guy was an actor—that explained a lot. The mob on the ferry. Everyone holding their phones to record the scene after the accident. Whispers of the nursing staff about tabloid articles. I really wanted to know what show he was on but didn't want to ask and seem even more clueless.

I was about to ask him if he wanted me to let his fiancée know what had happened—I mean, Ruby should be here, not me—when I heard a commotion outside the exam room. A different nurse, this one with no visible tattoos, rushed in to grab something from the cabinet. And through the open door, I saw two EMTs pushing a gurney down the hallway with what appeared to be a dog strapped to the top.

I blinked a few times. *A dog?!* As a patient in a human hospital?

Portia had said she owned a nail salon that did car repairs. Was this place a combination hospital/veterinary clinic? Was that even a thing? The island was small, yes, but was it *that* small?

The poor animal was whimpering and yelping as the gurney disappeared past the open door.

"What's going on out there?" Travis asked, straining to see.

"Car accident," the nurse replied, his arms filled with supplies. "A boy on vacation was hit while in his coyote form."

A boy in his coyote form. *His coyote form!* I would've questioned whether I'd heard it correctly, but the nurse was a good enunciator. My heart was pounding so hard right now that I barely heard what Travis was saying.

"Is it serious?" he asked.

"He'll be in good hands with Dr. Lasauvage," the nurse called over his shoulder. "So please be patient. It may be a little while until he can get back to you."

I turned to Travis. "What's going on?"

His eyes were at half-mast due to the drugs. "We've seen it happen all too often with tourists. Especially shifter kids. They're so excited they can roam freely on the island in their animal forms that they completely forget about traffic safety."

I tried to swallow, but there was a huge lump of WTF lodged in my throat.

Shifters. Coyotes. Then I thought about the dire wolves in the ferry line. The boy who asked if George was my son. Carlisle, the blood-sucking doctor. Travis and his wolf blood.

My cheeks were getting hot, the little hairs on my arm standing on end.

I was on Darkaway Island. *Where monsters come to play.*

"Daphne," Travis said groggily. "Are you...okay? You don't look so well."

I stared into his golden eyes, recalling his incredible strength and reflexes. His obsession with the moon.

Taking a step backwards, I slipped out of his reach, courtesy of his meds that had thankfully kicked in.

"I'm...I'm fine." My voice sounded far away, as if I were inside a darkening tunnel. I needed to get out of here. *Quickly.* I've fainted before, so I knew the feeling well. You couldn't talk yourself out of it, no matter how hard you tried.

Even though I was in a hospital, this was the last place on earth I'd want to pass out.

CHAPTER SIX

Daphne

I sat inside the coffee shop, cradling the ceramic cup as if it contained the elixir of life.

"I know, it must be shocking at first," Sister Mary-Francis said in that kind, no-nonsense tone you'd expect from a nun who co-owned a coffee shop called Unholy Grounds. She wore navy-blue slacks, orthotic shoes, and a nun's headscarf that only partially covered her gray hair. "But you're handling it remarkably well."

My hands, as well as my vanilla latte with a sprinkle of nutmeg, were shaking. I was also just this side of hyperventilating.

She thought I was handling it well?

Okay, so it wasn't every day you learned that monsters were actually real. That the incredibly hot guy you'd impulsively kissed for saving you—and your cat—was not only engaged, but was also a *werewolf*. Oh yeah, and his doctor was a vampire. Plus, the fact that you were currently trapped on an island with all sorts of other supernatural creatures.

But then, maybe the Sisters were simply referring to the fact that I hadn't had a serious cardiac event. Or become a drooling catatonic. Or gone stark-raving mad. All of which sounded semi-appealing right now.

I'd barely managed to exit Travis's hospital room, ignoring him as he called after me. Thankfully, the Sisters were in the waiting room with George, just like they'd promised. Given the ashen look on my face and my incoherent mutterings, they'd wasted no time bringing me here to the coffee shop to, in Sister Elenor's words, "chill and hang out."

I dipped a finger into my latte foam and stuck it into George's carrier at my feet. He licked it off with his sandpaper tongue. I wanted to snuggle him, but with customers going in and out the front door, I couldn't take the chance that he wouldn't want to be held and run off. That would throw a major monkey-wrench into my plans to get off the island.

The next ferry left in an hour, and I planned to be on it.

Sister Elenor set down a plate with a large cookie on a doily, then took a seat across from me. She also wore a simple scarf that framed the salt and pepper curls around her face, but unlike Sister Mary-Francis, she had on workout pants and running shoes. She reminded me of that nun who ran marathons.

"She sure *is* handling this well," Sister Elenor agreed brightly, pushing over the plate. She sounded so proud of me, which did make me feel a little better. Maybe I didn't look as terrified on the outside as I felt on the inside.

The cookie was as big as my head. And it was peanut butter —my favorite.

I broke off a piece and popped it into my mouth, savoring the delicious flavor in order to focus on something positive and good in my present situation. Tender, yet chewy, it reminded me of Gram's cookies—God rest her soul—only better because the Sisters used creamy peanut butter, not crunchy. Ever since I heard there was a government standard for an acceptable amount of rodent parts in peanut butter, I imagined the crunch being bones. Which was why I preferred creamy.

Nibbling on another bite, I looked around the coffee shop. Every inch of wall space in Unholy Grounds was covered in local artwork, gothic crosses, handwritten wooden signs with funny slogans, and posters advertising various community events. Once a month at the community center, there was a meetup for board game enthusiasts. A local yarn shop hosted a drop-in knitting circle, while a book club called *Books and Bikes* congregated here every Tuesday night. Then there was *Sinister Scooters*, which looked like a motorcycle gang of retirees, except they rode...motorized scooters? And then there was an upcoming festival called Monsterval that the EMT had mentioned.

It all seemed so perfectly normal, if not a little quirky. No wonder I hadn't picked up on anything being amiss until I got to the hospital and really started paying attention.

Several people stood in line to place their orders, including a middle-aged woman wearing a bikini coverup who was casually resting her hand on the head of—*gulp*—a huge leopard at her side. It was gorgeous with a shiny golden coat and black spots. No one was paying them any more attention than if they were a human couple.

Behind the counter was a purple-bearded elf barista with gauges in his pointy ears, a friendly Australian accent, and a smile that made you feel as if you were the reason he was so happy. Everything around me was charmingly mundane...if you ignored the eccentric, supernatural stuff.

I took a few more bites and sips and gained a little clarity.

It didn't actually *feel* as if I were in mortal danger. With this realization, the tension between my shoulder blades eased a little.

I had a lot of questions for the Sisters, of course, but I wasn't sure exactly where to start.

"So, you're witches?" I narrowed my eyes. "Isn't that, like, a conflict of interest considering you're nuns?"

They laughed. *Giggled*, actually.

"I'd always known there was something different about me," Sister Mary-Francis said, leaning back in her chair. "As a child, I could levitate small objects, turn lights off and on, do simple enchantments. That sort of thing. But it wasn't until I joined the convent as a young woman that my spell-casting powers really developed."

"Girl power," Sister Elenor declared, making a fist and giving it a little pump. "You know, like when women live together, they often have their periods at the same time."

Sister Mary-Francis gave an exasperated groan. "Do you mind?"

"Go on," Sister Elenor prodded. "Tell her the whole story."

"I was just about to until you interrupted me."

"No one's stopping you," Sister Elenor retorted.

The two nuns continued to bicker back and forth like an old married couple until finally Sister Mary-Francis turned to me again and vigorously cleared the frog in her throat. "As I was saying, I was kicked out of the sisterhood when I set a priest's robe on fire."

My eyes widened. "Are you *serious*?" I hoped she wasn't easily angered. I'd hate to be on her bad side.

"There had been rumors circulating about this priest for months, but nothing concrete. That is, until I caught him peeping into the women's restroom through a hole in the janitor's closet. What was I supposed to do?" One corner of her mouth twitched conspiratorially. "Ignore him?"

"He didn't die or anything," Sister Elenor quickly clarified. "Just scared the bejeezus out of him."

Sister Mary-Francis smiled ruefully. "When Mother

Superior learned what I'd done, that was the end of that. She kicked me out and told me not to come back. Because I was adopted as an infant, I didn't know much about my blood relatives. So, I did some genealogical research, got one of those DNA tests. Low-and-behold, I discovered I'm descended from witches."

That must've been *some* discovery, I thought wryly.

"What happened to the priest?" I asked, almost not wanting to know the answer. I was a lapsed Catholic, so I knew the church's history of turning a blind eye to priests behaving badly.

"He got the boot," Sister Mary-Francis said. "Last we heard, he was working at his brother-in-law's car wash franchise."

Although I had nothing against people who worked at car washes, this fall from grace seemed fitting.

I turned to Sister Elenor. "Did something similar happen to you?"

"Goodness, no," she said, shaking her head. "I'm human, just like you. Mary-Francis and I were best friends at the convent, so I was quite upset about what had happened to her. Frankly, she's a hero in my book, if you ask me. After Mary-Francis moved to Darkaway, which she'd heard about through her fox-shifter genealogy friend—what was his name again...?"

"Maurice," Sister Mary-Francis replied.

Sister Elenor shook her head. "His name started with a B."

"No, it didn't," Sister Mary-Francis said with a scowl. "*I* should know. He was *my* friend." She turned back to me. "*Anyhoo*, he was the one who told me about the Gifted Sisters of the Sacred Heart, a small convent located here on the island, so I thought I'd check it out."

Sounded like the name of a punk rock band, I thought, biting back a smile. This was serious business, after all, and I had no business finding any of it funny.

Sister Elenor nodded. "After she moved to the island, I came for a visit. Sure, the folks who live and vacation here can be a little strange from a human's perspective at first, but for the most part, they're just delightful." Her eyes sparkled with joy. "So, I decided to stay. And now, I couldn't imagine living anywhere else."

With nervous curiosity, I looked again at the leopard and his wife/girlfriend who were next in line. Were they tourists who lived on the mainland? Maybe the leopard was a banker on Wall Street. A heavy-equipment operator from Cleveland. Or a high school history teacher from Phoenix. I also wondered if he was getting a steamed milk.

"Let me get this straight," I said slowly. "In the real world, supernatural creatures live among humans just like they do here, only secretly?"

"This *is* the real world, my dear," Sister Elenor countered. "Just because it's secret doesn't make it any less authentic."

Point taken. "The *outside world?*" I said, correcting myself.

"Well, they hide it, of course," Sister Mary-Francis explained. "Except for a few special communities where they can live out in the open, like Darkaway Island. That's why the destination resort is so fun for creature folk. They don't have to hide their true natures here like they do at home. They can just be themselves. Let their hair down, so to speak."

I thought about Bettina's neighbor, Mrs. Baker. She knew about Darkaway. She'd mentioned honeymooning here, which meant...she had to be a supernatural creature too.

I reeled with that revelation because I'd spent a fair amount of time with her. Was she a witch? A shifter? A vampire? And what about her cowboy boyfriend? He'd mentioned visiting the island too.

Although I didn't have all the answers, a few more pieces of this strange puzzle were beginning to fall into place.

"I hope we haven't scared you more," Sister Elenor murmured. "It really is lovely here."

"Are there other humans on the island besides you?" I asked, more curious than anything. I had no plans to stay. *None.* The next ferry left in less than an hour now, so I wouldn't be here for much longer—but still, I was curious. "Being a supernatural isn't a requirement?"

"Goodness, no," Sister Elenor assured me, spreading her hands wide. "There are loads of us mere mortals here. The owners of the Midnight Cinemas, Marty and Celeste, are humans. Then there's Susan, a local glass artist who runs Arnie's Art Supply after her father, Arnie, ran off with a cat-shifter from Reno. Phyllis and Esmerelda own *Immortal You Yoga*, but don't tell Esmerelda I told you she's human. She moved here, hoping the island would awaken some hidden powers, but she's as human as they come. Then there's Bob and..." She continued to rattle off a dozen or more names. "Ugh. Who am I forgetting?"

Sister Mary-Francis stirred uncomfortably in her chair. "The...um...people who work in the crimson clubs. Can't forget them."

"*Crimson clubs?*" I asked cautiously, my gaze darting between the Sisters.

"Clubs where vampires go to feed on live human hosts," Sister Elenor explained. "They can't do that back home, of course, so it's something they...uh...look forward to when they come here. The atmosphere is a bit salacious, but it's very popular with the vampire tourists." At the horrified look on my face, she quickly added, "Don't worry. The blood hosts aren't recruited against their will, turned into vampires, or killed. From what I understand, it pays quite well."

Aware that my hands were cupping my neck, I forced myself to lower them. "So...it's not...dangerous here?" I asked, thinking about the dire wolves in the ferry line.

Sister Mary-Francis shook her head. "No more than in any other small town. Supernatural-on-human crime is not tolerated by the sheriff. Perpetrators are sent to Rocky Reach, a jail on one of the small atolls just off the coast. I'm involved in the prison ministry, so believe me when I tell you, it's *not* a walk through the tulips."

"Although you'll want to stay away from Wickedville," Sister Elenor cautioned.

I didn't need a warning to stay away, because I was counting the minutes until I could leave. But I couldn't help asking. "Wickedville?"

Sister Mary-Francis nodded. "It's a sketchy part of town that attracts miscreants."

I considered all of this for a moment then frowned. "With humans coming and going, how does the existence of Darkaway Island and its supernatural inhabitants remain a secret?"

"The island is charmed, of course." From beneath her athletic jacket, Sister Elenor pulled out a gorgeous pendant, a milky green stone in a filigreed setting. "It's made from moonstone sourced here on the island. When a human leaves the island and passes through the mist, if she's not wearing one of these personally charmed memory stones, she forgets everything about her time here."

I nodded slowly and dunked the last piece of the peanut butter cookie into my latte, contemplating every far-fetched thing they'd told me. However, since they were nuns, they had a lot of credibility.

What awaited me if I went back right now?

I thought about Pharma-Douche, who wanted me dead. I could continue to hide out at Bettina's place, sure, but I wouldn't be able to go anywhere. Or do anything that didn't involve a computer and good wi-fi. George and I would be stuck inside, ordering takeout and watching Netflix. Even though there were monsters here on Darkaway Island, at least they didn't want to kill me.

I stared out the window at the brilliant blue sky. Dozens of colorful kites swayed in the tropical sea breeze like waving, beckoning sentinels.

Welcome, Daphne.

Between the one-story buildings on the other side of the road, I caught a glimpse of the white sandy beach beyond them.

Come play, Daphne.

Back home, it was much colder than this and possibly raining.

Things were strange here, yes, but if I were honest, it didn't feel dangerous.

Whether I left now or stayed till the end of my vacation, I'd be none the wiser about the existence of supernatural creatures when I got home. But if I stuck it out here, I'd be safe from Pharma-Douche, more relaxed, and probably somewhat tanner.

I thought about Sister Elenor's comment about everyone being so delightful. The Sisters certainly were. So were Portia from the ferry and her cute son, Austin. And the vampire doctor with a good sense of humor.

Then there was Travis, of course, with his wolfish yellow eyes. But I wouldn't exactly call him delightful. No, that didn't quite describe him. More like dangerously hot, to be exact. And very much engaged.

After a bit more soul-searching and one more latte, I made my decision.

I was staying.

I checked into the hotel a short time later and took a long, luxurious bath with one of the bath bombs I'd had the foresight to pack. As I soaked in the swirling orange and pink water, the stress and tension from the Craziest Day Ever slipped away.

Had Scully and Mulder made any headway in the case? Except for the strange book that I'd tucked into the bottom of my bag, my life back there seemed like a world away.

When I was sufficiently pruned-up, I wrapped myself in a thick hotel robe and left the well-appointed bathroom with its clawfoot tub and waterfall-like faucets. I grabbed a piece of cheese from the tray of food that had been waiting in my room upon my arrival and strode into the large bedroom. A cool ocean breeze stirred the gauzy curtains framing the French doors to the small patio. Paintings by a local artist hung on the walls. A cozy book nook filled one corner and yes, I'd found a few books I wanted to read. No wonder Mrs. Baker had fond memories of this place. They really did treat you like royalty here.

Speaking of kings, George was stretched out on the humongous bed as if he owned the place.

"Are you having fun, mister?" I scooped him into my arms and snuggled him. He instantly started to purr. My boy could be a cantankerous kitty sometimes, but he was *my* cantankerous kitty, and I loved him to pieces.

At check-in, I had tried not to act shocked when the desk clerk mentioned having an animal whisperer on staff. She explained how cat charms had been placed around my villa so George could explore outside but not go too far. This was shaping up to be quite a unique vacation for both of us.

While audibly kissing the top of his head, something I could only do for a short time before he got pissed off, I noticed that a piece of paper had been slipped under my door during my soak in the tub.

I stooped to pick it up and nearly choked. This had to be a mistake—a terrible, awful mistake.

It was tomorrow's itinerary—for Date-A-Wolf contestants.

CHAPTER SEVEN

Daphne

At breakfast the next morning, I wasted no time tracking down the contest organizer, an attractive woman named Jada. She wore a floral print skirt and cowboy boots—a look I loved but not one I could pull off myself. She also had high cheekbones, a kind smile and a large day planner tucked under her arm.

"I'm afraid there's a problem," I said, pulling her aside.

"Why? What's wrong?" Her tone was genuine, but not overly concerned. Like a mother talking to a child who was upset because the seams on her socks were bothering her.

I glanced around to make sure no one was listening. "I'm human and didn't know about—" I gestured wildly "—any of this until I got to the island yesterday."

She frowned. "What do you mean?"

As I blurted it all out to her, Jada couldn't have looked more stunned than if I'd slapped her across the face with a wet fish.

She rifled through her planner, then poked her finger at one of the washi-tape adorned pages. "It says right here that you're a spirit medium."

It was my turn to be completely shell-shocked, and not just because this woman's planner pages were works of art. "A spirit medium? As in, I see dead people?"

She nodded apprehensively, a nervous smile creasing her face. "You do, don't you?"

I had no idea what she was talking about. "I've never seen a dead person. And I hope I never do. I'm just a regular, run-of-the-mill human, I'm afraid."

"Oh goodness. We've...uh...clearly made a mistake here." She apologized profusely and said something about their internet ad targeting. I could tell she really felt bad about the mix-up. "You're under no obligation to continue with the contest, Daphne. None."

I nodded with relief. The last thing I wanted was to be a part of some sort of weird paranormal dating ritual. I had barely come to terms with the fact that supernatural creatures actually existed. And that I was surrounded by them on this tropical island. Generally speaking, anything that involved me possibly getting killed was a hard stop in my book. I came here *not* to be killed.

"Is there any way I can ask you to go with the flow?" Jada asked, eyes pleading.

"*Go with the flow?*" As in, she didn't want me to quit?

"Just for tonight," she added, sensing correctly that I was about to tell her hell no. "Everything is set up for twelve contestants—all of our marketing materials, the staging, our graphics. I'll give you my personal guarantee you won't move forward in the contest after tonight."

I *knew* there had to be a catch to the whole you've-won-a-free-vacation business. I should've listened to my gut instinct that said I was being hoodwinked. I mean, come on. Who believes they can legit win stuff on the internet? But I guess I'd always dreamed of doing more. Being more. Filling out those quizzes and entering contests was a way of fooling myself that I was.

Jada spoke quickly. "You'll have a spa day today. Get your hair and makeup done. Then, after tonight's ceremony, you can go back and enjoy the rest of your vacation. On us, of course."

She made it sound so nice and normal. But she was probably some sort of supernatural creature herself. A shifter, perhaps, given the animal intensity of her eyes. Normal for her and normal for me clearly weren't in the same ballpark.

"Ceremony?" The word conjured up images of stone altars and witches dancing around a funeral pyre. "It doesn't...uh... involve things like sacrifices, bloodletting or evil incantations, does it?" Because that was where I drew the line between maybe-I'd-consider-it and fuck-no.

"No, no," Jada said hastily. "Nothing like that. Dark magic is strictly forbidden on the island. Have I mentioned that today you'll spend time in a gorgeous, award-winning spa right here in the hotel? It's made the top ten lists on a bunch of paranormal travel blogs—exotic oxygen facials, hot stone massages, paraffin pedicures, to name a few."

Given the cost of such treatments and my bank account balance, I rarely indulged in such pleasures. And I'd never even been to an actual day-spa, just strip-mall nail salons. I couldn't justify the expense. *Hmm.* Did they give you plush robes and green juice?

Maybe Jada was a witch, working a spell on me, or just really astute and knew what my hot buttons were, because I could feel myself caving.

No, this was madness! I couldn't participate in a dating contest with a supernatural creature. I *shouldn't* agree to this.

Jada was still talking. "Aromatic steam baths with locally sourced herbs and essential oils..."

Wait! What?

My head snapped up. *Locally sourced?* There were herbalists on the island? Did they grow their own plants in carefully tended gardens or forage for them out in the wild?

Taking a deep breath, I opened up the folded Date-A-Wolf itinerary again and noted how pretty the hand-written lettering was at the top. Had Jada done it herself, or had she bought the font online?

I rubbed my stiff shoulders, tense from—well, everything. I could actually really use a good massage.

Letting out the breath I knew I was holding, I said, "Well, okay, but I'm going to need something to wear."

CHAPTER EIGHT

Travis

"Stand up straight," Jada ordered as she adjusted my tie.

"I feel like a dog on a leash." I grumbled, trying to pull away from her, but had no luck. My sister was stronger than she looked, and if she made this thing any tighter, my head was going to pop off. "I don't see why we can't just postpone this. My knee hurts like hell, and I'm supposed to be on crutches for the next few days."

"You'll be fine." Jada examined me critically, brushing off a piece of non-existent lint from my lapel. "You're not an invalid. The women are here and ready to go. Unfortunately, we can't wait until it's a more convenient time for you."

I prickled with irritation. "This isn't about my convenience, Jada."

"The White Wolf Moon is—"

"I know when it is," I snapped. "That's all I've heard about since the reading of Dad's will—White Wolf Moon this, White Wolf Moon that. And the fact that it falls during Monsterval makes it even worse." If not for the popular island festival, most werewolf clans would celebrate the Moon on their own lands. But no, many would be coming here.

"Travis, listen," she said, her tone softening. "I've met the contestants. They're all very nice, and they're really looking forward to meeting you."

Great. I felt like a piece of meat. A prize everyone was vying for.

I hobbled to the mirror and loosened my tie a few inches, despite Jada's protests. It wasn't *her* neck being choked.

"I hope you know, the only reason I agreed to this contest was to save the ranch. As soon as I go through the official ceremony and sign over the ranch to you, I'm breaking off the fake engagement and flying back to Vancouver." The truth was, I didn't have the desire to be in any sort of relationship. Not now. Maybe never. They were too much work with too many expectations that I'd grow tired of trying to meet and eventually fail.

My sister looked at me in the mirror, eyes narrowing slightly. "What you do after you've signed the paperwork is your business. Just try not to break any hearts along the way, okay?"

Wasn't the whole point to get them to fall in love with me? Honestly, the whole dating contest idea was a ridiculous one. "Where did you find these women anyway? *1-800-I'm-Desperate?*"

Jada ignored the jab. "My IT guy created an extensive online questionnaire targeting single supernatural females. Thousands filled out the questionnaire, and we hand-selected the top twelve candidates."

Algorithmic and unromantic. Good. Love wasn't in the equation.

She explained how the evening would start with a meet and greet in the lounge, then some one-on-one time with each of the women on the veranda overlooking the pool. "That's to give you a chance to meet the contestants and get to know them a little better. Then, at the end of the night, you'll eliminate two of them by giving a charm to each of the ten women you want to advance to the next round."

I pinched the bridge of my nose, already feeling the beginnings of a headache forming behind my eyes. "What do they know about me? What have you told them?"

"Nothing, little brother," she answered, crooking up her neck at me. "They have no idea you're the star from *Secret Shadows*. Not yet, that is. They've seen no photos. All they know is that you're an eligible bachelor looking for that special someone."

I was somewhat relieved to hear that. No fame-seekers or gold-diggers, which was a real problem in my line of work. "And they willingly signed up for this madness?"

She cleared her throat and looked away. "Yep. They're all hoping to find their fated mate."

There she goes again with that fated mate bullshit. Such pairings were a romantic myth in our culture, but no one actually believed it.

"But I do have a request," she said with a smile that fell somewhere between wariness and guilt.

I eyed her suspiciously.

"One of the women has had...a change of heart. She no longer wants to participate. I told her I'd see to it that you wouldn't select her to move on."

"And what happens if the *bachelor* has a change of heart?"

My sister ignored me and continued. "I'll send her in last, so you'll know who she is. Then, at the charm ceremony, she'll be one of the two women you won't advance."

"Last contestant doesn't get picked. Got it." I snapped my fingers. "Okay, let's get this party started then. The sooner we do, the sooner it'll be over."

"For heaven's sake, Travis," Jade said, rolling her eyes. "It's not a root canal."

"Easy for you to say."

As I hobbled out of the door, someone from the hallway thrust a microphone and camera into my face.

"Fuck!" I pushed Jada back inside the hotel suite and slammed the door behind me, wrenching my knee again. At this rate, it would never heal. "What are the paparazzi doing here? How in the world did they find out about this?"

"Relax," she replied. "Those aren't paparazzi. They're my camera guys."

I glared at her. "Your guys? What the hell are you talking about, Jada?"

She gave me a sugary smile. "We're hoping to sell Date-A-Wolf to one of the paranormal networks when it's all over."

"*Date-A-Wolf?*" I sputtered. "Are you serious? You mean, like a reality TV dating show? You're going to televise this?"

"Who wouldn't want to watch their favorite actor from *Secret Shadows* find true love in paradise?"

I couldn't believe what was happening to me. At the hands of my own sister no less. "And you didn't think to inform me first?"

"Because I knew you'd say no, that's why." She opened the door again. "Sorry about that, fellas."

She flashed a grin at me over her shoulder. My older sister was having way too much fun with this, so I gave her my harshest scowl. If I were in my wolf form, I'd be flashing some serious fang.

"Oh, come on, Travis. Don't be such a grump. You have to admit—it's going to be great publicity for the island."

I closed my eyes for a moment, trying to rein in my anger. I should've known that Jada—the successful businesswoman that she was—would try to capitalize on every aspect of this insane contest. She was attracted to money-making ideas like a shark on chum.

"If you lose the ranch, I guess there's always reality TV

production," I grumbled as I reluctantly followed her down the hallway. I was only partially kidding.

"I'm not going to lose the ranch," she assured me. "The women are going to love you."

That was what I was afraid of.

CHAPTER NINE

Daphne

The Darkaway Island Resort Spa turned out to be much more beautiful than it was in the brochures. Not in a huge, opulent sort of way that would appeal to someone who was into flashy displays of wealth, but in a peaceful, luxurious way. I sat in front of my own lighted mirror along with eleven other women, while Portia made the final touches to my hair and makeup. She'd been thrilled when I called her to take her up on the offer to help.

While staring at my reflection, I had to stifle a yawn. I just had the best massage of my life, which made me want to curl into a ball and take a nap, but I also hadn't slept well last night. And not just because I'd been worried about this Date-A-Wolf business. George, who'd taken his standard spot on the pillow above my head, kept putting his paw with slightly retracted claws on my face as if to say, "Don't force me to scratch you." I really should look into all the cat-whisperer services the resort offered. Maybe he needed some therapy.

I was ashamed to admit, even to myself, that thoughts of

Travis had kept me awake as well. His incredibly protective nature even for a complete stranger. His nervousness in the hospital and how my presence had somehow made him feel better. It was charmingly sweet. If it was even possible to call a man that hot—*charmingly sweet.*

As I'd tossed and turned, I told myself to not let my thoughts go there. He was a supernatural creature and very much taken. But sometimes what you *should* think about and what you *actually* think about lived in very different places in your sleep-addled mind.

Sarah, the woman seated to my left, was a quiet, red-haired shifter of some sort. I wasn't sure if it was polite to ask what kind. Maybe paranormal creatures automatically just knew this about each other and asking would show my ignorance. Or maybe it wasn't something you asked someone. Not wanting to be rude, I kept my questions to myself.

She had luminous skin, green eyes and a narrow gap between her two front teeth. Given how many times she dropped something—her handbag, her phone, the rolled-up itinerary—I figured she was pretty nervous too. Which made me feel marginally better about my own anxiety that liked to hang out just below the surface. But being on my own for almost two years now had taught me I was stronger than my fears.

To my right was a gregarious half-vampire named Mia. Half because she was a daywalker, she'd explained to me enthusiastically when she introduced herself, clearly proud of that fact.

"My daddy is full-blooded and my mama is human."

Although I knew zilch about supernatural biology, I nodded as if I did. I didn't tell her that she was the second vampire I'd ever met. That I knew of anyway. It was weird to think that I could've run into other supernatural creatures back home without realizing what they were.

Mia turned around to examine every angle of her reflection in one of the full-length mirrors. She looked really pretty in that strapless, red cocktail dress. A bold move given how big her breasts were. No doubt, the bachelor would think she was smoking hot. I wondered if wolves panted while in their human forms.

"I hope there's food at this thing," Mia said, plopping down dramatically in her chair. "Because I'm *famished*."

I swallowed nervously, not sure how wise it was to be sitting next to a hungry vampire. But then, maybe half vampires didn't drink blood?

"The itinerary said drinks and heavy appetizers for a variety of dietary requirements," I told her.

What that meant for paranormal creatures, I had no idea. Instead, I recalled the nuns saying how everyone here was delightful and that crime against humans wasn't tolerated. I was fairly certain they weren't shitting me.

"Mr. Hotty McHotstuff better not get there right away," Mia said. "I hate eating in front of men."

I didn't have food hang-ups like Mia, but even if I did, I didn't give a hoot about making a good impression on the star of this show. I had no interest in dating a wolf—frankly, the idea was a little scary—so I wouldn't be going out of my way to impress him tonight. Kind of like sitting through a time-share presentation. I would go through the motions, then spend the rest of my vacation doing what *I* wanted to do.

Portia did my makeup with a variety of brushes she kept in a tool belt at her waist. Then she spent an agonizing amount of time on my hair, twisting strands around the barrel of a curling wand and spraying them. I'd never been able to achieve beachy waves like this myself. I liked the look, although it was too much work in my opinion.

"How long have you lived on Darkaway," I asked her as she painstakingly arranged a strand of my hair in the back.

"Born and raised," she replied. "I left for a few years, but I soon found my way back. The island—it kind of gets under your skin, you know? I couldn't imagine living and raising my kids anywhere else."

"There's no place like home," I said, but the sentiment rang hollow for me. I'd never felt attached to a place, so I couldn't relate. As a kid, we moved around a lot. And since breaking up with Gavin, I hadn't set down any real roots. I think I'd moved, like, three times.

"Ladies, are you ready?" Jada stood in the doorway, flanked by a cameraman and a woman holding a large, fuzzy mic. "It's almost showtime."

I steeled my shoulders that I was about to meet my second werewolf ever. Glancing around, I realized that some of the other women could be werewolves too.

There were a lot of excited yesses and murmurs of affirmation as we got to our feet and gathered around her.

Jada reached into a basket and gave each of us a small organza pouch. "Please put this bracelet on your left wrist. At the ceremony tonight, if you're selected by the bachelor to move on, he'll ask to put a charm on your bracelet. No matter how far you make it in the contest—" She gave me a pointed look "—you'll have a lovely token of your time here. The bracelet and all the charms have been handcrafted on the island by one of our talented artisans."

I wondered if Darkaway Island had many artists living here. And if so, did they have art walks or studio tours?

"She's talking about my friend," Portia whispered.

"Seriously?" I whispered back. "That's so cool."

Portia nodded. "Cassie was over the moon when Jada commissioned her to make the jewelry for Date-A-Wolf. But I wasn't surprised. She's very talented."

Inside the tiny bag was a delicate silver chain with one dangling charm. Portia helped me put it on.

"It's gorgeous." I twisted my wrist back and forth, watching how the light shimmered off the iridescent charm. It was stamped with the Darkaway Island palm tree logo. "Does your friend have a shop or studio on the island?" After tonight was over, I wouldn't mind getting a few more to add to this one. I'd always loved the sound of multiple charms jingling together on a bracelet. It reminded me that even little things had value and could bring you joy.

"Bobbles and Barrels. It's on Nightshade Avenue near the bakery. Follow your nose and they're right next door. She's a member of the local coven."

A witch made this. How cool, I thought, admiring the bracelet again and wondering if it was magical. I made a mental note to stop by her shop when I explored the town later. I loved supporting local craftspeople.

"Can you do mine too?" Mia held out her bracelet to Portia. She'd helped Sarah with hers, but Sarah couldn't return the favor because her hands were shaking too much. Which was weird. You'd think I'd be more nervous since she was a paranormal creature and this was *her* world.

"Sure. No problem." Portia opened the clasp and bent over Mia's wrist.

"Sooooo, any idea who the bachelor is?" Mia was trying to be casual but failing miserably. You could tell she desperately wanted to know.

Portia straightened. "I've heard a few rumors, but—" She mimicked locking her lips and throwing away the key.

As we filed out of the spa, she leaned close and whispered, "All I can say is that once you meet him, you may change your mind about staying in the contest." I'd told her earlier about my deal with Jada and that I'd be done after tonight.

"Fat chance," I said.

Portia smirked. "We'll see."

I tucked my bra strap back under my sleeveless blue dress

that I'd selected from one of the wardrobe racks. It wasn't a perfect fit, but it would do for tonight. I'd packed in hurry—I was running for my life, after all—so choosing the right lingerie to wear under formal attire hadn't crossed my mind.

The group stopped outside the doors of the Moonlight Lounge on the main floor of the hotel, and we listened as Jada spoke into her walkie talkie. "It's go-time here. Are you ready in there?"

"Ready when you are, boss," came the reply.

"That's my cue to hit the road, Jack," Portia said, giving me a gentle hug so as not to wreck my hair or makeup.

"Thanks for all your help," I said, returning her embrace.

"Good luck and have fun. You've got my number. Call me or stop by the salon and let me know how it went. I want to hear EV-REE-THING."

There wouldn't be much to tell, but I promised her anyway.

Jada clipped the device onto her belt and turned to face us. "Okay, ladies, we're going to do the first-meet one at a time so we can film each interaction. When I give the okay, you'll head through these doors, around the potted palm tree to the right and then straight back to the circle of lights." She paused, scanning the group with practiced calm, as if she'd done this dozens of times before. "We'll have a cameraman walking with you along the way and two others with our bachelor. Try not to look at the cameras. In fact, pretend you don't even see them. After you meet the bachelor, you'll go to the confession booth where you'll share your thoughts about him, how you're feeling, etcetera. Just thirty to forty seconds. No big deal. When you're done, head over to the bar area for food and drinks."

"It's so exciting that they're filming this," Mia whispered to Sarah and me. "I had no idea."

Yeah, real exciting, I thought dryly.

Sarah, on the other hand, looked like she was about to get sick.

"Had I known," Mia said, "I'd have had my teeth whitened."

"Had I known, I'd have told my family no," Sarah said with a humorless laugh.

Jada held up her hands to quiet the group down. "Ladies, we're going to put you in a certain order to go in. Lauren, you're first. Next up is Mia." Mia gave a little clap and took her place in line. Jada continued naming off everyone from a list on her clipboard. "Sarah, you're here, and then Daphne."

I was last in line. Just like she promised. Hopefully, the werewolf wasn't upset to learn I had no interest in dating him.

Ahead of us, Mia could hardly contain herself. She fidgeted and kept fussing with her hair and dress. When it was her turn to go, she burst through the doors, heels click-clacking on the tile floor, and a moment later, we could hear her squeal.

"Guess that's a good thing?" I murmured to Sarah.

"Yeah, I hope so," she replied.

The wait felt like *forever*. Every woman had to be talking to the bachelor for a long time. Were they confessing their deep, dark secrets and reciting the periodic table?

After a bit of small talk with Sarah about books—she was an avid romance reader like me—it was her turn to go. She glanced over her shoulder, reminding me of a deer caught in the headlights. It occurred to me that maybe she was a deer-shifter or some other prey animal. If so, I could see how meeting a wolf-shifter would be a little daunting.

I gave her a hug. "You're going to do great."

"I...I hope so," she said, hugging me back. "My family will kill me if I don't."

Okay, maybe not deer-shifters then. Her family sounded like actual monsters.

Now it was just me in the holding area alone. I mentally walked through what was going to happen. I would give the guy a curt smile and a business-like handshake that said I wasn't the least bit interested. No hugs. *Definitely no hugs.* I'd tell him it was nice to meet him, then I'd head for the confessional where they'd record my two cents. Easy peasy.

Hopefully, the whole thing would be over in time for me to attend the bonfire on the beach. According to a hand-lettered sandwich board in the hotel lobby, they hosted a big bonfire each night with hot chocolate and cocktails, a marimba band and fireworks.

Jada's walkie talkie crackled. "Okay, I'll send her in." She turned to me. "You ready, Daphne?"

I nodded.

"Listen," she said, that sheepish expression crossing her face again. "Since you're not continuing past tonight, don't be surprised if the bachelor doesn't talk to you much during the cocktail party. He'll be wanting to spend time with the other women to get to know them."

"Totally cool with me," I told her.

"Good." She looked relieved. "After you meet him, head to the bar and hang out with the others. The bachelor will start pulling a few of the contestants aside for one-on-ones on the veranda. Then we'll have the charm ceremony, and you'll be done."

"Perfect," I said, giving her dual a-okay signs, grateful the ordeal was almost over.

She took my hands in hers and gave me an earnest look. "You've been such a good sport, Daphne. I've got a tab at the hotel for you, so any resort activities you want to do while you're here, all your food and drink, it's on us. My family owns a dude ranch up-island, so if that's your sort of thing, let me know. And if you need anything during your stay here, you have my number."

Then the double doors opened in front of me. I flashed a jittery smile at the cameraman before remembering that I was supposed to ignore him.

The Moonlight Lounge turned out to be quite romantic in a

gothic sort of way. The place was dimly lit with tiny lights bobbing and twinkling overhead. Large, freestanding candelabras with dripping black candles stood amongst the marble columns and palms. Somewhere in the distance, a string quartet was playing a haunting rendition of a Coldplay song. Were they dressed in monster costumes like the pair near the ferry dock? It suddenly occurred to me that those guys on the street were probably the real deal.

It wasn't until I turned at the first potted palm that I realized the lights above me weren't twinkle lights at all, but actual little fairies flitting overhead. *Fairies!* No bigger than the palm of my hand with butterfly-like gossamer wings. Some of them blinked with clear light in time to the music, while others blinked blue, green and purple. Utterly mesmerized by how beautiful they were, I laughed with delight when one briefly alighted on my outstretched hand.

I hadn't realized I'd stopped in my tracks until the cameraman cleared his throat, breaking the spell.

Up ahead, I spotted the dark figure of a man silhouetted in front of blindingly bright lights.

The bachelor—the Date-A-Wolf bachelor. I swallowed nervously and hoped this was going to be quick.

And then the heel of my stupid, borrowed shoes caught on the uneven tile floor, and I nearly tripped.

Nice move, Grace!

Even though I was getting cut from the contest tonight, my falling in front of the leading man would definitely make the blooper reel. How embarrassing would that be? And a little hilarious, if I were being honest. But then my goal of not making an impression, even a bad one, would be toast.

I kept my head down and picked my way forward a little more carefully. I didn't want to watch the dude watching me. I'd probably trip again.

But at the sound of muted, yet angry voices, I looked up. The first thing I noticed was a pair of crutches leaning against a low wall. And then, standing in the circle of lights, surrounded by cameras was a tall, broad-shouldered man. A very *familiar* tall, broad-shouldered man.

Omg! Travis?

My jaw dropped and my mouth went dry.

Travis Monroe was the Date-A-Wolf bachelor.

My mind swirled with confusion. This had to be a mistake. Or a joke. Wasn't Travis engaged? Where was his fiancée? Did she *know* about this? Maybe Travis had an identical twin brother. But then, how do you explain the crutches? Werewolves weren't polyamorous, were they? No offense to the polyamorous community, but that wasn't really my thing.

Stepping into the circle with him, I tried to make light of the situation with an awkward little wave. "Hey, Travis."

He glared at me, arms crossed, brows pinched together over golden, very wolfish eyes. "What are you doing here, Daphne?"

I was taken aback at his grumpy response. *He* was ticked off? Because of…what? *Me?*

Anger prickled at the back of my neck, and I could feel my cheeks getting hot. He thought this was *my* fault? "I should be asking you the same thing," I snapped.

Travis opened his mouth to say something to me, then evidently changed his mind, because he turned abruptly and stepped out of the circle. "Cut the cameras, Jada. I want a word with you. In private."

I stood there, not knowing what to do. Was this some sort of joke? Was I being punked? If Ashton Kutcher popped out right now, I was seriously going to hurt someone.

"Why don't you head to the confessional," said the cameraman, interrupting my chaotic thoughts.

I managed to cobble something together for the cameras, then I proceeded to the bar, squeezed between Sarah and Mia, and ordered a mango margarita. At this point, I honestly didn't care about my proximity to a hungry vampire, although I assumed she'd eaten something by now. "Make it a double, please."

With a flick of his wrist, the bartender set a margarita down in front of me. He had a sweet smile despite the sinister-looking patch over his left eye. Holding the tiny umbrella to the side with a finger, I wasted no time taking a huge sip. It was strong, but very mango-y. Perfect.

Mia fanned herself with the happy hour menu. "I had no idea we were going to be dating Drake Valentino, did you? It literally felt like a stake to the heart when I saw him."

"*Drake Valentino?*" I was more confused than ever.

Mia looked at me as if she'd never seen me before. "Do *not* tell me you don't watch *Secret Shadows*."

"I...I'm afraid I don't." I wasn't sure if admitting that was breaking some sort of paranormal code. I chugged down another gulp of liquid courage and decided I didn't care. "Never heard of it."

"Girl, are you serious?" Mia held up her hands as if blocking herself from my ignorance. "I can't even!"

"I don't watch it either," Sarah admitted, clearly emboldened by my truthful admission of my cluelessness.

Mia looked equally disappointed in both of us. "Hello! *Secret Shadows* is only the hottest show on the Paranormal Network. Travis plays Drake Valentino, a sexy werewolf cowboy who is renovating an old hotel in Deception Harbor. He was an Army Ranger, stationed overseas and has all kinds of PSTDs now after being injured."

I bit my lip to keep from laughing. I didn't have the courage to tell her she'd mixed up the letters. At least I hoped she'd mixed up the letters. If not, that would be a show I wouldn't care to watch, no matter how hot the leading actor was.

She continued without taking a breath. "He was dating this

skanky ho for a while. She cheated on him left and right. I'm so glad he dumped her."

I wasn't sure where the line between Drake stopped and Travis started.

This explained everyone's reaction to him around town. Their hometown boy literally *was* a celebrity.

I took another sip of my drink. "Listen. I...uh...thought Travis was engaged. In real life."

"Engaged?" Mia raised an eyebrow. "Why would he be doing Date-A-Wolf then?"

Guess it meant werewolves didn't have a social structure involving multiple partners. I was mildly comforted by that. "I heard someone mention they'd read it in one of the tabloids."

Mia flicked her hand. "That's old news. He's single now."

So, the guy *was* engaged, but not anymore, and now he was dating in the most public manner possible. Okay, then. Who was I to question the dating habits of supernatural creatures?

I was about to ask Mia where the food was—I was starving—when a deep, masculine voice behind me stopped me in my tracks.

"Can I talk to you out on the veranda?"

I turned to find Travis right behind me, and I nearly knocked over my drink. He wore a light gray suit, a dress shirt open at the collar, and tan loafers without socks. The tailored jacket clung to his broad shoulders, barely caging his raw masculinity. I'd been too distracted earlier to notice these details, although I seemed to recall he'd been wearing a tie then. Damn, he was hot.

I stood up quickly, teetering on my borrowed heels. "Sure."

"I meant Mia," he said gruffly.

With a squeal, my fellow contestant jumped off her barstool, and he led her away without a backward glance.

I sat back down again, my cheeks flaming hot with

embarrassment. The asshole acted as if he and I had never met before.

He'd been nice in the hospital, sure. But he'd also been drugged.

I'd dated men who thought they were all that and a bag of chips. Having been engaged to one, I had neither the patience nor the desire to do that again. And given the fact he was a werewolf? Well, multiply that no by a hundred and one.

The next hour slogged by like a tortoise on Valium. Travis continued to pull other contestants away for tete-a-tetes on the veranda, including Sarah who'd been as nervous as I'd ever seen her. She returned a short time later, saying he was nice, but that she didn't think they had a love connection. Sarah seemed both relieved and worried about this, which I found somewhat perplexing.

"If you're disappointed about being sent home tonight, don't be," I said. "I plan to spend the rest of my time on the beach and —" I snapped my big mouth shut.

I hadn't told her I was here by mistake. My arrangement with Jada to stay on the island and finish out my vacation was probably unique to my situation. When the other contestants left the contest, they might really leave the island.

"That's not it," Sarah said. "Well, I mean, Travis seems like a nice enough guy, but I don't *like* him like him. I'm...I'm worried about how my family will react if I'm sent home."

She'd mentioned them earlier. "What does your family have to do with this?," I asked, narrowing my eyes. "What will they do?"

Sarah hesitated, staring at her hands as if trying to decide how much to share with me. "I come from a wolf clan with a long history of arranged marriages, but unfortunately, no suitors have shown an interest. My family saw this as the perfect opportunity to fix that. They're going to be very, very unhappy if this doesn't pan out."

My heart went out to her. Everyone should be able to decide who to love—or not love. No one's family should force them into doing something they didn't want to do. No wonder Sarah seemed so apprehensive about being here. I wasn't all that thrilled to be here either, but at least it was a combination of my own actions combined with poor internet targeting.

Surely there had to be a happy medium between families who forgot your last birthday and families who wanted to control you.

Finally, after what seemed like forever, it was time for the charm ceremony. *Good.* I couldn't wait to get back to my hotel room, change into shorts and flip-flops, then head down to the bonfire and chill out. Or maybe I'd just crawl into bed, read for a bit, and start my vacation fresh in the morning.

At Jada's direction, the twelve of us formed two semicircles under a vine-draped trellis. The sound of the ocean roared in the darkness just beyond the veranda while the hotel's bonfire crackled and burned like a funeral pyre out on the sand. Thankfully, I didn't spot any dancing witches.

With a heavy limp, Travis emerged from the shadows and took his place in front of us.

As if on cue, fireworks went off behind him, illuminating the beach and water in brilliant flashes of color. A few of the women, including myself, *oohed* and *ahhed.* It really was spectacular.

Travis cleared his throat and called the first woman forward. "Lauren, may I put this charm on your bracelet?"

"Oh, my goddess, yes!" Lauren rushed to him and held out her wrist. After he attached the charm, she gave him a hug and returned to the group.

Then he called Mia's name, and I literally thought her boobs were going to bounce clear out of her dress. Thankfully, they stayed put. "Mia, may I put this charm on your bracelet?"

"*Yes, yes, yes,*" she squealed. It sounded like she was having an orgasm. Unlikely, sure, but not impossible.

Travis continued calling women forward, including a very surprised Sarah, until the only ones without a charm were a cat-shifter named Lillian, an elf named Carmen, and yours truly.

Thank goodness it was almost over. My feet were killing me from standing around in these heels. On the way back to my room, I was going to check out the various beach cabanas and decide where I wanted to try getting a spot in the morning. I'd have to get there early. The good ones probably went fast.

Then Travis called out the last name. I started to turn toward Lillian to congratulate her until I realized it wasn't her name he'd called.

It was mine.

I was so shocked, I couldn't move, my feet were frozen to the floor. Someone literally had to push me forward.

I moved toward Travis haltingly, searching the darkness behind the camera lights for Jada. What was going on? She'd specifically said this wasn't going to happen.

His golden eyes sparkled in the moonlight as I stopped in front of him. I stood there searching his face for some sort of explanation, but all I got was a practiced, camera-ready smile.

"Daphne, will you accept this charm for your bracelet?"

I was so confused. And not because he'd slightly changed the wording of that catchphrase. "But I thought I was done tonight. I'm not supposed to be moving on," I whispered.

"There's been a change in plans," he said through gritted teeth.

"But Jada said—"

"I don't give a shit what my sister told you," he snapped, shooting a withering glare off camera to his right. "This is my decision and mine only. Not hers."

What the— Jada was his sister? His own sister created...*this*?

She groaned from the wings. "Travis, please. We're rolling."

"Then cut and edit the footage later," Travis replied. His expression softened when he turned back to me and held out the charm. "May I?"

I clasped my hands behind my back, moving the bracelet out of his reach.

Not so fast, buddy.

I wasn't about to let him off the hook and fawn at his feet. I didn't care that he was a fancy movie-star and always got his way.

"You were a real jerk back there at the first-meet. And you showed zero interest in me during the cocktail party, basically giving me the cold shoulder. You're bad boyfriend material, Travis, and I deserve better than that." I cringed inwardly at the word *boyfriend*, but this was Date-A-Wolf, and I wasn't about to pussyfoot around. "Why in the world would I want to date someone like you?"

I lifted my chin and steeled my spine, expecting him to react poorly. After all, no one likes to be called out for being bad at something. Particularly a man when you're talking about his dating prowess. They think they're hot shit and hate it when you point out they're not.

I was surprised when Travis threw his head back and howled with laughter.

"What? So, you're mocking me now?" I seethed. "Like this is some sort of game to you?" Which it was, but that was beside the point.

"Not at all. I'm sorry, Daphne," he said, wiping his eyes. "Really. You're absolutely correct."

He said it with such sincerity, but he was an actor, so I wasn't sure if I trusted that assessment. He couldn't *really* be agreeing that he was bad boyfriend material. Could he? It would be a strange admission for someone who was the prize in a dating contest.

Travis pulled me away from the cameras and prying eyes, which I really appreciated, then turned to face me on the other side of a nearby potted palm. "Listen, Daphne. You were the last person I expected to see paraded in front of me tonight. Especially after what happened at the hospital with you not being ITK."

That sounded like a personality test—INFP? ESTJ? I'd taken plenty of online quizzes, but that acronym didn't ring a bell. Why would he be bringing it up now? "ITK?"

"In The Know. A human who knows about the supernatural world and creature folk. I realized at the hospital that you were clueless."

I bristled. I didn't appreciate his word choice.

"I figured this was a mistake—or someone's idea of a joke. And to be perfectly honest, I wasn't sure how to handle the whole cocktail-and-mingling thing. It was so...awkward and confusing." He swallowed hard before continuing. "Jada said you wanted to go home, so I was trying to respect that and focus on getting to know the other women instead. But I shouldn't have flat-out ignored you. It was a dick move on my part."

I couldn't argue with that.

An angry glint flared in his eyes, and I was glad it wasn't directed at me. "I'm so pissed at my sister. None of this—" he spread his arms wide "—should have happened to you. It wasn't fair or right for her to put you in this situation."

We were in agreement there too. "Then why are you choosing me? Why not just let me go?"

"Let you go?" He frowned, as if the idea was preposterous to him. "Because I want you to stay."

One minute he couldn't stand that I was in the contest and

now he wanted me to continue? His sudden reversal was giving me a serious case of whiplash.

"I don't know how it works in your world, Travis, but in mine, dating is a two-way street. What if *I* don't want to stay?"

He looked taken aback. As if he couldn't fathom someone not wanting to date him—a hot-as-hell, famous celebrity, desired by women everywhere.

"Fair enough," he said, squaring his shoulders as if he thought I might punch him. "You're absolutely correct." Then he looked at me—*really* looked at me, as if peering through the shadows around my heart. "But I really wish you would."

I'd like to say that I weighed my options carefully, that I assessed the pros and cons with a calm and rational mind. Rewarding bad behavior was never a good thing. It ensured you'd get more of the same.

And the man was a werewolf, for heaven's sake. *A werewolf!*

But my mother would tell you I could be impulsive at times —that I didn't think things through from beginning to end. Too rash and hotheaded. Just like my father. She also referred to him as a monster on more than one occasion.

Despite all reason and my better judgment, I thrust out my wrist at him. "Okay. Fine. Give me the charm."

He tried to hide a smirk at the corner of his mouth, but it only accentuated his infuriatingly cute dimple. As he attached the charm to my bracelet, his fingers grazed the inside of my wrist, shooting electricity up my bare arms.

I ground my teeth together, doing my best to ignore the sensation.

This man was trouble. I'd be smart not to forget that.

CHAPTER TEN

Travis

I propped my boot on the lower rail of the fence, leaned on the top rail, and looked around my family's property. Darkaway Ranch was located a few hours outside of town, in the shadow of the Mystic Mountains. These lush acres of rolling pastures and forests had been in my family for generations.

Hell, if I was going to let a half-brother I just met have this place. My father's will was a sham, signed by a confused, angry old man. I wasn't about to stand by and let the chips fall as they may.

"Glad to see you're heeding my advice."

I nearly jumped out of my skin at the sound of my best friend's voice right beside me. Correction—*asshole* best friend. He loved doing sneaky vampire shit like this.

"What the fuck?" I glared at Alexander who was casually looking up at the crescent moon rising on the horizon.

"Getting plenty of moonlight is going to help that knee heal faster," he said, ignoring my biting tone. At the hospital, he'd described it like humans getting vitamin D from the sun.

I chuffed. "Ever thought of calling first before materializing —or whatever the fuck you call it—out of thin air?"

"It's called *fading*, but I didn't. I flew here." Alexander stretched out his arms, and his shoulders cracked. "Long day in the ER, so at nightfall when my shift was over, I decided to go flying. Thought I'd pop in and see how the contest was going."

The doctor came from a vampire lineage that could turn into bats, ravens and owls, but not all the undead had this special skill. Some could turn into wolves, others to smoke. And some couldn't shift their forms at all.

At the thought of shifting, I gripped the top rail tighter. I yearned to run through the woods, feel the earth beneath my paws, and howl at the moon. But Alexander had advised against changing into my wolf form for the next few days to give the injury time to heal. It was like seeing a cupcake on the kitchen counter after a workout. Knowing I shouldn't have something made me crave it even more.

"I should revoke your invitation," I growled to Alexander.

He grinned, flashing some fang. "That only works for buildings, my friend, not land."

"How's that coyote shifter pup doing?" I asked, changing the subject. "The one who was hit by the car." The boy had been on my mind ever since he was brought to the ER and rushed on a gurney past my room. Alexander was a talented doctor, but he couldn't perform miracles.

My friend's expression softened. "It was touch and go for a while, but he'll be fine. Looks like the family will be spending their vacation in the hospital, though, instead of on the beach."

A cheer went up from inside the main barn, and Alexander cocked his head in that direction. "Find the future Mrs. Monroe yet?"

I'd confided in him earlier about my father's will and Jada's ridiculous contest. He knew my goal wasn't to find an actual wife. Just a fake fiancée to satisfy the mating ceremony requirements, thus saving the ranch.

"Not yet."

My thoughts strayed to Daphne again. The bit of attitude she gave me at the charm ceremony had made my inner wolf perk up and want to play. I'd been a total dick to her, yet she held her own against me. I respected the fuck out of that.

"I'm glad you're going this route instead of hiring a Cupid," Alexander said. "I dated one once, and it didn't end well."

Just one? I stifled a laugh. I'd known him for a long time. The guy was a total fuck-boy and had probably dated dozens from that fairy lineage over the years.

"They're doing the first part of the Ranch Challenge now, which is supposed to show their aptitude for ranch life," I said with finger quotes. "Not that I plan to live here when this is all over, but that's irrelevant."

Alexander snorted. "And they call *me* a cold-hearted bastard."

I ignored the insult. "They formed teams, and each team member has to perform a certain ranch task. Right now, they're in the barn cleaning stalls and bucking hay. The team with the highest number of points is safe from elimination tonight and has a group date with me tomorrow night."

Alexander nodded his head approvingly. "Niiiice. Where are you taking them for that? The group fantasy suite? Going to have an orgie so you can assess their prowess in a group setting?"

"What I wouldn't give for a stake right now, and I'm not talking about the kind you can eat." Easy for him to joke about all of this—it wasn't his family's land and livelihood on the line.

We watched as the women, flanked by cameras, exited the main barn. They headed into the corral where four horses were saddled up and ready to go, one for each team.

I scanned the group and quickly found Daphne. Unlike the other contestants who'd clearly primped and prepped, which struck me as a little silly considering they knew they were coming to the ranch to work, she wore a pair of slim-fitting jeans tucked into old cowboy boots and had pulled her silky brown hair into a messy ponytail. She radiated a no BS attitude that said she wasn't trying to impress anyone.

Least of all me.

Beyond her initial shock at the hospital, she hadn't reacted to this new world in fear, but with a sense of awe and wonder. If the situation were reversed, I reckon I'd have gotten drunk off my ass and taken the first ferry back to the mainland, so props to her for sticking it out.

Her reaction to the fairy-sprites was charming as hell. I recalled the look on her face when one had landed on her finger. Having grown up on the island and now working on a show where almost everyone was some sort of magical creature, I didn't see my world the way she did. It was...interesting.

She'd looked stunning in that blue dress too. Then I imagined how she'd look beneath me, her loosened hair spread out on my pillow—

"Ladies," Jada's voice boomed through a bullhorn, jerking me away from my carnal thoughts.

Heaven's Moon, I had no business thinking of Daphne this way. I wasn't here for a love match. Or a fuck buddy.

"I see you've picked your horses," she said. "Have you chosen which teammate is going to ride?" She waited for the nods and affirmations. "Okay, then. Helmets on, butts in the saddles. I'm going to walk you through the next challenge. Come on, right this way. Chop-chop!"

"Your sister is a pint-sized combination of Jeff Probst, Chris Harrison and T.J. Lavin," Alexander remarked.

I nodded. "Except meaner and more demanding."

Mia had been chosen to ride from Daphne's team, and she sprang into the saddle like she'd done it a million times. But rather than watching her ride, I found myself watching Daphne instead.

Why was I so bewitched by this human—someone who had no place in my world?

She and Sarah were laughing about something. Actually, Daphne appeared to be acting out some sort of goofy story. I strained to hear her above the sounds of the horses and riders getting into position, but even with my wolf senses, I was too far away. I watched as she did a silly dance, pulsing her arm up and down.

What on earth was she doing? One of the other contestants shushed her, and the two of them clamped their hands over their mouths.

That was when Daphne caught my gaze and that fierce heat ignited in me again—a wild, primal surge that set my blood on fire. But to my surprise, she didn't seem to feel the same spark. Instead, the amusement in her expression instantly faded, and she inclined her head in acknowledgement, all business-like again. I nodded back, perplexed and frankly, a little disappointed. My attention normally got the opposite reaction from women.

She whispered something to Sarah, who looked over at me, eyes wide, cheeks bright red. Daphne elbowed her, and Sarah gave me a little wave.

Well, wasn't that interesting? Daphne wanted me to notice Sarah instead. Didn't she care I was noticing *her*?

Jada pointed to a series of obstacles set up in the arena. "One at a time, you'll ride your horse over the bridge, weave in and out of the poles, then go through that freestanding gate, closing it behind you. Then you'll gallop around the barrels at the far end of the arena. Fastest time from start to finish wins this part of the challenge. Any questions?"

Alexander let out a low whistle. I turned, assuming he was

ogling Mia and her shapely figure atop her horse, so I was annoyed to see him looking in Daphne's direction.

"Isn't that the human woman who was with you in the ER?" he asked, his gaze lingering a bit too long for my liking. "I didn't know she was a contestant."

"Neither did I," I replied. "Not until last night, that is." I explained how Daphne had come to the island thinking she'd won a singles trip then learned she was a contestant in a dating contest.

"And yet, she still agreed to take part," he said, nodding with respect. "She's sure handling it like a champ."

I agreed. "However, Jada's mad at *me* that Daphne is here today."

"Why?" Alexander asked, his brow knit in confusion. "That was *her* fault, not yours." Like a true friend, the guy had my back.

"You're fucking right, it is." I carefully flexed then rubbed my sore knee. "She promised Daphne she wouldn't advance in the contest. Told her if she participated in the first meet, she'd see to it that I wouldn't give her a charm, and her participation in Date-A-Wolf would be over."

"But you gave her a charm anyway," Alexander mused. "Way to show your sister who's boss. She can't tell you what to do."

I threw him a dark glance, not sure if he was mocking me or not.

He cleared his throat. "So...uh...are you sending her home tonight then? If her team doesn't win, of course."

There was something in his tone that I didn't like. Actually, *more* than a little something. "Why?" I asked warily.

"No reason." He gave what was supposed to be a nonchalant shrug, but I wasn't an idiot. Nothing about vampires was ever casual. They were far too calculating for that.

Arms crossed, I tapped the toe of my boot, waiting for the truth to come.

"She's really... attractive," Alexander said. My spine stiffened, and he continued. "If you were planning to send her packing, I thought maybe I'd go over there and say hi. Reintroduce myself."

My inner wolf roared to life, and I had to clench my fists to keep my fingers from turning into claws.

"Stay away from her," I growled. At this moment, I didn't give a shit that the guy was my best friend. He wasn't going out with Daphne.

"Down, boy," Alexander said, holding up his hands. "Possessive, much? If you're not giving her a charm, why do you care? It's not like I bite on the first date."

"I mean it," I said through gritted teeth, trying not to envision my soon-to-be-ex-best-friend sinking more than just his fangs into Daphne. "Stay the fuck away from her."

"Relax, Travis." Alexander had one of those beguilingly sweet tones that come naturally to vampires. "I guess that means you *are* giving Daphne a charm at the next ceremony."

"No, I'm not, but—"

A scream from the arena interrupted our conversation. We turned to see Kiana, an elemental witch from Paris, falling off her horse. She hit the ground at an awkward angle and grabbed her arm. We ducked through the fence and raced through the corral. Well, Alexander did. I hobbled as best as I could. He was in full doctor mode by the time I got there.

"I'm afraid it's broken," he told her after a quick examination. "We'll need to take you to the ER."

Kiana looked at me, tears in her eyes. "I am so sorry, Travis."

I was caught off guard at her reaction. Why was she apologizing to *me*? She was the one who was hurt.

"There's nothing for you to be sorry about," I assured her. "Alexander is a doctor and he'll—"

"You don't understand," she wailed then muttered something

in French. "I came here, hoping to find love. Now that...that is not going to happen."

Her hovering teammates tried to console her with gentle hugs and words of encouragement.

I stepped back, shocked at how much this contest meant to her. I wasn't expecting that reaction. Not at all. To be honest, I hadn't even thought about what the contest meant to any of them.

A pang of guilt twisted in my gut at that realization. Unlike me, each of these women came here with the genuine hope of finding love. Maybe not forever but certainly beyond the final charm ceremony. And here I was leading them on like a fucking douchebag, making them believe I was into this as much as they were.

Although I played a hero on TV, I was the villain in this story.

"Jada, I need to speak to you. Privately." Once we were out of earshot on the far side of the corral, I turned to my sister. "I can't do this."

I speared a hand through my hair and cast a longing glance toward the edge of the forest, wishing I could shift without risking my knee and go for a run. I needed to clear my head of this bullshit.

Jada frowned. "What do you mean? You want to quit? *Now?*"

"It's all fun and games until someone gets hurt," I told her. "And I'm not just talking broken bones. These women are legitimately hoping to fall in love with me, and that I'll love them back. I can't lead them on like this, only to drop the winner after the fake mating ceremony at the White Wolf Moon. Sure, I'm an asshole, Jada, but I'm not a total dick."

Jada leaned against the top rail of the corral. "I was afraid of that."

I eyed her suspiciously. "Afraid that I would suddenly get a conscience and couldn't go through with it?"

"You're a decent guy, so it doesn't surprise me." She tapped her lip with a forefinger and studied me with narrowed eyes. "Under what circumstances *would* you be okay with it?"

"Leading on a girl and making her believe I loved her?" I turned away from my sister and gazed up at the moon. "Jeez, sis. You really do think I'm a monster."

When she didn't reply right away, I turned back around to see her watching Mia over by the barn, taking a bunch of selfies from a variety of different angles.

"Did you know Mia recently changed her occupation on all her social media profiles from accounts payable specialist to social media influencer? And that Lauren sells online fitness videos?"

I gave her a terse look. "And your point is...?"

She cocked her head at a few of the other women. "Alice is a songwriter, trying to break into the music scene, and Samantha is documenting the renovation of her condo online, trying to get some brand deals."

"Okay," I said slowly.

I think I knew where she was going with this, but evidently, I wasn't catching on fast enough because Jada was staring at me with that trademarked exasperated expression of hers that I knew well. I'd seen it a lot from her over the years.

"What I'm *saying*, Travis, is that many of these women are not here to find love either. They're here for the exposure. And if the show sells to a network, their social cred will go way up. They'll get scores of new followers. Brands will want to work with them. People will check out what they're doing and buy what they're selling. They'll get free travel, clothes, makeup, sponsorships..."

I rubbed my jaw and let that sink in. So, in other words, if several of us were using the contest as a means to an end, what was the harm in that?

"Basically, they'd be using me as much as I'd be using them."

"Ding, ding, ding. Give that boy a gold star," Jada said.

The trouble was, where did Daphne fit in?

I looked back at the women just as Daphne was handing Kiana a tissue. She said something that got the woman to smile, then Kiana threw her good arm around Daphne's neck and kissed both of her cheeks.

Not only was this woman gorgeous, she was also kind, considerate, and had a tender place in her heart for others. Even when those *others* were part of a paranormal world that she'd only just learned about.

"She's not like them, Travis," Jada said quietly, following my gaze. At least we agreed on that. "And not just because she's human. Promise me you'll send her home the next chance you get."

CHAPTER ELEVEN

Travis

After Alexander and Kiana piled into a ranch vehicle and headed for the hospital, Jada considered canceling the riding competition altogether, but the contestants took a vote and wanted to continue tomorrow.

It wasn't a surprise to anyone that Mia had the winning time the next day. She navigated the course like an expert. Apparently, she'd grown up on a ranch in Texas and used to barrel race.

For the last part of the three-part challenge, we gathered near one of the bunkhouses. Four tables were set up in front of the smoker with identical sets of ingredients, utensils, and pans, including a portable burner.

"Ladies," Jada said, "in case you haven't guessed it, this challenge involves food. Barbeque, to be exact. The thing about Travis that you may or may not know is that he *loves* barbeque."

The women looked over at me for confirmation, and I nodded. "It's true. I love a good 'que."

"Chicken, ribs, brisket, salmon," Jada continued. "You name

it. If it can be grilled and Travis is in his human form, he'll eat it. In his wolf form, though, he prefers raw meat." She paused to give them a chance to laugh at her dumb joke, which a few of them did. "So, for this part of the challenge, you'll be making your own barbeque sauce from scratch. Those of you who did the earlier challenges can give input to your teammate, but the measuring, mixing and cooking will be done by her alone. The ribs are almost ready, so Travis will taste your sauces in a blind taste test and choose the winner. Remember, the team with the highest overall score from all three of the challenges will be safe from elimination and go on a group date with Travis tomorrow night."

Jada handed out several Darkaway Ranch aprons, a different color for each team.

Daphne and the others took their places behind the tables.

"Ladies, are you ready?"

They nodded.

"Okay, go!"

There was a flurry of activity as the women started grabbing ingredients and dumping them into pans and bowls, while their teammates shouted instructions.

"Start with the ketchup!"

"Ack! That's too much vinegar!"

"Turn on your portable burner!"

"Use more garlic! He's not a vampire."

Everyone went into a mixing and measuring frenzy. Everyone, that is, except Daphne.

Totally focused, she stood there and took stock of all the items in front of her. She picked up a bottle of something, chewed on her lip as she read the label, then carefully set it back down. Her teammates were yelling at her to get going, but Daphne seemed oblivious to them. She was in her own little world.

Intrigued, I kept watching as she sniffed a jar of spices and sprinkled a little on her hand. Taking a taste, she looked over at me, cocked her head and narrowed her eyes, as if she were trying to figure out if this flavor was something I would like. She did this with virtually every ingredient on her table. Unconventional, yes, but the way she picked up each bottle with her pinkie finger extended was so fucking adorable. And every time she looked at me, I felt the heat of her stare. Unable to keep my eyes off of her, I barely watched the others.

"*Come on*," Mia screamed. "*Get moving!*" I thought the woman was going to pop a blood vessel.

But Daphne clearly wasn't one to be rushed. When she finally started mixing the ingredients she'd assembled, she did it slowly and methodically. She put the pan on the burner, adjusted the heat, and took a taste. Then her eyes locked on mine again, a thoughtful expression on her face. She reached for a jar, hesitated, then grabbed another, sprinkling a little of whatever it was into the pan before stirring again. This went on a few more times—taste, adjust, stir—until finally, Jada was counting down from ten to one.

"*Time!*"

The women threw their hands in the air and stepped away from their tables.

Jada made a show of shooing me away so that she could arrange the sauces into a blind taste test. As I walked off with a cameraman trailing behind, I overheard Mia berating Daphne for not listening to her—something about the wrong ratio of ketchup to vinegar. I bristled at her caustic tone, but Daphne told the woman to zip it and held her ground.

Good girl. She wasn't about to let someone else second guess her. Not even a vampire.

While I was sequestered on the far side of the barn, one of the producers asked for my opinion about what made the perfect barbeque sauce so they could get it on camera. Honestly, I hadn't given it much thought. I just liked what I liked. So, I made up some bullshit about it having to be the perfect amount of tangy and sweet.

I returned to find a table covered in a red and white tablecloth, four plates of ribs slathered in sauce, each marked A, B, C and D.

"They all look delicious," I said as I sat in the hot seat. "How am I going to pick just one?"

The women laughed, some a little too exuberantly.

I tucked a napkin into my shirt and began sampling the ribs. They were fall-off-the-bone tender, thanks to the ranch's longtime cook, a bear shifter named Elvis Marsh.

"Elvis," I called to the old man standing behind the grill. "You've outdone yourself again."

He tipped his hat to me.

The barbeque sauces were all very different from each other. One was cloyingly sweet with a gritty texture, like the sugar hadn't completely dissolved. Another was too tangy, almost sour, with an overpowering vinegar flavor. The third? It was just plain odd. I couldn't place why...only that I didn't like the taste. Too many strange, competing flavors. This sauce was probably Daphne's.

Only one of them was a good combination of tangy, sweet and spicy. I took another bite. It was really delicious.

I filled out the form and handed it to Jada before I changed my mind. Part of me wanted to choose Daphne's sauce so that I wouldn't have to send her home tonight. Even though it was the right thing to do in the scheme of things, I still felt pretty shitty about it.

Jada looked at the form then shot me a withering glance.

"*What?*" I mouthed.

She gave her head a curt little shake then she held up the bullhorn. "The winner of the barbeque challenge *and* the overall Ranch Challenge is..."

When the show aired, this was the part where they'd cut to

clips of the women waiting nervously for the results as tense, dramatic music played in the background. The producers would draw it out, panning over each woman to catch every chewed lip and worried look on camera. Maybe they'd even go to a commercial break first.

The only one who didn't seem to be holding her breath was Daphne. She was licking her thumb, trying to clean off a splotch of barbeque sauce on her purple apron, as if that was her most pressing concern at the moment.

"...*the purple team!*" There were gasps and shrieks. "Congratulations, ladies. You're safe from elimination and will go on a group date with our bachelor tomorrow."

Daphne's head jerked up in surprise. "We won?"

Mia pulled her into a bear hug. "I knew you could do it."

"Good going, Travis," Jada muttered under her breath as I studied the winning plate of ribs again. *This* one was Daphne's? Given the unconventional way she'd made her sauce, I'd assumed the bizarre-tasting one was hers.

I'd geared myself up that I would be sending her home tonight, but now two other women would be leaving instead. The reality was she could be taking the place of someone who would've been my perfect temporary mate.

No wonder Jada was ticked off at me.

I glanced over to where Daphne stood with her teammates. Smashed against Mia's chest, she was smiling awkwardly and giving Sarah a high-five. The other teams gathered around the three women to congratulate them.

When the camera focused on me again, I gave a thumb's up, then took another bite...and another. These ribs really were delicious.

Although it made no sense, none whatsoever in the scheme of things, I was secretly relieved. This woman intrigued me on so many levels. And it wasn't just because her barbeque sauce was the shit.

No, I wasn't ready to say goodbye to Daphne yet. Even though a part of me knew I should.

CHAPTER TWELVE

Daphne

After we got back to the hotel, we had little time to change and meet back down at the Moonlight Lounge for the cocktail party and charm ceremony. Jada had us on a tight turnaround since yesterday's schedule had been cut short when Kiana got hurt.

"You know what the bad thing is about winning immunity?" Mia asked, adjusting her bodice.

"Not getting the chance to be eliminated?" I said, only half joking.

Although the Ranch Challenge had been a lot more fun than I'd been expecting, I just wanted the competition to be over. Dressing up and parading in front of cameras, vying for a man's attention, really wasn't my thing. As I'd prepared the barbeque sauce, the weight of Travis's gaze had been unsettling, but I refused to let it rattle my concentration.

Mia wrinkled up her nose as if she smelled something foul. "Very funny, Daphne. No, it's because Travis will be spending his time with the other girls to help him decide who to send home. That's what's wrong with it." She grabbed her phone. "Come on, ladies. Group selfie."

Sarah and I obliged and gathered around Mia. She took a few snaps, changing the angle of her phone each time, then proceeded to post her favorites to social media. It should've ticked me off she had cell coverage on the island and I didn't, but I was enjoying my digital detox. It made me feel insulated from whatever was happening back home.

"See? Look." Mia pointed.

I followed her gaze and saw Travis leading Samantha, a water nymph from Minnesota, to a cabana on the beach. Sheer fabric was draped over the canopy and billowed gently in the ocean breeze. A tray with two glasses of champagne sat in the middle of the mattress. It looked cozy—and *very* romantic. Well, except for the cameras.

Mia slumped in her chair. "That definitely won't be any of us in a windswept tête-à-tête tonight. Heavy sigh."

I bit back a laugh. I'd never met anyone who verbalized their visceral reactions.

Watching Travis and Samantha getting comfortable in the cabana, I felt a twinge of something in the middle of my chest. But it wasn't jealousy or envy. It was just that it looked really... comfortable. That's all. It would be nice to be sitting there, sipping on a glass of champagne and listening to the ocean surf.

With Travis.

No, no! Not with Travis. Just in general.

Sarah clinked the ice cubes in her drink. "How many contestants is he sending home tonight?"

Mia took a long sip of her Bloody Mario through a thick straw and held up two fingers. Hopefully, the drink was in name only.

Nodding, Sarah turned to me. "Where do you think we're going on our group date tomorrow?"

"I have no idea," I replied a little sheepishly. "To be honest, I kind of forgot about it."

"Why am I *not* surprised?" Mia wasn't even trying to hide her exasperated tone anymore. "I hope he's taking us on his private plane. He's a pilot, you know."

I didn't know where Mia got all her information, but she sure seemed well informed.

"If that's the case," I told them, "I won't be able to go."

"Why not?" Sarah sounded truly disappointed.

"I don't have a memory stone, so I can't cross through the island's charm." At her confused expression, I added, "I'm human, remember? I'm not a supernatural creature." I'd told them the truth yesterday at the Ranch Challenge. It was too draining to lie all the time.

"Well, I'm sure Jada has something else planned then," Sarah added with a kind smile.

Mia played with her straw. "What a shame. I'll have to suggest a plane ride when he takes me on a one-on-one. Because I, for one, would *love* to fly with him."

Sarah's eyes widened, the panic in her expression obvious. "He's taking *each* of us on one-on-one dates?"

"Not everyone." Mia deftly removed a stalk of celery from her glass using long, dagger-like nails. "Just the ones he wants to get to know better. Which is why I know he'll choose me."

While I appreciated confident women, I found this attitude of hers a tad much.

A short time later, Travis escorted Samantha back to the veranda then asked Lauren to accompany him. That cozy little cabana was sure seeing a lot of action.

Mia made a gagging sound. "I can't stand her. Barf."

"Who?" I wasn't sure which woman she was referring to.

She pointed to Lauren. "That." As if Lauren were a thing. "I *hate* her."

Hate was a pretty strong word for someone you just met. "Do you know her?" I asked.

"No, I don't *know* her," Mia said. "But I know *of* her. Let's just say, her family and my family go waaaaay back."

Sarah leaned over and whispered, "Lauren comes from a family of supernatural vampire hunters."

Mia's animosity toward the woman made a little more sense now.

"She said she's falling in love with Travis," Mia said, rolling her eyes again. "She's talked to him maybe ten minutes tops, so that's a crock of baloney."

Compared to Mia's fifteen minutes.

Mia crunched on her celery stick. "Besides, he's mine."

I wondered if all vampires were this possessive. It wouldn't surprise me, though. They certainly were in all the romance books I'd read.

"Anyone want anything?" I asked, rising from my seat. I wasn't comfortable with this conversation. Ragging on other women wasn't my thing. We needed to support each other, not tear each other down. Life was hard enough as it was without adding more to the drama pot. "I'm going to get a drink."

"Nothing for me, thanks," Sarah said.

Mia handed me her empty glass. "I'll take another Bloody Mario."

I held it gingerly and quickly deposited it on an empty tray on my way to the bar. I didn't want to inspect the red residue too closely in case it was the real deal.

At the bar, I heard footsteps coming up behind me and cringed. I turned, expecting to see the camera crew. They were interviewing the contestants to get our reactions before the charm ceremony, and they hadn't gotten to me yet. I was doing my best to avoid them.

Turned out, it wasn't the camera crew, but Travis. The crew followed a few steps behind.

My heart skipped a beat. Not because of Travis, though, I told myself. Being on camera wasn't my thing. I didn't like thinking about how I looked all the time and if a certain angle was unflattering. Lab coats, hair in a tight bun, and dorky safety glasses were more my style.

"Care to join me?" He held out a hand to me. "There's something I want to show you."

I took it tentatively. "Um. Yeah. Sure." I hadn't been expecting to spend any time with him this evening given what Mia had said.

His hand was very warm as it enveloped mine, and I couldn't help wondering if he had large paws while in his wolf form. I'd been wishing I'd brought a lightweight sweater—the breeze coming off the ocean was chilly tonight—but not anymore. I was plenty warm now.

Sarah smiled over at me and held up her crossed fingers as we passed them. I loved how supportive she was even though we were technically competing against each other for the same guy. Mia, on the other hand, looked pissed—and it probably wasn't because I'd forgotten her Bloody Mario.

When we got to the beach, I had some difficulty walking in the sand in these heels. Travis paused and crouched in front of me. I assumed he meant for me to use him as support so I could remove my shoes.

"Climb up," he said.

I blinked, wondering if I understood him correctly. "On your back?"

"Unless you'd prefer I shift into my wolf," he said teasingly. "Which, according to the doc, I'm not supposed to do yet, but I think I could manage."

The thought of seeing him as a wolf both terrified and exhilarated me. His human form I could handle all day and twice on Sundays. But his *wolf?* A shiver cascaded down my spine.

At my hesitation, he added, "Or I could throw you over my shoulder and show you what a brute I really am."

I gave a nervous laugh. Why did part of me get turned on by feral caveman shit? "Aren't we just going over to the cabana?"

Since it wasn't more than a dozen steps away, this seemed liked overkill. I hadn't seen him do that with anyone else. But then, maybe it was dramatics intended for the screen. He was an actor after all, and the cameras were literally right here.

"No. I'm taking you somewhere else."

I looked around. "Where?"

"You'll see." He made a clucking sound to hurry me up, like you do to a horse. Except that *he* was the horse, and he wanted me to ride him.

Keeping my mind out of the gutter and my ass covered (no one needed to see *that* moon), I held my skirt and climbed aboard.

"Good girl, now that's more like it." He hooked his arms under my legs, straightened to his full height, and took off down the beach at a good clip.

His knee must've been healing well, I thought, as I tried to ignore how his praise heated my insides and that the hottest part of me kept rubbing against him.

God, he smelled good. This time like fresh cut grass and sunshine. I had to keep myself from burying my nose in the nape of his neck and breathing him in. However, when he hopped over a narrow channel of water, my lips accidentally brushed his ear. I couldn't be sure, but it seemed as if his body vibrated beneath me like a tuning fork. Had he just *growled*?

It was surprising how intimate a piggyback ride from a very attractive man was.

Soon enough, we were no longer in front of the hotel, and the beach here was dotted with rocky sea stacks. Although it was pitch dark, you could see their imposing shadows rising from the sand.

Travis headed toward one of the largest ones and set me down next to it. "This is Fairy Rock."

I pulled off my heels and sank my bare feet into the cool sand. Cranking my head up, I estimated the sea stack's height to be 150 or 200 feet tall. "Why is it called that?"

"Come on. I'll show you." He grabbed my free hand and led me around to the backside of the rock where it was low enough to climb up. "Here. Put these on first." Travis reached into his pocket, unrolled an object and handed it to me.

They were two objects, actually. "What are these?"

"Rubber swim booties. The barnacles on the rocks can hurt. They help with traction too, so you won't slip."

"Well, well, aren't you a Boy Scout," I said. "Always prepared."

"I try," he said with a wry smile. He'd brought a pair for himself too.

After we slipped on our booties, Travis helped me onto the rock. We picked our way over the barnacle-covered lower section, careful to avoid the little tidepools scattered about the surface.

When we reached the ocean side, he paused. "You go first."

I stepped around him, and what I saw took my breath away.

Colorful tiny lights flitted in a cylindrical pattern from the base of the rock up to the star-strewn sky. Fairy-sprites. *Hundreds* of them. Like the ones at the Moonlight Lounge. So, this was why it was called Fairy Rock, I mused, as tingles of delight skittered along my skin.

"Oh my gosh, Travis, they're beautiful." I was vaguely aware that he was watching me and not the spectacular show of twinkling lights. He'd probably been to this place many times before. "Why are they here, flying like this?"

"You know how an eagle will find an updraft in the sky and just hang out for a while, circling higher and higher?"

"Mmm hmmm," I answered, not daring to take my eyes off

what I was seeing. If I blurred my eyes just slightly, the fairy lights formed continuous neon lines spiraling upward.

"At low tide in the evening, there's a thermal updraft here that the sprites enjoy playing in. We have them all over the island actually. I thought you might enjoy seeing this one."

"I...I love it," I said, my voice suddenly thick with emotion. I was overcome by how thoughtful this was. He'd actually noticed and remembered how entranced I was when I saw the little creatures for the first time at the Moonlight Lounge, and he wanted to show this to me.

The back of his hand brushed mine, then he shoved them in his pockets as if he wanted me to have this experience on my own. But he was the one who brought me here. It was a gift to me.

Hooking my arm in his, I leaned into his warmth and let his steadiness keep me balanced as I watched the magical twinkling lights above us. One of the fairy sprites came close to my face, and I laughed with delight. I may have toppled over if not for Travis's hand suddenly at my back, steadying me. With the sound of the surf crashing around us, I could've stood here beside him forever.

But then a voice cut through the darkness like a buzz saw. "Travis? Daphne? You up there?" It was one of the camera guys. "These rocks are really sharp."

Travis sighed and I stepped away from him.

"Guess they should've brought their rubbers," I whispered.

A laugh burst from his throat. "Coming," he called back to them, shooting me a devilish smile that made me snort with laughter.

I hated to leave, but everyone was waiting for us. Correction: everyone was waiting for *Travis*. I fidgeted with the charm bracelet around my wrist. I wasn't sure what time it was, but the ceremony had to be starting soon. Had our bachelor figured out who he was sending home? I had to admit, I was glad I was safe from elimination, that it wouldn't be me.

At least, not tonight.

Travis held my hand as we picked our way back over the barnacle-covered sea stack. It came as no surprise to see the lights and cameras rolling when he jumped onto the sand. He turned and reached to help me down, his large hands splayed around my waist. But when I landed, he didn't let go of me. Instead, he pulled my hands behind him, making the fronts of our bodies collide. He was all broad shoulders and big, strong muscles. And, if I wasn't mistaken, he was more than a little excited. Which I found pretty thrilling, to be honest.

I lifted my chin. "Thank you for bringing me here, Travis. That was such a thoughtful—"

Without warning, his mouth crashed over mine, my words lost on his lips. A hand tangled in my hair, another cupping my nape. It was one of those sexy, made-for-TV kisses that every girl dreams of. His tongue invaded my mouth as he kissed me deeper, and I think I moaned just a little.

Okay, so the theatrics were for the sake of the cameras, but I didn't care. I slid my arms around his neck anyway and arched into his sexy embrace.

Right now, I wasn't worried about whether or not kissing a werewolf was a good idea. Because in this moment, it definitely was.

CHAPTER THIRTEEN

Daphne

The morning sun rose over Midnight Beach and cast a warm, peachy glow through clouds stretched thin on the horizon. Above them, the sky transitioned to a brilliant, clear blue, promising a day of island fun. Despite its name, there was nothing dark or melancholy about this place.

Up early to stake a claim at one of the cabanas, I tossed down a towel and a copy of Paranormal Paradise to save my spot.

Our group date didn't start until nightfall—Jada wanted all the Date-A-Wolf activities to be as vampire-inclusive as possible, even though none of us tonight were light sensitive.

Which meant my daylight hours were free.

On the agenda: catch some rays, read, eat and repeat. Maybe a nap. *Ah, heaven.*

But first, I needed to run a few errands.

I consulted a map of the downtown that I'd grabbed from the hotel lobby. The illustrations inside were coloring-book style, which explained the basket of mini colored pencils that had been placed on the table with the maps. I'd just assumed the island golfers were into color-coding their score cards, so I didn't take one. On my next trip through the lobby, I'd have to grab a few. It would be fun to color in the map later.

I located the places I'd already been to as points of reference. Then I slung my beach bag over my shoulder, adjusted my sunnies and headed for the boardwalk.

At last night's charm ceremony, Travis sent home a vampire from Cleveland and a bear shifter from Missoula. Both had been pretty upset about it. He'd taken a fair amount of time walking each woman out and helping her into the waiting limo. Somberness hung over him like a dark cloud when he returned. Ignoring the champagne that Jada had poured for him to toast the remaining contestants on camera, he excused himself and bade us goodnight. His sister hadn't been too pleased about him leaving. Something about a missed photo-op.

If you'd have asked me earlier how I'd feel to still be part of the contest today, I'd have said disappointed...and probably a little apprehensive.

But that was before Travis had taken me to Fairy Rock.

Goosebumps prickled my skin as I recalled how the sprites had twinkled and frolicked upward in the night sky. It clearly hadn't been a scripted part of the show with the camera crew scrambling to keep up. Mia was right—Travis had ignored reality dating show standards to use his limited time with the women who were at risk of being sent home. Instead, he had spent it with me.

And then there was that kiss—that toe-curling, panty-melting, steal-my-soul-away kiss. Although I had to keep reminding myself it was all just for show and he wasn't actually the man for me, I couldn't help being drawn to him as if he were. Animal magnetism had a whole new meaning.

That kiss, though unscripted, would definitely make for

good ratings. But if I let myself believe it was anything other than that, I was a fool.

Even though it was still fairly early, a lot of folks were already out and about. I passed three women with toned arms and surfboards heading to the beach. Teenagers who weren't sleeping till noon were spreading out blankets next to the volleyball nets. Families with toddlers were building sandcastles, and those with older kids were flying kites. It wasn't until I was on the boardwalk that I realized most of them, if not all, had to be paranormal creatures of some kind.

Stepping around a watercolor artist and his easel, I nearly ran into a couple holding latte cups and the leashes of five little dogs. They were that breed you see in televised dog shows—the ones with dreads that make them look like happy-go-lucky mops. I'd never seen one in person though, not to mention five.

They didn't bark at me, just wagged their mop-tails. But when a sizable group of gray-haired cyclists cruised past, they barked up a storm at them, hopelessly tangling their leashes and spilling their owners' lattes.

I quickly learned that none of the roads in this strange little beach town were straight. They twisted and curved every which way, and many of them seemed to just dead-end and go nowhere. I was thankful I'd had the foresight to grab a map, although I don't know how helpful it was. There seemed to be subtle changes to it every time I looked.

I turned down what I thought was a side street, and the road opened up onto Nightshade Avenue, one of the town's main drags. Despite the ominous name, it had vintage street lights, brightly painted shop doors, and lush pots of hanging flowers everywhere you looked. The city gardener clearly had a green thumb.

Nothing about the island or its inhabitants was congruent. None of it made sense...and yet it all seemed to work.

A multitude of interesting shops lined both sides of the

cobblestone street. Dark Tarts sold questionably named hand pies from a walkup window where people were waiting in line to be served: Kill-Him-Tomorrow had a filling of pineapple and corpse berries; Teacher's Pet was made with lemon and crab apples; and Hide-the-Body was a chocolate cream. The young woman in line with glasses, yoga pants and a computer bag looked like a writer. She was probably getting a Dark-Night-of-the-Soul.

A little farther down was Atwater's Surf Shop. They sold beach wear and fishing licenses, rented beach equipment and, according to the posters in the window, offered various water excursions.

I paused in front of Island Candy, mesmerized by the taffy puller machine in the window stretching and folding long ropes of candy. If someone offered a meditation class where all you did was sit cross-legged and watch a machine pull taffy, I'd sign up in a hot minute. Especially if they gave you samples at the end.

I popped inside and bought a small bag of their Island Princess mix from an elegantly dressed woman with sleek gray hair and rainbow-colored irises. Given the Island Candy logo, I strongly suspected she was a unicorn. I had to do some meditative breathing to prevent myself from blurting out my childhood fantasy of wanting to own one of her kind as a pet. I doubt that would have gone over well.

On the other side of the street, just before a bend in the road, was an old-fashioned movie theater, its marquee advertising a noon showing of *Night of the Living Dead*. I shivered and hoped that some monsters were still fictional.

Midnight Garage and Nails turned out to be as strange and eclectic as I'd imagined. A scalloped black awning hung over the front entrance, and a wood placard with grungy pink script dangled underneath. As if you happened to be strolling down the street, saw the sign and decided, hey, I think I'm going to take my car in for servicing *and* get my nails done. The same scripted font was also prominently painted in the front window. It was designed to appeal to women…and men who weren't afraid of a little pink. I loved it immediately.

The garage doors were open, and two cars were up on the lifts. Noticeably absent were the sounds of power tools and noisy compressors, even though mechanics were busy working inside. It took me a moment to realize the garage must be charmed. A spell had been placed to filter out the loud noise. I smiled to myself. I was getting better at this.

As I reached for the handle, the door opened unexpectedly, and I nearly bumped into a mom and two girls coming out.

"So sorry," the woman said with a bright smile. She wore a beach coverup and those thin salon flip-flops you get when you forget to bring your own. The girls were in one-piece swimsuits and jelly sandals. "You know what it's like herding cats."

That made me think of George. I hoped he was having fun exploring the charmed area outside our little villa.

Wait. Cats?

I looked at the woman and her girls again. All three of them had unruly blonde hair that framed their faces. Lion-shifters, maybe? A split second later, I had my answer as the girls shifted into cubs right there on the cobblestones. One minute they were human, then *poof*, they were little lions with sparkly pink claws.

"Girls, stay close," their mother called.

I stood there for a moment, awestruck as I watched them go, and wondered what it would be like to see Travis turn into a wolf.

Inside, an impressive chandelier of gleaming chrome car parts and crystals hung from the ceiling, and the reception desk was made from the front half of a muscle car. To the left were several mani-pedi stations, and to the right was a large window looking into a tidy garage. The waiting area chairs on the salon side were upholstered in pink leather, while the ones on the garage side were black. Car and fashion magazines were stacked on the side tables.

The receptionist/service advisor behind the car-desk was a beefy, tatted-up guy with a fade cut and multiple piercings. If it weren't for the school-age girl sitting next to him painting his nails black, he'd look pretty gruff.

"How can I help ye?" he asked in an accented, pack-a-day voice. He didn't smell like cigarettes though, so maybe his smoking days were behind him.

"Dad!" the little girl scolded. "Hold still. You're going to make me mess this up."

"Sorry," he said, giving me a look of mock horror over the top of her head.

I bit back a smile and held up the boots. "Is Portia here? If not, can I leave these for her?"

Before he could answer, heels clicked on the tiles, and Portia rounded the corner. She wore stylishly ripped jeans, animal print stilettos and a fair amount of eye makeup. She was one hot mama. "Daphne! I thought that was you."

"Thanks for letting me borrow these," I said, handing her the boots.

Her eyes twinkled. "So…did they bring you good luck?"

Good luck?

Heat rose to my cheeks, and I threw a hard glare at the Tony Lamas. Had a spell been placed on the boots to get me to fall for Travis? Or to compel *him* to fall for me? Was that why he was suddenly so thoughtful and perceptive and had taken me to Fairy Rock? Pre-cowboy boots, he'd been rude and standoffish. Post-cowboy boots, he was a whole different animal.

"Why? Are they charmed?" It would also explain why I was wildly attracted to someone I shouldn't be. Someone I should be scared of. Someone who—

"O.M.G. no," Portia said vehemently, saying the letters not

the words. "They're just good old-fashioned cowboy boots. Promise."

I relaxed again, but only a little.

Was I really starting to have feelings for Travis? Actual romantic feelings?

No and no.

Okay, so maybe I was crushing on him. I mean, how could I not be? The man was unbelievably hot and could be really considerate.

He was also a werewolf.

Charmed boots or not, given my track record of falling for men who turned out to be trouble, I didn't trust my instincts. Not anymore. If anything, I was just a star-struck fan of a handsome celebrity.

A little voice in the back of my head annoyingly pointed out that I hadn't known he was a celebrity. I hadn't watched *Secret Shadows* before bingeing a few episodes in my room last night, so I couldn't be considered a fangirl of his work. I ignored it.

"Ah, look at the feckin' time," the receptionist exclaimed, jumping to his feet. I noticed he was wearing a kilt.

"Dad! Language."

"If ye miss the bus again," he told the girl, "yer ma will kill me." With his daughter and pink backpack in tow, he rushed out of the salon, calling something unintelligible over his shoulder as the door slammed.

I raised my brow quizzically and wondered if Portia understood that.

She shrugged. "Angus shares custody of his daughter with his ex and does this almost every day when he has her."

I looked around again. Pendant lights over the manicure stations were constructed from gears, vintage glass and filament bulbs.

"I love your place," I told her. "The colors. All the details. It's got a great vibe."

"I couldn't have done it without Viktor," she said, blowing a kiss toward the garage. "I just tell him what I want him to make, and he makes it."

I remembered seeing her with a handsome, burly guy on the ferry. "Your husband is very talented."

"He is. Very." The way she said this implied more than just his skill at repurposing car parts. "So…how did things go?"

I started to bite a hangnail then thought better of it considering where I was. "Well, I'm not leaving the contest, if that's what you're asking."

"Nice! And…?"

"And my team won the Ranch Challenge. We're going on a group date tonight."

"Yes!" She pumped her fist and did a little jig, clicking her heels on the tile. "I want to hear all the juicy Travis details."

Despite my protests that I didn't *have* any juicy details or want to get my nails done, she ushered me to a manicure station. She wouldn't make my nails too long, she assured me. Just tidier and less susceptible to biting. She tried to talk me into their signature colors, fuchsia with black tips, but I went with pale pink instead.

As she buffed, filed and polished, she made me rehash what had happened in the contest so far—who went home, who remained, who wore what, and who said what to whom.

When she was finished, I had to admit my nails looked a lot better.

"Are you sure I don't owe you anything?" I asked. "You've already done so much for me."

"Nope," Portia said. "My treat."

Just then, there was a loud crash from the garage followed by a slew of cursing. So much for the *silence charms*. I could see Portia's husband through the viewing window stomping around, a dark expression plastered on his face.

"Is...uh...everything all right in there?" I asked, glancing at Portia.

She didn't seem concerned. "Everything's fine. He's been a grouchy bear since coming out of hibernation and learning I wasn't pregnant." She gave me a sly grin. "Not for a lack of trying, however."

She already had two littles, I thought, remembering her young son and her baby on the ferry. My science-loving head filled with all sorts of questions about hibernation, gestation, and the mating habits of bear shifters, but I held them in check.

"Oh, I almost forgot. I have something for you." I started to reach into my beach bag, but Portia stopped me.

"You'll mess up your polish," she said. "I'll get it."

"It's at the bottom." I held out the bag to her. "A jar of lotion from my online apothecary shop. A little token to say thank you for all your help. I honestly don't know how I could've made it through these last few days without you. You've been a godsend." Although I hadn't made it specifically for her, I had a feeling she'd like the sage-mint scent, so I'd popped one into my bag from my stash at the hotel.

"Honestly, Daphne. You didn't need to—" Portia reached inside, then instantly whipped out her hand as if she'd been bitten by a sharp-fanged spider. "What. Is. That?"

"What is what?" I asked, confused.

Wide-eyed, she pointed to the bottom of my bag. "That... that book."

I'd completely forgotten I'd brought along the leather-bound tome. I figured I could page through it on the beach if I tired of my book or the copy of Paranormal Paradise I'd swiped from the lobby.

"It's from back home. I picked it up in my boss's office by accident. Ex-boss, actually. I probably don't have a job anymore. It's a long story—he's possibly a murderer. I tried giving it to the authorities, but when that didn't work, I..." My voice trailed off as I remembered how I hadn't been able to tell Scully and Mulder about the book. How I'd thrown up in front of them.

So how was I able to talk freely about it now? Was it because *I* hadn't told her myself? That she discovered it without me?

Portia's gaze bounced between me and my beach bag. "Is your ex-boss a dark wizard?"

"*What?*" I nearly choked.

"Your ex-boss. Is he a…a dark wizard?"

Images of Sauron, Voldemort, the Night King, and the Lord Ruler came to mind. *Fictional* dark wizards, but still fairly disturbing.

"He's a horrible man, yes, but I don't think Pharma-Douche is…is a wizard." But even as I said the words, I couldn't be so sure.

I knew now that paranormal creatures lived secretly in the outside world. Was it possible that Pharma-Douche was one of them? Was he a supernatural CEO? But he'd hit on me, and I'd rebuffed him. If he were a dark wizard, wouldn't he have cast a spell that made me say yes to his advances?

Portia scribbled something on the back of a business card and thrust it at me. Just an address. No name.

"Go here. They'll know what to do."

"Is this your friend Cassie?" I asked, recalling Portia telling me about her friend who made the Date-A-Wolf charms.

Portia looked horrified. "Cassie? Why on earth would you think that?"

"Didn't you tell me she's in one of the local covens?" I twisted my wrist and made the bracelet jingle.

She was quick to correct me. "No, no, not her. Cassie and her family don't…uh…do that sort of work."

Before I could ask what sort of work that was, she was ushering me out of the salon. A mix of worry and confusion churned in my stomach as Portia glanced nervously up and down the street.

"You didn't tell anyone you were coming here with...that, did you?"

I shook my head. "The one time I tried to tell someone about it, I puked. I don't really want to do that again."

"Okay, good."

I didn't know what was good about puking, but I didn't press further.

"That's some bad juju, Daphne. I can feel it, and I'm not even a witch."

CHAPTER FOURTEEN

Travis

I pressed the elevator button in the hospital lobby then checked my phone.

Nothing.

I was expecting to hear some news from my new attorney. Alexander had recommended her—said she was a real bulldog, which I could respect. Although I'd just retained the woman, her findings couldn't come fast enough. But then, patience wasn't exactly a virtue of mine.

Where was that blasted elevator anyway? I didn't have all day. I flexed my knee. *Maybe I should've taken the stairs.* I jabbed at the button several more times.

"Do you think that's going to help?" said a female voice behind me.

My inner wolf jolted to life, and I turned to find Daphne standing a few feet away.

She was gazing at me expectantly, a half smile on her lips. I blew out a long, slow breath, the air between us crackling with electricity. Heaven's Moon, she was a sight.

With a pair of cheap Darkaway Island sunglasses perched on her head, a beach bag slung over her shoulder, and a colorful sarong tied around her hips—still with the price tag on—she was far too imperfectly perfect for my own good. My baser instincts didn't see that as a problem whatsoever and gave a low growl.

Down, boy.

I was rarely at a loss for words—I was an actor, for gods' sake, and made a living saying them. But around Daphne, it seemed I had little more than a picture-book vocabulary. "Hey."

She jutted a chin at the elevator button. "Does the elevator say to itself, forget those people on four. There's a guy in the lobby who's in a real hurry."

I chuckled. "What brings you here?"

"Just checking on Kiana," she said. "I heard she had to have surgery."

I pressed my lips together and gave a solemn nod. "Yeah, I heard that too." Guilt tugged at my insides yet again for the part I played in her injury.

She glanced at my leg. "Are you here for a checkup? Is Carlisle, um, Dr. Lesauvage, looking at your knee?"

I shook my head. "No, I'm visiting Kiana too."

Her eyes widened with surprise. "You are?" Then an expression crossed her face that I couldn't read.

The elevator doors opened. I motioned her inside, but she hesitated.

"That's okay...I don't want to intrude." She clutched the strap of her beach bag with both hands. "I've got other errands to run and can just come back later."

Intrude? With Kiana? As in, she thought I had a thing for her and wanted to spend time with her? Alone? I needed to dispel that misconception before it took hold.

"Come," I demanded. "We'll see her together. I was planning to visit the coyote shifter boy too. Remember him?"

I held the door along with my breath, not wanting a chance meeting with Daphne to evaporate into nothing more than passing niceties.

The elevator gave an annoying buzz. In or out, it demanded.

"Okay," Daphne said after a moment and stepped inside.

A thrill of satisfaction coursed through me, and I pressed the button for Kiana's floor.

"He's the boy they brought into the ER when you were there, right?" she asked, repositioning her beach bag and giving me a spectacular view of her breasts.

"Yes." I flexed my hands as I thought about cupping those silky soft mounds and drawing first one nipple, then the other, into my mouth.

Eyebrows raised, she looked at me inquisitively. Had she said something? Fuck. Had she caught me gawking? I cleared my throat, dragging my mind out of the gutter. "What?"

"Did you meet his family?"

"Briefly. Since they're spending their vacation in the hospital, I thought a visit from Drake Valentino might cheer them up." I rubbed a hand on the back of my neck. "I know that must sound pretty egotistical."

"You're a celebrity," she said. "I get it. Never discount the value of something that brings joy to someone, Travis. Something that takes their mind off the pain, if only for a while. You know, like good genre fiction."

I raised an eyebrow. "A book?"

She squared her shoulders and stood a little taller as if she were readying herself for a fight. "You know—romance, horror, fantasy, science-fiction.... Oh sure, those books often get crapped on from high falutin' skeptics, but there's nothing better to whisk you away from reality than reading a page-turning novel."

She was obviously very passionate about the subject. As an actor in a supernatural soap opera, I could relate. I was used to getting dogged by so-called critics too. But I liked what I did and it made people happy, so fuck the naysayers.

"Let me get this straight," I said. "You're comparing me to a *book*?"

"Consider that a compliment." An impish smile played across her lips. "Although from what I gather, Drake Valentino is kind of an asshole."

I scoffed. "Depends on your perspective."

"He slept with someone while his fiancée was in a coma. That's pretty dickish, Travis."

Someone's been binge-watching Secret Shadows in her hotel room. I smirked, secretly thrilled that she was stalking Drake Valentino.

"Well, she did try to run him down with her car," I said. "That's how she got into the accident in the first place."

Daphne flipped her hair behind her shoulder, which made her sunglasses slide off her head. She gave a little yelp and caught them before they hit the floor. I couldn't help but smile —yet again—at her adorable awkwardness.

She put the sunglasses back on her head and scowled at me. "Sounds like he may have deserved it."

"True, but *technically he* didn't cheat on her until after she tried to kill him. Not to give away any spoilers, but he'd been pining for his best friend's little sister for a long time."

"Affairs of the heart can be just as devastating as physical ones." There was some venom in her voice, which made me wonder if she had some real-world experience with someone who cheated on her. Anger stirred inside me at the thought of anyone causing her pain.

When we got to Kiana's room, the woman was happy, if not a little surprised to see us. Other than calls from Jada and Sarah, she hadn't heard from any of the other contestants. Daphne offered to take a few pictures of me, Kiana and her mom, who had flown in as soon as she got the news about what had happened. I promised to check in with her again after her surgery.

Daphne acted as the photographer when we visited Elliott too, who was—I was glad to see—sitting up and talking. After signing a few autographs for his family and sharing some behind-the-scenes stuff about *Secret Shadows*, we said our goodbyes and left.

As soon as we stepped into the elevator again, Daphne burst out laughing. She'd clearly been holding it in.

"What's so funny?" I asked.

She grabbed the railing as if it might keep her from falling to the floor. "You know what you signed, don't you?"

I looked at her, confused. I'd signed so many things I honestly didn't remember.

Daphne wiped her eyes. "That plastic container Elliott's grandma gave to you."

"The water bottle?" The older woman had been looking around the room for something for me to sign and grabbed it from the windowsill next to Elliott's bed. To be honest, I'd signed stranger things than that, so I hadn't really thought much about it when she handed it to me.

"It wasn't a water bottle, Travis. It was—" She erupted in more fits of laughter. "It was a portable urinal."

"A *what*?!"

"You signed a freaking urinal!"

Now that I thought about it, the lid had been spout-shaped. With my wolf's keen nose, however, I'd have detected the smell of pee if it had been used before.

But that didn't stop me from raising my hands over my head like claws and pretending I was going to touch her with my urinal-infected fingers. She shrieked and spun out of my grip. I was just about to grab her when the elevator dinged. We stopped our childish antics as the doors opened onto the lobby filled with people.

Red-faced and out of breath, we rushed out, ignoring the stares.

Once outside, I turned to her on the sidewalk. Even though I'd be seeing her on the group date tonight, I wasn't ready to go our separate ways just yet. The chemistry between us was undeniable, and I wanted to spend more time with her. Just the two of us—away from the cameras and the contest. The calls to my agent and my lawyer could wait. "Let's go grab a bite to eat."

She fidgeted with her beach bag, shifting it to her other shoulder.

"Poe's Kitchen is a favorite among locals," I cajoled. "It's right around the corner."

"Edgar Allan Poe," she said under her breath. "Figures." She twisted her hands together, looking pretty conflicted.

It seemed like she wanted to say yes, and yet she was hesitating. Why?

Earlier, I'd have said it was the whole werewolf/human thing, but I knew that wasn't it. We'd kissed twice, and she didn't seem the least bit scared. Okay, so the first time, she technically was the one who kissed me, and it was before she knew about my true nature.

Could I be giving off scary-werewolf vibes and just not know it? I thought about Fairy Rock, the hospital visit, and her goofy elevator antics. No, I was certain she wasn't afraid of me.

"I...can't," she said, looking away. "I've...um...got some errands to run."

"No problem. We can run your errands together and then have lunch. There's plenty of time before nightfall."

"No," she said quickly, eyes widening, the playful spark in them gone. "You can't— I've got— No."

If this part were being filmed, this was where they'd add the screeching sound of brakes.

She pointed back to the hospital. "That was fun. You were

really good in there and made a lot of people happy. But I'll...
uh...see you tonight, okay?"

I was an alpha-male, not an alpha-hole, so I wasn't going to
press the matter further. Even though my inner wolf was
pushing me to "alpha-up" and *make* her do my bidding.

Before I could answer, she spun on her heel and left, the
price tag on her sarong flipping against her leg.

I stood there on the sidewalk, mouth agape, not entirely sure
of what had just happened.

For one thing, I had just been turned down for a date. That
sort of thing didn't happen often. Not to me.

Was she not attracted to me? Had I read her wrong? That
first night, she did say I was bad boyfriend material. Maybe she
still felt that way. But then why had she said yes at the charm
ceremony?

And later—when I'd kissed her at Fairy Rock—why had she
responded like she was as into it as I was?

I rubbed my neck and headed off in the opposite direction.

Or maybe... Was she hiding something? Did Daphne Dupree
have secrets of her own?

CHAPTER FIFTEEN

Daphne

As it turned out, our group date wasn't all that memorable. Since I knew we were going to be strolling through the carnival on the boardwalk, I wore a pair of breezy palazzo pants paired with a crocheted tank and flats. Sarah dressed sensibly as well with a cute patterned skirt that swirled around her knees, a graphic tee and tennis shoes. Mia, on the other hand, dressed to impress, with a body-hugging red dress and sky-high heels that made her look like a supermodel. Had she not realized we were going to be doing a lot of walking? I hoped she wouldn't get blisters.

After Travis and I had parted ways at the hospital earlier, I'd spent the rest of the afternoon trying, in vain, to find the address Portia had given me. But every time I thought I must be getting close to the place, I turned onto a street and realized it didn't match up with what the map was telling me.

Then it occurred to me it might be the map. When I'd confronted the hotel concierge about it, the blue-skinned woman with two tiny horns at her temples had told me it was because the address was in Wickedville and that the hotel's maps were family-friendly.

I'd been more than a little irritated at that. Portia's talk about dark wizards and bad juju had really shaken me up, and I wanted to get rid of the stupid book as soon as possible.

The concierge had told me it wouldn't do any good trying to go there during the day, anyway. Most of those shops were only open after dark. I'd have to go another time.

Now, with the camera crew in tow, Mia did everything she could to monopolize Travis's time. She hooked her arm in his and wouldn't let go, looking into his face with stars in her eyes, relegating Sarah and me to following along behind them like puppies.

Which gave me a prime view of his ass, though. God, the man was beautiful. From the front *and* from behind.

He wore the kind of trousers that were cut like jeans but not denim, a collared shirt that showcased his muscular chest and arms perfectly, and leather shoes with athletic-shoe soles. He could be both an actor in a popular TV show and a CEO in a boardroom. Or, if my ovaries had their way, a hot dad who'd be ready to jog after his small child on the boardwalk if he had to.

He was with Mia, though. Her child? I balled my hands into fists at the thought.

The Ferris wheel loomed up ahead, a colorful contrast against the inky-black sky and the darkness taking root inside me. Although it had gondola-like cars big enough to hold all of us, Mia pushed Travis on ahead of her and shut the door.

"Sorry, girls," she whispered to us through the grate. "With the camera crew, there's not enough room for all of us." When the car started moving, Mia called out disingenuously for it to stop, that two of us hadn't made it on yet. To Travis's credit, he spun around and asked the ride operator for help but was told the Ferris wheel couldn't go backward. So, we were stuck riding in the next car.

Despite all of our obvious differences, Sarah and I turned out to have a lot in common. We talked about books, our pets and our collective anxiety. Unlike my family, which wasn't involved much in my life, hers was all up in her business, having put some serious pressure on her to conform to their expectations. Surely, there had to be a happy medium when it came to one's relatives. She was supposed to get married and start having babies, but she wanted to adventure travel and wasn't sure she even wanted kids.

"If I can "land" Travis," she said with air-quotes, "I'll be redeemed in their eyes. So far, I've been a disappointment."

Fuck that, I wanted to tell her. But she'd been homeschooled and probably wouldn't appreciate any vulgarity. "What kind of adventure traveling do you want to do?"

"Anything to do with rocks," she said dreamily, a far-off look in her eye. "Rock-hounding, rock-climbing, spelunking."

"Spelunking? Did you know there are sea caves on the north end of the island?"

Sarah's head snapped up. "Are you shitting me? Here? On Darkaway?"

Guess she didn't mind a little vulgarity after all. "I read an article about it in Paranormal Paradise. You've got to time it just right with the high and low tides, but it looks amazing. They mine moonstones up there too. And there's good herb foraging. Maybe when we have some downtime, we can head up there and spend the day." Assuming I'd have dealt with the book by then.

Her eyes sparkled with excitement, and we fist-bumped. "Deal."

The group date didn't improve much after the Ferris wheel. When Travis won a stuffed animal at a target shooting game,

Mia plucked it from the attendant's hands, assuming Travis had won it for her. And when we stopped to listen to some Scottish street musicians, one of whom was the guy from Midnight Garage and Nails, Travis's gaze met mine expectantly. It seemed he was about to ask me to dance, but then Mia suddenly pulled him away. With the cameras rolling, the crowd clapped in time with the beat as they twirled around on the cobblestones.

It was really cute, really romantic. If you were into that sort of thing.

I don't think Sarah or I said more than a few words to Travis all night, although we both got charms at the ceremony. Because we were closet bitches, she and I secretly hoped he was sending Mia home—we were so over her—but alas, he bid adieu to Shannon and Cora instead.

"These reality dating shows need to have a villain," Sarah muttered to me as we stood on the vine-draped veranda when Mia's name was called. "I've heard it makes for better ratings."

Afterwards, Jada announced Travis had some business on the set of *Secret Shadows* and would be flying up to Vancouver. That meant all official Date-A-Wolf activities would be suspended the next day. She didn't seem at all happy about it.

Sarah turned to me, a hopeful look in her eyes. "Tomorrow?"

Although I didn't want to let my new friend down, that creepy book was really weighing on me. I needed to figure out what the heck was going on. Who knew when I'd get another chance like this? "Unfortunately, I've got some important errands I need to run."

From the way she slumped her shoulders, I could tell she'd been let down a lot and that she expected it. Which, to be honest, made me feel pretty shitty. I vowed to make it up to her.

"Another time then," she said, her gaze not meeting mine.

"On our next free day, I'm totally down for it." I'd never been spelunking and was truly excited to go.

She smiled, but I could tell she didn't quite believe me.

As I made my way back to my villa, I should've been relieved to have an unexpected day off from the contest, but I wasn't. Not exactly. I couldn't help thinking how it would've been fun to spend a little more time with Travis.

CHAPTER SIXTEEN

Daphne

In the morning, I headed to Unholy Grounds for an iced latte and a peanut butter cookie. I found a spot at a corner table and lazily worked on the Daily Epitaph's crossword puzzle as various supernatural creatures came in for their caffeine fixes. I could really get used to this chillaxing island life, considering what awaited me back home. But then, doesn't everyone on vacation wonder what it would be like to live in paradise? I sure hoped Scully and Mulder were making headway on the case because it's not like I could stay here forever.

I'd toyed with asking Sarah about spelunking—her hurt expression still weighed on me—but the caves were several hours away and I needed to go to Wickedville at nightfall. I didn't want a set time when I needed to get back since I couldn't exactly tell her why.

I ate the last bite of my cookie and tried not to think about Mia's one-on-one with Travis tomorrow when he returned to the island. She'd been beyond excited when she'd opened up that date card this morning. He was taking her flying in his private plane and then having a romantic picnic lunch somewhere. The nice part of me hoped they had a great time, but the mean part wished the plane was grounded, their bread was stale, the cheese was moldy, and their wine was corked.

I was definitely getting in touch with my dark side on Darkaway Island. Twirling my pen, I didn't want to admit, even to myself, that I might be developing feelings for Travis. Sure, the man was extraordinarily beautiful. And thoughtful. And so fucking funny, as I thought about him chasing me in the hospital elevator.

It'd be downright foolish to fall for him. I'd been a fool for love before, and I wasn't about to do it again. And that was with someone who lived in my world and *wasn't* a monster. At least, not in the literal sense.

With an exasperated sigh, I stared at 4-down. "Wolf-like" wasn't *Travis*, but without a working phone, I couldn't exactly google it.

"Do you happen to have any more jars of that special cream?" Sister Elenor asked, interrupting my dark thoughts and setting down a freshly baked cookie. I couldn't remember ordering another one, but I wasn't about to complain.

Yesterday, I'd noticed that she'd burned her hand pretty severely while making a batch of peanut butter cookies, so I'd given her a small jar.

"I'm afraid that was my only one," I told her. "You need more? Do you think it's helping?"

"I'll let you be the judge of that." She showed me her hands. The burns were completely gone.

A warm tingle of pride rushed through me. I loved that one of my concoctions had worked so well.

"One of the ladies in my book club said it helped with their arthritis," she continued. "And another said it helped with her asthma. They each want their own jar of what they're calling

Daphne's Miracle Cream. One of the gents even said it helped with his chafing." She put a hand to her mouth as if she were telling me a secret. "I didn't ask what was being chafed, however."

Arthritis, asthma, chafing? If I could speak to each of them individually, maybe I'd be able to tailor something better. But if my generic cream was doing the trick, that was even better. I told her I'd be happy to make more and asked where I could purchase supplies.

She gave me the names of a few farmers' market vendors who might be able to help. Unfortunately, the market was closed today, so I'd have to go another time.

At sundown, I successfully found the entrance to Wickedville—yay me—but the city was doing some road construction and it was completely blocked off.

"Sorry, you'll have to go around to the other entrance," one of the workers said as a dump truck with gravel rumbled by.

This was the only way I knew how to get here. Given what had happened the other day when I got lost, I didn't think I'd be able to find it.

I peered through the wrought-iron gate. "Can't I just go in through there?"

"Not until after midnight." Then the guy waved me off and barked some orders to his coworkers.

Dang it. I didn't want to come back that late.

With a heavy sigh, I shifted the beach bag to my other shoulder, trudged back to my hotel, and vowed to return tomorrow.

After all, I had another free day. I could still hear Mia squealing when she opened up that date card.

CHAPTER SEVENTEEN

Travis

After shooting some *Secret Shadows* promo up in Vancouver yesterday, I'd been hit with a huge bombshell in my attorney's office. Not only had she found a loophole in the will, allowing me to be named Alpha at the White Wolf Moon with or without being mated, but she said there was a high-probability one of the contestants was a mole, put in place by a rival clan to undermine my family's stake on the island.

"There are several wolf shifters," I'd told her, thinking of Sarah and Alice. "But they're from mainland packs, with no claim to the island."

My attorney shook her head thoughtfully as only a psychic could. "To be honest, it could be any of them. A vampire, for instance, could just as easily be swayed by money as anyone else."

Money.

The Crutchfields had to be behind it. Their pack ran a seedy casino in Wickedville and had always wanted to expand their territory. A schism in the Darkaway Island pack could do just that.

When I'd shared this news with Jada and told her we could cancel the contest, that it wasn't necessary anymore, she insisted we continue. She'd had some real interest from the networks and didn't want to stop now. I figured she'd refuse, but it was worth a try.

I didn't know who the mole was, but I was hellbent on finding out. If the Crutchfields wanted to play games, then *game on*.

Now, as I banked the aircraft around the south side of the island, Mia sat in the passenger seat and yammered on about a *Secret Shadows* plot line. I turned down the volume of my headphones.

If only Daphne were with me on this one-on-one. Her excitement would be real. Not some fake bullshit. But I couldn't risk letting her fly; piercing the island's veil of charm might cause irreparable harm to her memories of the island. And of me.

"Hey," Mia shouted, waving her hands to get my attention, and I surreptitiously turned the volume of my headphones back up.

"That looks like a volcano," she said, pointing inland to Mystic Mountain.

"That's because it is," I said woodenly. "It's dormant. Hasn't erupted in centuries." I should try to be more conversational, but I just didn't have it in me.

"Well, it better not erupt while I'm here." Mia huffed. "Volcanoes and earthquakes terrify me. That's why I live in Texas. Although I'll have to get over my earthquake fear because I'm planning to move to California when this is over. You live there, don't you? I mean, when you're not filming *Secret Shadows* in Vancouver."

I grunted a *yes* and wondered which tabloid she'd been

reading. It was true that I owned a condo in LA and split my time between there and Vancouver. Darkaway Island *should* have been where I stayed while the show was on hiatus—it was just a short plane ride away—but it hadn't felt like home in a long time.

Damn. I needed to shake this foul mood.

Maybe Mia would like to see Mermaid Cove. I banked the plane and soon we were flying over the white cliffs and emerald green water of the cove. I expected to get some sort of reaction from her, but all she seemed to care about was taking selfies and asking about my co-stars.

I rubbed my temples and let out a low sigh. If Daphne had come instead, I'd have landed in the cove and we would've eaten the fancy lunch my sister packed for us down there on the water. But I just didn't have it in me with Mia.

According to Jada, the rest of the contestants were having a free day.

What was Daphne doing with her spare time today? What had she done yesterday while I was up in Vancouver? Had she explored the shops and everything Darkaway had to offer? Was she having fun on the boardwalk...without me?

I decided to wrap things up early with Mia then go find Daphne.

Was she was sitting on the beach right now, wearing a tiny bikini? One that would be easy for me to slip a finger under. I'd pull the cabana curtains closed and—

I shifted in the pilot's seat, not wanting Mia to notice my sudden erection and think it had anything to do with her.

CHAPTER EIGHTEEN

Daphne

George and I had slept late. So, after a light lunch, I headed to downtown Darkaway to kill time before nightfall. I'd browsed through the shops, and bought some cute earrings and another bag of saltwater taffy.

Last thing I wanted was to be on the beach, hear a seaplane, then look up and wonder if it was Travis and Mia. No. I didn't want to subject myself to that kind of negativity. I had enough on my plate already.

Now, as I passed under the wrought-iron sign to Wickedville with the tagline *Enter at Your Own Peril*, I felt the temperature drop significantly. Another thing I noticed, other than my goosebumps, was that the cobblestone streets were narrower here, the buildings much older and seedier than in the other part of town.

A gloomy mist swirled in alleyways and dark corners. Streetlights, the ones that were actually working, did little in the way of exterior illumination. I was glad I didn't have far to go.

At the clip-clop sound of hooves, I looked over to see a

carriage being pulled by two enormous black horses. It stopped in front of a pub adorned with stone gargoyles. From this angle, I couldn't see who—or what—was getting out.

This had better be worth it, because this entire place was giving me the creeps. Before I could change my mind, I set off for Nightmare Alley, which was supposed to be a few blocks down on the left. I'd waited long enough to get some answers about this stupid, mysterious book.

I passed a junk dealer, a pawnshop, a bail bondsman, and a shabby haberdashery that sold "capes and canes for the distinguished vampire gentleman." It felt as if I'd stepped into another time and place. An eerie version of London at the turn of the last century, perhaps.

The back of my neck prickled a few times, and not just when I passed a shop that sold coffins. I glanced around but saw nothing out of the ordinary—if *ordinary* included people wearing robes and/or capes, a lion, two panthers, and several dogs that probably weren't actual dogs.

Sudden movement over my shoulder drew my attention. I turned to see a dark figure darting into a nearby doorway. Another chill raced up my spine. Was someone following me?

I hugged my beach bag tight to my body and quickened my pace, wishing for a parka and a can of pepper spray. Although I didn't know if the latter would do any good warding off monsters if one happened to be following me.

Up ahead, I spotted a post with crooked signs pointing in various directions: Transylvania (6150 miles), Tower of London (4920 miles) and Nightmare Alley (10 steps).

I proceeded with caution into the narrow alleyway.

Music pulsed from an open door where a couple was locked in a romantic embrace. *Wait.* That was no kiss, I realized with a shiver, noting the curve of a woman's neck. Must be a crimson club. I tried not to stare and forced myself to keep going.

I didn't get more than a few feet when a figure stepped out of the shadows and blocked me.

"Well, hello there." Despite the high-pitched voice, he was a rather large-girthed man with bleached blond hair, shifty eyes, and a red-lined cape that drug on the ground. Though I didn't know much about vampire fashion, it seemed a bit long for him. He could easily trip over that thing.

I swallowed nervously, clinging to the hope that what the Sisters had told me about paranormal-on-human crime was accurate. That it didn't happen often.

Reaching into my beach bag for something I could use to defend myself, I tried not to make eye contact with the vampire and stepped out of his way. However, the man moved with me and wouldn't let me pass.

He lifted his chin and sniffed the air. "You're a virgin, am I right?"

"*Excuse me?*" Anger coursed through my veins like a flash flood. I took a step forward and jabbed him with my room key right in his flabby chest. "Who do you think you are, talking to me like that?"

Stumbling backward, the man cried out in pain, which gave me a smug sense of satisfaction.

"You staked me!"

He was being overly dramatic. My room key was still lodged between my knuckles. But I wasn't about to argue with an outraged vampire.

Before I could turn on my heels and get the heck out of Dodge, a large animal brushed past me and knocked the man to the ground. A huge dire wolf, bigger than the ones I'd seen at the ferry, stood on the man's chest and snarled. His silver fur glistened in the pale light, as did his razor-sharp fangs that were inches from the guy's neck.

"Hey, you two," said a stern female voice. "Break it up." Her tone had the casual authority of someone who saw a lot of bullshit and wasn't about to put up with more.

Saliva dripping from his fangs, the dire wolf didn't move and was still poised to rip out the guy's throat. I covered my eyes because I didn't want to see any carnage, but I peered through my fingers because I was genuinely curious about what was going to happen.

"You." The no-nonsense voice belonged to a middle-aged woman with a septum piercing who stepped into view and pointed at the vampire. "I'll call your Maker. And you." She pointed to the wolf. "I'll call your Alpha."

Much to my utter shock, the dire wolf morphed before my eyes into a furious Travis.

While I stood there, questioning all of my life choices that had led me to this, he yanked the vampire to his feet and shoved him against the brick wall. "You stay the fuck away from her."

Travis in his human form was just as deadly as his wolf.

"I didn't do anything," the guy whined, his voice a bit higher pitched than it had been a moment ago. "I swear."

"I heard what you said, you piece of shit."

The vampire laughed nervously. "I can tell she's never been bitten. Didn't see any harm in pointing that out."

Travis bared his human teeth, and I swear, they still looked canine.

"Okay, that's enough, you two," said another authoritative voice. This time, a burly, bald man in a sheriff's uniform strode toward us. After a brief word with Travis, the sheriff hauled the vampire away.

Travis brushed off his clothes and stalked toward me, the golden glow of his wolf-eyes both enrapturing and extremely menacing.

"W-what just happened?" I asked.

He ran a hand through his messy hair and glowered down at

me. "You almost became a snack for a hungry vampire, that's what happened."

I didn't mean *that*. What I meant was I couldn't believe I had just seen him change from his werewolf form into his human form. One minute he was a wolf, and then *poof*, just like that, he morphed back into a human. Fully clothed. Not at all like the gruesome transformations in pretty much every werewolf movie I'd ever seen.

This was...almost *magical*.

"What are you doing skulking around Wickedville, Daphne?" Travis's tone was entirely too accusatory.

"*Skulking?*" The warm and fuzzy thoughts I had about him rescuing me from that sleazy vampire evaporated. "For your information, it's none of your business what I'm doing here."

He closed his eyes for a moment, and when he opened them, the yellow was gone. "In case you hadn't noticed, this isn't the best part of town."

Okay, he had me there. But *skulking?*

I chewed my lower lip. I really wanted to tell him what brought me here, but as I clutched my beach bag, heavy with the spell book inside, bile rose in the back of my throat.

Although I didn't want to lie, I couldn't tell him the truth either. The last thing I wanted was to get sick in front of Travis. Our relationship wasn't exactly at the hold-my-hair-out-of-my-face-so-I-don't-barf-on-it stage. Surprising how intimate a little vomit could be.

CHAPTER NINETEEN

Travis

"I need you to be a real jerk right now."

"That's an odd request." I frowned at Daphne over the rim of my IPA. She was looking back at me rather intently. I couldn't imagine why she was asking this, or what she wanted me to do.

After her close encounter with the vampire, we came to Rover's Shed, an unmarked speakeasy around the corner from Nightmare Alley. You had to know the special knock to get in. Although it had been years since I'd been here, I was glad I still remembered it.

I took another large swig and wiped the foam from my mouth with the back of my hand. I needed to tread lightly here. If she learned I'd been tailing her through Wickedville—*and why* —she'd know just what kind of asshole I could be.

I cared about what she thought of me. *Stupid, I know.* But I didn't want her to think I was an asshole. Even though I was a giant one.

She truly didn't seem In-The-Know when she got to the

island, but maybe I was wrong. Jada had blamed bad internet targeting, but was it possible that Daphne, or someone she was in cahoots with, gamed the system in order to get her into the contest?

I didn't want to believe she was the mole, but I hadn't forgotten how strangely she'd acted outside the hospital, either. Her nervous smile. Her sudden inability to meet my gaze. I doubted it was because she didn't want to have lunch with me. Paired with what I'd learned from my attorney, it was obvious she was hiding something. And I was determined to find out what.

Daphne plopped her beach bag on the table with a *thunk* and shoved it at me, almost knocking over my pint. "Ask me again why I came to Wickedville."

Her eyes blazed with fiery determination as she focused all of her attention on me. My cock thickened in response. I may not understand her, but fuck, the woman unleashed something wicked in me.

"Okay," I said slowly, playing along with whatever this was. "Why did you come to Wickedville, Daphne?"

"I can't tell you that." Clutching the fabric of her beach bag right over the printed slogan *Finding My True Nature On Darkaway Island,* she jerked it forcefully off the table. "You're an actor. I need you to act like a major jerk, okay? What do you really want to do right now?"

Bend you over this table and—

I needed to get a grip and muzzle my inner wolf better. He'd been much more aggressive lately.

"Come on, Travis," she said, completely oblivious to my feral thoughts. "Think. WWDVD. What would Drake Valentino do?"

He'd want to fuck you too.

Heaven's Moon! I gritted my teeth and vowed to call the pack together for a group run as soon as possible. This was ridiculous. My knee was healed enough. My ability to shift with no adverse consequences had proven that.

She shoved her bag at me again, and this time it *did* knock over my pint.

Swearing loudly, I sprang to my feet, but not before beer poured onto my lap. I grabbed her bag so it wouldn't get soaked too.

Damn, it was heavy. Much heavier than I'd been expecting. For a moment, I forgot about my wet crotch. "What the hell is in this thing?"

"I'm not telling you anything, Drake. Give it to me." She had an oddly expectant look on her face as she reached for the bag but didn't quite touch it.

Drake? What was she—? And then I got it. Or at least, I think I did. She wanted me to do what Drake Valentino would do.

I gave her a crooked smile. "Oh no, you don't, darlin'." I jerked it out of her reach. "What do we have here?" I stuck my hand inside and pulled out...an ancient leather-bound book with a rusty metal clasp.

Daphne gave a little fist pump. "Yes!"

I prided myself on being fairly intuitive when it came to women. Daphne, however, wasn't like most women. "Why are you hauling this thing around? It's got to weigh almost ten pounds."

"I was waiting for you to do that."

"If you wanted to show me, why didn't you just tell me? Why all the games?" I felt like I was auditioning for a top-secret part knowing nothing about the show or the role.

She lowered her voice. "Because I didn't want to barf on you."

I raised a brow, more confused than ever. She certainly didn't look sick.

"Sit back down." She snapped her fingers at me, and I felt my mouth quirk. No one had ever snapped their fingers at me. I doubt I'd tolerate it from anyone other than her. "I have something I can tell you now."

Taking a seat on her side of the banquette since my side was wet, I dabbed at my crotch with a few napkins.

Her hands shook as she told me how she'd picked up the strange book in her ex-boss' office by mistake, how her supervisor had been killed, and how she'd gotten sick whenever she tried to tell someone about the book.

I wrapped an arm around her and pulled her close, my protective nature rising to the surface again. "To think I'd assumed that being an unwitting Date-A-Wolf contestant and learning that the world is filled with supernatural creatures were the most stressful things you'd experienced lately."

She nestled in closer, and I tucked her head under my chin. I'd have pulled her onto my lap if not for my wet crotch.

"I actually feel pretty safe here," she murmured.

I hoped *here* meant 'here with me' and not just 'on the island.'

"What *were* you doing in Wickedville, Daphne?" I asked, breathing in her scent and acutely aware of my erection straining at the seams. Maybe it was good I didn't have her on my lap after all. I'd be liable to take her right here in public.

"I was trying to find the address of someone who may know something about that dumb book." She sighed. "It sure feels good to say that to you without worrying about tossing my cookies."

A huge weight lifted from my shoulders that Daphne's strange behavior was because of a book and not because she was in cahoots with the Crutchfields. It was a relief to switch gears from a suspicious asshole to a determined one, wanting to help her get some answers.

"Come on," I said, grabbing her hand. "You'll be safe with me."

Once we returned to Nightmare Alley, we soon found the address she'd been looking for. I pushed open the door of a dusty little shop called Dismal Devices and stepped aside to let her in first.

Wobbly stacks of manual typewriters, adding machines, rotary phones and phonographs stretched to the ceiling. We followed a pathway through the stacks, taking care not to bump into anything. At the end, sitting behind a gargantuan desk, was a skinny man with tiny round spectacles and an oversized handlebar mustache.

To spare Daphne from getting sick, I'd planned to do the talking, but she stopped me with a hand on my arm. "This feels...different. I think I can do it."

"Are you sure? Because I don't mind."

She gave me an appreciative smile that stirred me up again. "Positive."

The man—Dr. Eisenhorn, according to the business cards on his desk—cleared his throat impatiently and squinted at us through his thick lenses. "Why are you here? Did you not see the sign? By appointment only."

Daphne squared her shoulders at his rudeness and retrieved the book from her beach bag. "My friend Portia sent me. Said you'd know what to make of this."

He inhaled sharply when she plopped the ancient-looking book down in front of him and stared at it for a moment. Then he pulled out a pair of white cloth gloves from a desk drawer and began to examine the tome.

"What do you think it is, Dr. Eisenhorn?" I asked. "And why—"

"Stop with the interruptions!" He thrust a finger at his business cards without looking up from the book. "Can you not read? Or do you just choose not to? It's Dr. Eisenhorn THE THIRD."

Daphne and I exchanged a quick glance. This guy was really something. Per that same business card, he was also a professor at the Darkaway College of Magical Arts. I was glad I'd attended school elsewhere.

He asked Daphne a variety of questions that she dutifully answered, and he recorded it all in a dot-grid ledger.

Who had the book before her? Was Mr. Griffin born on a Tuesday or a Saturday? Did she recall what time of day, down to the minute and second, it had come into her possession? What had she eaten for breakfast that morning? Was she right-handed or left-handed?

Finally, Dr. Eisenhorn the Third removed his specs and rubbed his eyes. "This is a dark magic spell book. Very powerful. The likes of which I can't say I've ever seen before."

Daphne brightened. "Great! You can have it then. I am so ready to be done with that darn thing."

The professor shook his head. "No."

Her face fell and she took a step back, looking as if she might cry.

Anger rushed through me, and I put a hand on her shoulder, but I held my tongue so she could say what she needed to say. I wanted to convey to her that I had her back.

Her hip brushed mine in acknowledgment. "Why not?" she asked. "I'll just give it to you. For free. It came into my possession purely by accident. Portia says there's some really bad juju in there."

"There is," the man said with a condescending laugh. "But I can't take it."

Can't or won't?

"See here, Dr. Eisenhorn the Third," I interjected, unable to stay silent any longer. "The spell book clearly makes Daphne uncomfortable. You're the expert in these matters. She isn't."

The man pursed his lips, which made his mustache appear to be sitting on his chin like a small rodent. Then he handed the spell book to me and told Daphne to leave. Walk to the door by herself.

"Why?" I asked.

He glared at me. "Do you want my help or not?"

The minute Daphne disappeared around one of the stacks, the book jerked in my hands as if being tugged by an invisible rope or a fish on a hook.

"Now hold it even tighter." Eisenhorn the Third instructed me to crisscross my arms, pinning the book to my chest. To Daphne he called, "Open the door and step outside."

I heard the creak of the heavy wood door. Almost immediately, I lurched forward, unable to remain where I was standing. If I hadn't been holding the book as tightly as I had, I'm sure it would've flown from my hands.

"Okay, come back," Eisenhorn hollered to Daphne. Then he muttered to himself and jotted more notes in his ledger.

"What happened?" Daphne demanded when she returned. "What did I miss?"

The professor set down his fountain pen. "As I suspected, the book has taken a fancy to you. It won't let you go without it."

"That's ridiculous," I scoffed. "Books don't have crushes on people."

Eisenhorn stared at me over the top of his tiny glasses. "You teach Magical Studies at what college again, Mr. Monroe? And where did you receive your doctorate in the History of Magical Books and Incantations?"

A muscle ticked in my jaw. Fine. The man was an expert in these matters, but that didn't make me any less frustrated.

"I don't understand," Daphne said. "I've been able to go out and not take it with me. I've left it in my hotel room many times."

Eisenhorn scratched the tip of his nose. "Probably because the chain of command wasn't broken. It doesn't think it's being pawned off or given to someone else."

I leaned on the edge of his desk to think, but he cleared his throat and I straightened back up. "Okay, okay. But what can we do about it? Daphne can't keep living like this."

The man adjusted his glasses as he stared at the book. "Several of my colleagues are coming into town for Monsterval. Between the three of us, it's possible we can break the affinity spell."

"What is she supposed to do until then?"

"Sorry," the professor said with a nonchalant shrug, making it obvious that he really *wasn't* sorry. "Not my problem. She's on her own."

Like hell she was.

I could be a patient man when necessary, but not when it came to Daphne. The woman had gotten into my bloodstream —what affected her also affected me.

I stuffed the damn book into the damn beach bag and slung it over my shoulder, nearly knocking over Eisenhorn's damn business cards.

"Come on." I grabbed Daphne's hand. "Let's get the hell out of here."

CHAPTER TWENTY

Daphne

O n the way back to the hotel, we stopped several times for Travis to sign autographs and take pictures with fans who recognized him. He'd wanted to order food at the speakeasy, but after learning about the book, we went straight to the dismal shop instead, so I knew he was hungry.

Not once did I see him roll his eyes or sigh in frustration when someone recognized him. Did the man not get hangry? Either that or he had an infinite amount of patience with his fans.

Although I didn't get the answers I sought tonight, I didn't feel quite so alone anymore, either. And that was worth a lot. Being able to share everything with Travis had lifted a huge weight from my shoulders, and it wasn't just because he was carrying my beach bag with that heavy-ass spell book inside. I hadn't liked keeping this secret from him.

"I read in the Daily Epigraph that you're filming a reality dating show here," said a red-haired woman rather excitedly, her gaze bouncing between us. She had a cardigan draped over her arm and a black t-shirt that said *Touch Your Dark Side on Darkaway Island*. "Are you guys on a one-on-one or something?"

Travis shifted the beach bag to his other shoulder and started to answer, but another woman piped in, cutting him off. A glittery cat-ear headband sat atop her head, making me wonder if she was some sort of feline shifter or if she just liked the look.

"Why would you do a dating show?" She gave him the once-over as if he were a tasty morsel. "I can't imagine you'd have trouble finding dates."

Travis didn't seem to notice. "It's a favor to my sister. Good publicity for the island and Darkaway Island Ranch, which my family owns."

"I read about that place in the guidebook," whispered a third woman as she elbowed a fourth woman. "Cookouts, cowboys and Drake Valentino. I'm all in."

Travis started to tell them he spent little time there, but the women seemed more interested in taking selfies with him than listening to what he had to say. I frowned, watching these interactions. It had to be frustrating for him to be treated like a commodity like this. Which made me wonder how he'd gotten into acting. He sure was a natural.

One resourceful fan even had him hold up a blank piece of paper so she could use the photo at their gender-reveal party. "If it's a boy, we're naming him Drake," she said.

"Good luck," he told her. I wasn't sure if he meant good luck with the birth or good luck raising a kid whose namesake was a man-whore.

During one particularly long interaction, I popped over to Dark Tarts and bought several handheld chicken pot pies made with fresh herbs and vegetables.

"Thank you," he said as we continued down the cobblestone street a few minutes later. He took an enormous bite, covering his mouth while he chewed. "How did you know that Cluck You is one of my favorites?"

I shrugged. "Lucky guess."

We snacked on our delicious hand pies and headed down a set of twisty, winding stairs toward the marina. From this vantage point, we could see the Ferris wheel in the distance and some of the boardwalk.

"How did you get into acting anyway?" I asked, wiping some crumbs from my chin.

"Purely by accident," he replied. "As you know, we get a lot of tourists here. One summer, I was home from college, working at a pizza joint in town and trying to stay out of my dad's orbit, when I met the casting director for *Secret Shadows*, who was on vacation with her family. She encouraged me to audition, said I was perfect for a new character they were casting, and the rest is history."

"Drake Valentino's origin story."

That made him laugh. I liked the sound of it and how it made me feel all melty inside.

"Even though Drake can be a total asshole," I told him, "you really are a fantastic actor."

He laughed again. "I can't tell if that's a compliment or not."

"It is." I hip-bumped him. "Hey, thanks for going to bat for me back there with Dr. Eisenhorn. I really appreciate it."

He turned to me with a hand on his heart as if I'd committed a moral sin. "The Third."

I snorted out a laugh so hard I had to grab his arm, his *very muscular* arm, to keep from toppling over. "That guy was something else," I said, swiping at my eyes and hoping my mascara hadn't run.

"Yeah, a total asshole."

"And his dismal shop with all those cobwebs." I shivered. "I kept looking around, expecting to see a giant spider crawling around the corner."

I suddenly had a horrifying thought and gripped his arm again, nearly knocking the Cluck You out of his hand. "You don't have giant spider shifters here, do you? Please tell me there is no such thing. And don't lie to me either."

Who knew what sorts of monsters existed here? While it had been manageable so far, I drew the line at big-ass sentient spiders.

He chuckled. "No giant spiders."

"Okay, phew." My heart rate slowed to something manageable again. Letting go of his arm, I side-eyed my beach bag. "So, how far off is Monsterval again?" I couldn't remember what the poster at Unholy Grounds said.

The amusement on his face disappeared. "It's seven weeks away. The festival falls on the same weekend as the White Wolf Moon."

I turned away, took another bite and did the calculations. That was a month after the end of the contest and the end of my free vacation. I didn't exactly have the money to cover that sort of expense on my own. And although Travis and I were really hitting it off, I didn't want to make any assumptions that I would be the contest winner. Speaking of dismal, I was reminded of my track record in accurately predicting a man's intentions.

A few large yachts bobbed out in the harbor, their lights glittering on the dark water, while others were moored at the docks. At the end of one of them, people and various creatures were boarding a shiny black and red pirate ship. Probably a booze cruise.

"It must be amazing to call this place home," I said, changing the subject and wiping a few flaky crumbs from my face.

I wasn't sure if he'd heard me—or if he wasn't going to answer—until he finally said in a low, gruff tone, "This place hasn't felt like home in a very long time."

One of the women boarding the pirate ship got her heel

stuck in the dock boards, and a large brown bear was trying to help. Not having any success, the bear changed into his human form and used his opposable thumbs to wrestle it free.

I turned my attention back to Travis. It was hard not to get marginally distracted around here. Everything was so spectacularly strange and wondrous. "But you grew up on the island."

"Growing up in a pack is...complicated. Particularly with an Alpha like my father." His dark brows converged, and I got the sense that he was recalling something specific. "This is *his* home, *his* place. There was never any room here for me."

A boulder lodged in my throat, making it almost painful to swallow. I wanted to put my arms around him to ease the memories of his childhood trauma but wasn't sure if that would help or not. I knew nothing about actual werewolf families or politics except what I'd read in paranormal romance books, and those were fictional.

"But I thought your father passed away," I breathed.

"He did."

Recalling how his touch had comforted me several times today, I rubbed his shoulder anyway, hoping it would help and show how much I cared.

"Who's the Alpha now?" I asked.

He exhaled slowly and leaned into me, but his gaze remained far off and glassy. "That would be me."

CHAPTER TWENTY-ONE

Daphne

The next few days of the contest were filled with various competitions and group dates. I still hadn't had my one-on-one with Travis yet, but he kept giving me charms, so I guess he wanted me to stick around. I didn't want to know how I'd feel if he didn't.

He had the same air about him as he had that day in Wickedville when fans were asking for autographs, like it was simply a part of his job, his duty to perform.

Maybe that was why he had a private plane, beyond the obvious convenience, because he loved flying where he was far above the chaos of his world. I felt a twinge of sadness that I couldn't see him doing a thing he enjoyed so much. And I saw red when I remembered that Mia had.

I wasn't jealous by nature but with Travis...it was different. I felt almost territorial.

After the latest charm ceremony, Sarah and I realized we weren't needed for anything the next day, so we decided to finally go rock hounding and explore the sea caves on the northwest side of the island.

I didn't think she believed me at first, that I really wanted to go, but I looked her square in the eyes and told her, "Girl, we're going!"

At dawn, with our backpacks loaded, we headed out in a rental car and got to the top of the trailhead a few hours later.

The hike down to the sea caves was steep but not too treacherous given the well-constructed stairs, landings, and hand railings. Regardless, we made our way carefully. Twisting an ankle when we had a lot of walking to do would ruin our plans for the day.

The constant roar of the ocean, screeching of gulls and the smell of the fresh sea air had me smiling from ear to ear. I loved the feel of the energy here and wished I could bottle it up and take it with me. At the thought of going home, a pit formed in my stomach, but I shoved it away. I was determined to find joy in the here and now, and not worry about all that.

When we got down to the rocky beach, Sarah consulted the map she brought, which wasn't the stupid one from the hotel, and pointed to the left.

"There's supposedly a small stream that dumps into the ocean just to the north of that sea stack. People find a lot of moonstones there. Wait—hold on." Consulting the map again, she pointed to the right instead. "It's that way."

I didn't care where we went. We were going to have an adventure regardless.

"And what about the caves?" I was looking forward to the rockhounding, but even more excited for the spelunking. "Maybe we should do that first since we won't be able to once the tide comes in and blocks the access."

Sarah pulled out a small tide book from the front pocket of her cargo shorts. "The tide is still going out. Let's check out the stream bed since it's on the way to the caves and then we'll go back to hunt for stones later if it looks good."

I nodded eagerly. "And I heard there's a great sea glass beach somewhere around here too."

Sarah grinned, reflecting my excitement. "Sounds like a plan to me."

Picking our way along the beach, we arrived at the mouth of the little stream that flowed from the gap between the two sea cliffs. Then we followed it up about twenty paces to a rockfall and— *Oh Lordy, the stones!* I was the first to find one and nearly screamed when I spotted a milky white oval nestled among the gray. Delicate rose and blue mineral veins spread across the surface. Like hunting for sharks' teeth or foraging for mushrooms, once we knew what to look for, they seemed to jump out at us left and right.

We'd each collected maybe ten or twelve of them of various sizes and colors when I remembered that this was just supposed to be a quick look. "Hey, should we go to the caves now? We can come back to this later and not be rushed." The last thing I wanted was getting trapped inside a cave at high tide.

Sarah was washing off a moonstone in the stream and stood up. "Yeah, you're right. I could literally do this all day. Look at this one."

She showed me a milky pink stone with veins of blue and purple.

"Gorgeous!"

We made our way along the beach, just below the line of seaweed marking high tide because the traction was better on wet sand than dry. Just beyond a particularly large sea stack, we spotted the craggy opening of a cave, and my heart lurched. I doubted there'd be stalagmites and stalactites, but I still couldn't wait to get inside.

I wondered if Travis had ever been here. Surely, he had since he grew up on the island. He and his friends probably got into all sorts of trouble exploring the caves.

"How much more time do we have?" I asked, recalling the warning signs at the bottom of the stairs, telling visitors to be mindful of the tides.

Sarah looked at her watch. "About an hour. Plenty of time to find a treasure chest or two."

We scrambled over a few boulders and then we were inside. I was grateful my new friend had told me to dress warmly, because it was frigid in here. The cave opening was about twenty feet tall and curved around into the inky darkness.

Sarah brought us both a head lamp, so I fastened mine like a headband, clicked it on, and illuminated the craggy walls around us. The cavern was fairly narrow, its damp walls covered in slippery moss. Not a stalagmite or stalactite in sight —but that didn't make it any less amazing. There were a few rocky ledges on both sides and the remnants of a few campfires. Guess the cave didn't go completely underwater at high tide.

"Is the whole coast dotted with these sea caves?" I picked my way carefully over the rocks embedded in the sand. I liked the way our voices sounded in here. Muffled and echo-y at the same time.

Sarah nodded, her headlamp bobbing up and down. "The dragon cliffs are still several miles up the coast, but they're very territorial. Non-dragons venturing too far will get singed. Not that we'll go that far, but hopefully they've got it well marked."

Spotting a piece of trash on a nearby ledge, I climbed over a large boulder to retrieve it. I hated when people didn't pick up after themselves. "I haven't seen a dragon yet," I told her. "Do you know if they come into town much?"

"I'll bet you have seen one just didn't know it. They're shifters too."

I gave a low whistle. "Amazing to think I could've walked by an actual dragon and not realized it. I hope that's not being rude or obtuse," I added quickly.

"Don't worry. It's not." Although she was slightly in front of me and I couldn't see her smile, I could hear it in her voice. "I keep forgetting this is all new to you. Full moon is coming, so I'll probably see if I can join one of the local packs when they go for a moon run. Although I don't necessarily like being with a group of people I don't know, I'm not comfortable lone-wolfing it in a place that's not familiar to me, either."

Being in the contest must be challenging for her given that she was so introverted, which made me all the madder at her family for forcing her into this. "Can you ask Jada? Or Travis? Maybe you can go with their pack."

"Nah."

My head snapped up in surprise. "Why not? I'm sure they'd be happy to have you."

"It might be a conflict of interest."

Then it was a good thing I couldn't tell her about the book and being in Wickedville with Travis the other day. "I'm really glad I met you. I just wish..." I swallowed, searching for the right words. "...that all of this wasn't temporary."

"Yeah, me too," she replied softly.

We hadn't gone too far—there were so many things to look at—when the alarm on Sarah's watch went off. "Time to turn around and head back," she said.

"You set an alarm?" To say that woman was prepared was an understatement. She'd ordered our lunches, arranged for the rental car, and checked out our gear from the hotel.

My headlamp illuminated her face, and I saw her big grin. She was loving this as much as I was. It was fun to see her so happy for once. "I didn't want us to get too distracted and get caught in here at high tide."

"Good thinking."

But when we made our way back to the entrance and rounded the last corner, we both gasped. The water had risen so much that it almost completely covered the entrance.

"Oh, my gods! How could this happen?" Sarah grabbed the tide book from her cargo shorts. "It says right here..." Her voice trailed off, then she got all choked up. "I must've read it wrong. I'm such an *idiot!*"

"Let me see." Trying not to panic, I took it from her and could totally tell how she had confused the high and low tide times. One was light blue and the other was dark blue. "You're definitely not an idiot."

"Let me see if I can get out and go for help," she said, ignoring my protests and removing her backpack. But as she scrambled over the rocks, she slipped and came down hard.

"Are you okay?" I asked, rushing over and helping her up.

"Yes." She vigorously rubbed her elbow. "I'll be fine."

But I could tell she wasn't. "How can you do that?" I pointed to the submerged entrance.

"I'll just shift into my wolf form—that won't scare you will it?—and go for help."

"But your arm." I remembered the warning Travis's doctor told him. "It won't heal properly."

"The moon's energy is waxing toward full moon. It'll actually heal more quickly."

I continued protesting that we could just wait it out here, but Sarah was having none of that. "This is *my* fault. I won't have you suffer because of me."

"I'm not going to suffer, Silly. Besides, you drowning isn't going to help."

"My wolf is a strong swimmer," she assured me. "I'll be back as soon as I can."

Realizing I couldn't talk her out of it, I climbed onto the highest ledge I could find. When I turned around, she'd already shifted into her wolf form. She had a beautiful, shiny red coat and was about half the size of Travis's wolf. With a short bark, she jumped into the dark water. I stood rooted to the spot, heart pounding in my throat, and watched as she swam through the mouth of the cave.

And then she was gone.

CHAPTER TWENTY-TWO

Travis

After a boring-as-hell one-on-one with a fox shifter from Florida—I wasn't interested listening to the time when she and her friends chased a bunch of chickens, I looked around the hotel for Daphne and learned that she and Sarah had gone hiking. A frisson of unease shot through me. Although the Crutchfield's territory was on the northeast tip of the island, far from the sea caves, I didn't like the idea of her possibly running into one of those assholes.

At the thought of being out in nature, my inner wolf gnawed at me like a leashed dog, and I realized I hadn't run in days. Not since my injury, which seemed ages ago now. I called the pack together before my wolf got even crankier.

Unlike my father who ordered everyone in the Darkaway Island pack to attend, I sent out word that if anyone was available and wanted to go for a group run, we were meeting at the ranch at moon rise. Jada and Matthew were in, of course, along with my little brothers, and some cousins, including a few pups who were on their first runs. Once we shifted into our wolf forms, we wrestled a bit in an upper pasture, then I led the pack through the dense forest and up the mountainside.

Surrounded by family, I ran through the trees, over ferns and felled logs. Wind rushed through my fur, energizing my spirit, the ground solid and sure beneath my large paws.

Heavens Moon, I *missed* this. A run through Stanley Park with a few co-workers from the set of *Secret Shadows* didn't hit the same.

We eventually got to a large clearing where we gathered in a circle around the littles and howled at the moon. The sound of my family rang like a chorus in my ears, and it occurred to me that this was the first time I'd led the pack since my father's death. It was both odd and strangely comforting at the same time.

The air smelled of rain and was charged with electricity. A thunderstorm, though rare on the island, must be rolling in. I hoped Daphne was back from her hike and drinking hot chocolate at the hotel by now.

I was mindful not to keep the group out too long. While the young ones wouldn't mind getting caught in a downpour, their parents wouldn't want to deal with all that wet fur. It was the complete opposite of what my father would do. He'd keep the pack out till all hours, rain or moon shine, forcing them to listen to him yap about this or that. The man loved to hear himself talk.

I let one of the younger pups lead the group back down the mountain while I brought up the rear. We had just crossed another creek, this one teaming with fish, when I scented another wolf.

Someone not part of our pack.

While the Darkaway Island pack was the oldest pack on the island, it certainly wasn't the only one. I stopped, braced myself for a confrontation, the hairs on my neck standing on end.

A small red-coated wolf stepped out of the trees. A female.

Clearly exhausted. Though I couldn't read her thoughts, I could tell she was in some sort of distress. She shifted into her human form. *What the fuck.* It was Sarah. She'd been running hard and leaned on a nearby tree trunk to catch her breath.

I shifted into my human form as well. Not being from my pack, I couldn't communicate with her otherwise. "What's wrong?" I demanded, glancing around. "I thought you were with Daphne."

"I was, but—"

The blood in my veins turned to ice. "What happened? Where the hell is she? Is she hurt?"

If the Crutchfields had anything to do with this, I was going to rip those assholes to shreds.

"No, no," she said, reassuring me. "She's fine. But the two of us got trapped in one of the sea caves at high tide."

Fresh panic gripped me—Daphne was alone and in trouble—and the drive to go to her became my singular focus. I needed to shield her from danger before it was too late.

Protect her.

"It's all my fault," Sarah said, wiping the tears from her eyes. "I read the tide table wrong. Then, in my rush to get help, I lost control of the car and it went into a ditch."

A rookie move for sure, but not unusual. And then there was the unexpected storm rolling in, which undoubtedly contributed to the tidal surge. "Stay here. I'll send someone for you."

Without waiting for a reply, I shifted back into my wolf form and charged through the trees.

Jada!

Where are you? I thought you were right behind us.

Through the bond, I told her about Sarah and where she could find her. *Take her back to the ranch. I'm going after Daphne.*

Want me to send someone to help you?

No, I'll be fine.

And frankly, I didn't want to wait for reinforcements. I *couldn't*. I needed to get to Daphne—now. If anything happened to her, I'd never forgive myself.

I was still a few miles from the coast when I scented them— three wolves from the Crutchfield pack on the other side of a small clearing. Coming to a halt, I lifted my muzzle and inhaled deeply. Thank fuck, I didn't detect Daphne's scent on any of them, otherwise this encounter would be a blood bath.

The oldest, a scrawny twenty-something named Leon, shifted into his human form. I wasn't an idiot, however, and remained as a wolf. Individually, I was bigger and stronger than each of them, but it was still three against one.

"Hey, Travis," Leon said, daring to look me straight in the eye. "How's the contest going? Find a mate yet? A cute little filly to fuck?"

One of his packmates gave a little yip.

"Shut up, Ed," he snapped.

I gave a low growl, all the hairs on my back raised, ready to spring into action. Although I was unable to verbally communicate with him, he understood me perfectly.

I dropped my head slightly, took a menacing step closer, and his two brothers backed away.

Leon ran a hand through his mullet. "I heard you need to be mated by the next White Wolf Moon. What a shame you could lose the ranch."

Who the fuck told him about the will? Merrick? His wife?

Teeth bared, I lunged at them, sending his little brothers running off, their tails between their legs.

Leon tried to shift, but I was faster and had him by the throat. The will wasn't an issue anymore, but it pissed me off these assholes knew about it in the first place.

"I was just curious," Leon rasped. "That's all."

I bit down, enough to leave a mark, then let go and pissed on his leg.

"Asshole," he said as I bounded into the trees.

By the time I reached the coast, the rain slashed in sideways and gray mist had turned the sea stacks into faint shadows. Although the storm had washed away Daphne's scent from the beach, it didn't take me long to find her. There were only so many caves along these cliffs, and my wolf had a very powerful nose.

Huge waves pounded the shore as I leapt into the surf and swam to the opening about fifty feet away. Dark water and foam churned around me as the current tried to batter me against the rocks, but the moon had healed my knee, and I easily made it through the mouth of the cave.

Once inside, Daphne's scent was stronger, and I prayed I got to her in time. Sarah had said she was okay when she left her, but that was a while ago. A lot could have happened since then.

When my paws touched the ground, I bounded out of the surf and found Daphne huddling on an upper ledge, alone. My thoughts had turned dark on the way here as I imagined what I'd do if I found the rival pack had been here, but I smelled none of them.

"Daphne!" I shifted into my human form and scrambled over the rocks to her. "Are you hurt?"

Huddled on the cold rock, knees to chest, she lifted her head. "Travis?" She squinted into the darkness, teeth chattering. "What are—? How did...?"

I dropped to her side, waves of relief coursing through me as I pulled her onto my lap. I needed to feel her sweet, soft body against mine to ensure she was okay. Thank the moon, I didn't smell blood or see any bruises. Wrapping my arms around her, I rubbed her back vigorously. "Are you okay? Are you hurt?"

"I'm f—f—f—fine now. Just a little f—f—f— frozen."

That would *not* do. "Would it scare you if I shifted back to my wolf form and curled around you? He runs hotter than me."

I recalled how scared she'd been that day on the ferry dock seeing the Crutchfield boys.

She burrowed her face into my chest and made a soft sound of contentment that went straight to my balls. "Your wolf doesn't scare me, Travis. I saw him in Wickedville, remember? He's...magnificent."

A frisson of heat rushed through me. She wasn't afraid of me —the man, or my wolf.

My inner beast swelled with pride at the compliment as did my cock, and my thoughts immediately turned carnal. I tried to imagine how it'd feel to be deep inside her. Now *that* would be magnificent. She was smaller than me, of course, but not petite, with sturdy hips and lush curves. In a word, *perfect*. I'd go slow at first, keeping my primal nature tightly constrained so as not to hurt her. Then, once inside, I'd let go.

Closing my eyes, I inhaled deeply, drawing her scent into my lungs. She smelled of salty sea air, cedar and something sweet. I wondered how she'd taste.

"W—why aren't your clothes wet?" she said against my chest, pulling me out of my X-rated thoughts, but just barely. My inner wolf was still there. Right below the surface, pacing like a caged animal.

"Shifter magic," I explained. "My fur was definitely wet, but as soon as I shift back into my human form, my clothes are as dry as when I started."

"How nice," she said, and I nearly snorted. This woman was so accepting of me and my world even though it had been completely foreign to her a short time ago.

As I contemplated making good on my earlier offer to shift back into my wolf form, I hesitated, unsure it would be enough. This rocky ledge was ice cold, and it wasn't getting any warmer.

And then I remembered the hiker's cabin I'd passed on the way here. The island's nature guild kept the popular trails maintained and the cabins well stocked for hikers. It would have a fireplace, wood, provisions and blankets. Perfect for cold, wet hikers who got stuck in a storm.

I told her my idea, promising to keep her as dry as possible. Once we got to shore, it was maybe a five-minute run up the coast. She was game.

"After I shift," I said, removing my leather belt, "put this around my neck and it'll give you something to hold on to besides my fur. If I leave it on, it'll just disappear with the rest of my clothes."

"Like a collar?" she murmured, lifting a brow, her beautiful eyes sparkling. Was she being a smartass or was this a sexual innuendo? Either way, I loved it.

I cocked my head at her. Two could play that game.

"Are you ready for me?" I meant—*for me to shift into my wolf form*—but I was thinking along other lines.

She gave me a pointed look like she knew what I meant. "Yes."

I reached for the moon's energy. Although it was hard to make yet another change under the same moon, I managed.

She slipped the collar around my neck, climbed onto my back and buried her face in my fur. And as I bounded into the surf, her legs wrapped tightly around me, I imagined a similar, but different scenario. One that also involved her legs wrapped around me but with me burying my face somewhere else.

But first, I had to get her to safety.

CHAPTER TWENTY-THREE

Daphne

Travis in his dire wolf form was even more magnificent than I remembered. His silvery coat glistened as he towered over me, his back level with my shoulders, yellow eyes locked onto mine. He did a downward dog so I could fasten the leather belt around his thick neck. Unable to help myself, I gave him a little scratch behind his ears.

He nuzzled my palm then flashed me a sharp look that said, *Get the fuck on*, so I obeyed him.

I clung to his back as he surged through the frigid black water and tried to ignore how cold it was. The hiking cabin wasn't far, he'd said, and I trusted him to keep me safe. I wasn't so sure about my heart, however.

The surf was relentless, but Travis's wolf was incredibly strong and we soon made it to shore. Good thing, because I was wet and cold as hell when we got there. I repositioned my hands —one on the leather belt and the other holding a fistful of his fur. I was mesmerized by the feel and rhythm of his powerful muscles as he shot up the stairs and into the dense forest.

I didn't remember how we got to the cabin, just that we ran through the trees and were suddenly there. It was possible I'd lost consciousness at some point along the way, because the next thing I knew, I was in a bed wrapped in blankets, while a fire crackled in a nearby fireplace. A shirtless Travis, wearing low-slung jeans, was adding another log to the fire.

That perfect physique of his held my attention like super glue. Even if I wanted to, I couldn't tear my eyes away from how the firelight reflected on the bulging muscles in his back and arms. And the man had abs for days and days. No wonder his wolf was able to cut through the powerful current like nobody's business.

He threw a glance over at me, then hesitated when he realized I was awake and watching him.

Busted. I smiled awkwardly. "Um, I thought your clothes didn't get wet when you shifted."

His brows drew together. "They don't."

"Then where's your shirt?" I asked.

"You're wearing it."

And that was when I realized I was naked under these blankets, wearing nothing but this man's flannel shirt.

Heat crept to my cheeks. How had I not been aware when he undressed me? I saw my clothes now, including my sensible bra —not a lacy, cute one—and my granny panties, draped over a chair near the fire. I frowned, pissed as hell at myself for my lingerie choices this morning.

But how was I to know that a gorgeous man was going to be undressing me later that night, after rescuing me and taking me to a cabin in the woods—I glanced around—with only *one* bed?

"What's wrong?" he asked, concern marring his ruggedly handsome face. Then he was at my bedside. "I thought you were warming up."

"I...I am." But just as I said it, I realized I was still very cold, like my bones were frozen from the inside.

It was possible I may have let my teeth chatter a little more than was necessary though, because he wordlessly climbed onto the bed and got under the covers with me, wrapped those strong arms around my body and pulled me close. Had he done this earlier? Surely, I'd have remembered if he had.

"Mmmmm." He was soooo warm...and this felt heavenly.

"Better?" His lips brushed the edge of my ear and I shivered. He must have thought it was from the cold because he held me even tighter.

"Much." I nestled the back of me to the front of him, quite aware that my ass was pressing against a very hard part of him. I mean, all of him was hard, but you get the picture.

With all this rustling around, the shirt I was wearing—his shirt—had scrunched up past my hips. If I were a good girl, I'd pull it back down, putting one more barrier between us. It would be the smart thing to do—the *sensible* thing to do.

But I was not a good girl and left it exactly as it was.

"Was it worth it?" he murmured, lips against my hair.

For this? A laugh burst from my throat. It was hard not to think that it wasn't. "Well, I did find some beautiful moonstones."

He chuckled. "I'll take that as a 'yes' then."

I softly elbowed him and took the opportunity to snuggle in deeper. "How did you know I was even trapped in that cave?"

Travis explained how he'd been on a run with his pack when a bedraggled Sarah had stepped out of the woods. "I wish you two had read the tide table better," he said, a light note of reprimand threading through his husky tone. "You could have been hurt. Or worse."

I stiffened. "Have you seen that little booklet? It's extremely confusing."

When he didn't immediately agree with me, I pressed my cold feet to his bare ankles and he jumped.

"Heaven's Moon, woman! Your feet are like ice cubes."

I snickered. Served him right. "Then admit it."

"Okay, okay, it's confusing."

I started to move my feet away, but he hooked his foot around mine and kept them close.

At some point, his warm, broad palm had slipped to my hip, my *bare* hip. If I twisted just so, his hand would be right there. My breath caught in my throat as he grazed his thumb over my skin like he was waiting for something to happen and was just biding his time.

Meanwhile, liquid heat was building up inside me, and I realized I wasn't cold anymore. "Your guidebooks on this island are something else."

"*My* guidebooks?" He chuckled again and the sound rumbled through me. "Don't blame your poor map-reading skills on me."

So, we were back to that, were we?

Indignant, I turned to face him. His lips were inches from mine, and something dark moved behind his eyes, igniting more warmth between my legs.

"It's nuts you're supposed to remember that the light blue section means low tides and the dark blue section means high tides. Or maybe it's the other way around. I mean, they're both blue, for goodness sake. And don't get me started on that map from the hotel."

A corner of his mouth turned up in a smirk and the strand of heat inside me curled tighter. He thought this was *funny?*

I continued. "As the king of the island, you really should do something about this."

His laughter shook the entire bed. "*King of the island?*"

"King of the pack. Whatever you want to call it. Everyone fawns over you like royalty. The island's favorite son." I poked a finger into his ribs to make my point, and he jerked like he was really ticklish. I filed that away for later.

"It's called Alpha," he said, enunciating the word slowly as if I had the IQ of a turtle. "And there are several packs on the island.

Not just mine. Oh, and let's not forget about Drake Valentino. He's quite famous, you know."

"Oh, heavens no, how can we possibly forget about *him*?"

He gave me a narrow-eyed look—like he wasn't sure what to do with me, but his grip on me never wavered.

Truthfully, I rather liked teasing him like this. Getting under his skin like he'd done to me. I exhaled slowly in a futile effort to control the rapid beating of my heart.

I wanted this powerful, dynamic man. Needed him like I needed air to breathe. And unless I was reading the signs wrong, he wanted me too. I considered that for a moment. If I gave in to him, I knew I could lose my heart. Was it worth the risk? After all, I was just a lab technician, here temporarily, and he was a werewolf celebrity. Our worlds couldn't be more different.

Still, he did nothing.

Was he waiting for *me* to make the first move? I decided to do a little experiment.

He let me push his shoulder back against the mattress, confirming my suspicions. This powerful werewolf Alpha was letting *me*, a human woman, take charge of him in bed.

Was it because of my weakened physical condition? Out of respect for the obvious power imbalance? Or maybe he didn't want to frighten me in case I changed my mind? Whatever the reason, it was *hot*.

I straddled his legs and caged him between my forearms.

"Would Drake Valentino stand for poorly worded guidebooks?" My still-damp hair cascaded around his face and I stared at his full lips, desperate to kiss him again.

"Drake doesn't do a lot of readin', darling," he said in the cowboy drawl of his alter ego, making me laugh.

"Then what would your wolf do?" Tracing the tip of my finger along his jaw, I heard the rasp of his stubble and wondered how it would feel against my inner thighs. Then I quickly dashed that thought away. "Would he let something like this happen?"

"My *wolf?*" Travis growled and yellow flashed in his eyes. "He'd be sick of all this talking and would be fucking you by now."

CHAPTER TWENTY-FOUR

Travis

"Really?" she rasped, her warm breath fanning over my chest as she looked at me, eyes dark with intent.

Daphne's mouth was soft against mine when she leaned down and kissed me. *Finally*. It had been sheer torture for my wolf and me as we waited for what felt like *forever* for her to make a move.

I'd been with human women before, but no one who knew my true nature. It was...liberating to be myself with her.

I fisted a hand in her tangled hair, thrust my tongue past the seam of her lips, and ran the other hand over her hip and down her bare thigh. She made a soft, feminine sound that shot straight to my cock, making it even harder. Heaven's Moon, the way she looked wearing my shirt should be illegal.

"Something tells me you need to be warmed up on the inside," I told her.

"Really? How did you know?" She was kissing my neck now. I hissed in a breath as she sucked on my earlobe. Then she tried rather unsuccessfully to unfasten my jeans.

"Such an eager little thing."

"Well, I'm very, very cold, and that was an excellent suggestion."

She still hadn't figured out the top button. *Enough.* My wolf and I were done being patient. She may have started this, but I could take it from here. She gave a little gasp as I suddenly rolled us over, swapping positions. Me on top, her beneath me.

I shucked off my jeans and retrieved a condom from my wallet before tossing it to the floor.

"Mmmm," she said against my mouth. "I see you came prepared."

"You never know when you'll need to rescue a beautiful woman from imminent death and she'll be so grateful that she wants to fuck your brains out."

Daphne snorted with laughter until tears streamed from her eyes. "Oh my God, Travis, are you always this insufferable?"

"Normally, I'm much worse."

I unbuttoned my shirt she wore and kissed my way down her exquisite body. I gently grazed my teeth over one nipple before drawing it into my mouth, making it peak even further. She arched her back and moaned. Heaven's Moon, she had beautiful breasts, full and lush...and I couldn't wait to see them bouncing in my face as she rode me. But that would have to wait, I told myself, as I slid lower.

Her fingers dug into my shoulders. "What are you doing?"

"What's it look like I'm doing?" I growled, kissing her belly and pushing her thighs apart even further.

"I didn't know wolves were into that sort of thing."

I lifted my head and peered up at her. "Darlin', I'm into everything. Why would you think I wouldn't be?"

Worry lines creased her forehead. Something was wrong. I stopped what I was doing and drew myself up again. She'd mentioned the fact that I was a werewolf. Maybe she was having a change of heart. "Is this too much? Because I'll stop in a heartbeat if it is."

Her cheeks colored and it took a moment for her to reply. "It's not that. It's just that..." Her voice trailed off, and she blinked a few times. I wasn't sure if she was collecting her thoughts or if she didn't want to share them. I kept quiet to give her room to think. "It's just that Gavin—my ex-fiancé—wasn't really into...it. Said it grossed him out."

"*It?* You mean oral sex?" I kissed her forehead, her cheeks, her temples, trying to take away her shame. "That's his fucking problem. Not yours."

"Well, he *was* into it. But just the receiving end. It was me he wasn't into like that."

A white-hot rage rushed through me. If I ever met that selfish asshole, I'd throat-punch him then rip his head off. "How long were you together?"

"A few years," she answered softly.

"And before him?"

"There were a few guys before him but I'd..." Her words trailed off and she wouldn't meet my gaze.

"Never had an orgasm that way," I finished for her.

She bit her lip and nodded, unleashing something deep inside me.

I twirled a finger around her nipple and nuzzled her neck. "Would you be game to try? Because I'd love nothing more than to pleasure you like that. But only if you want me to."

Her eyes were bright as she searched my face. "Okay," she said tentatively, as if she wanted to believe me but still wasn't sure.

My inner wolf surged with pride that she trusted me like that.

I would need to be slow and gentle. Take my time with her. Show her with my actions that I was just as into it as she was. I didn't know how much time I had with Daphne here on the island, but I intended to make the most of it.

In fact, I had an idea. "Are you warm enough now?" I asked.

She rubbed her foot against the back of my leg. It wasn't cold anymore. "Yes, very. But that doesn't mean I want you to stop trying to warm me up."

I got out of bed and heard her sharp intake of breath. I glanced over to see her staring at my admittedly large erection jutting out in front of me, and my wolf preened.

"What are you doing?" she asked, nostrils slightly flared.

"You'll see." After stoking the fire again, I headed to the basin and removed the scratched mirror from the wall. I carried it to the bed, propped it on a nearby chair and adjusted it. Then I climbed back under the covers with her. "I want you to watch what I'm doing to you. And then I want you to tell me if you think I'm enjoying myself or not."

She quirked her lips. "Are you giving me homework? *Oral sex* homework?"

I shrugged. "You have a problem with that?"

"No, not at all."

"Good. Because I would like to give you an A."

"Don't you mean an O?"

Such a little smartass. I growled at her and got started.

CHAPTER TWENTY-FIVE

Daphne

Travis was an absolute *beast* in bed. He'd clearly done this a time or two. He pushed my thighs apart, glanced in the mirror, then adjusted my legs again.

"Can you see okay?" he asked. "I know that's a really crappy mirror."

I nodded, not trusting my voice.

"Heavens moon, you're beautiful." He said it with such raw, unfiltered sincerity that my cheeks flushed with heat, and I had to force myself not to look away.

He kissed the sensitive skin of my inner thighs and, yes, his stubble felt amazing. Opening me with his thumb and forefinger, he lowered his mouth. I arched my back in pure bliss when he pressed his tongue to my clit and moved it skillfully back and forth, and when he gave it a soft suckle, I nearly lost my mind.

"You taste so good," he said, voice low and rough. "Think you can let go for me?"

I wasn't sure if that was a rhetorical question or not, but I answered it anyway. "Yes."

He propped my legs on his shoulders, repositioned me for better access, and lowered his head again. I gripped fistfuls of his hair and moved my hips to the rhythm of his very wicked tongue. I was close already. *So close.* Hardly a build up from zero to 60, the man drove me like a sportscar. He slipped two fingers inside, then three.

"You're so wet for me." His breath was hot against my sex. "I can't wait until my cock is right here." He curled his fingers just so and licked me again.

Okay, that did it. My inner muscles tightened around him as he drove me off the edge. An explosion of pleasure shot out from my core, sizzling every nerve ending in my body, as he continued to stroke and suck me. I was pretty sure I just screamed his name, because he made a deep masculine sound in response.

The pleasure was so intense, so powerful, it was almost too much. Sensing this, he lifted his mouth, but kept his fingers inside, letting me ride out the most spectacular orgasm I'd ever had.

"Gorgeous," he said, almost to himself.

A quick glance in the mirror showed he was stroking himself. A self-satisfied thrill shot through me. He really *did* like doing this, I guess.

"Here. Let me help with that." I reached for him, trying to pull him up.

"Uh uh," he said, pressing his thumb to my swollen and extremely sensitive clit again, making me suck in a breath through my teeth. "Not yet. I want you to have another one like this, but with just my fingers. I plan to use my mouth for other things. Think you can do that for me?" He was peering up at me from between my legs, his dark eyes a beautiful wolfish yellow now.

I swallowed. *Another* one? I was pretty sure I'd break apart first, but I trusted him and realized that I wanted to do what he asked of me. At least for right now. Tomorrow was another story. "Okay. I'll try."

He kissed my inner thigh. "That's a good girl. You're going to get an A for sure."

My laugh quickly turned to a soft moan as he slid partially up my body to pull one of my nipples into his mouth. It felt so good as he suckled and teased one pebbled tip, while gently pinching the other one between his thumb and forefinger. I rocked my hips forward, trying to remind him I had a void inside that needed to be filled by him.

If he wouldn't give me his cock, then I wanted his fingers. *Now.* But he ignored me, sliding up further to kiss my mouth, and I tasted myself on his tongue. I reached between us to wrap my fingers around him, but he jerked his hips back and his heavy erection slipped from my hand.

"Not yet," he commanded, finally pushing his fingers into me again. "Just you."

Then he did this thing with his thumb, combined with his tongue flicking my nipple, and I was coming again.

I cried out and gripped his shoulders to keep him in place as my inner muscles tightened around him.

How had I never experienced something like this before? He made it seem so easy, so effortless as he turned my world upside down and inside out.

As I spiraled back to a somewhat vague sense of normalcy—whatever normal was now—he had a dark grin on his face. "There, little prey. I think you're ready for me. Now, where did I put that condom...?"

CHAPTER TWENTY-SIX

Travis

At the ranch a few days later, I watched Jada *caligra-fy* a Date-A-Wolf date card as I bounced my little niece on my shoulders. Although I was still frustrated with how things had ended with Daphne in the cabin, I tried not to snap at my sister. I didn't want to be a grumpy-ass uncle in front of the girls.

But Jada had the nerve to tell me I was spending too much time with Daphne and that I should give the other women a chance. So, I had to remind her I always made a point to talk to everyone at the various Date-A-Wolf mixers and cocktail parties, to which she said, "Yes, but the whole time, you can't keep your eyes off of Daphne. It's like she's a magnet, you're a pile of iron shavings, and everyone else is an afterthought."

Okay, so this *really* irritated me. And not because she compared me to a pile of anything instead of something manlier like an iron anvil.

"It's really very simple," I told her as I trotted my niece around the room, trying my hardest not to use any swear words. "I don't have the same feelings about the rest of the women that I have for Daphne." Jada started to protest, but I stopped her. "Last time I checked, *I'm* the Date-A-Wolf bachelor who gets to pick who *I* want to date."

Jada capped her pen and blew on the date card to dry the ink. "It's because she's *not* like the others, Travis. That's literally my point."

"Who are you dating, Uncle?" my niece asked, resting her chin on the top of my head. It surprised me she even knew what that was, but given all this Date-A-Wolf chatter, Jada must've explained it to her at some point. "Is she pretty?"

"Very."

Daphne *definitely* wasn't like the others, and despite this ridiculous contest, I had developed real feelings for her. It had started well before the cabin, I just wasn't ready to admit it then, but I liked who I was around her. Calmer, less chaotic, more grounded. And I liked how she made me see my world in ways I'd never noticed before.

When she'd been in danger, it brought out a side of me I'd never felt, either. The primal urge to protect her, fierce and unyielding, had surged through me—drowning out every pack instinct, every duty—as I raced to get her to safety that night. In fact, I hadn't even thought of them as my sole focus had been on her.

"You're right," I told my sister, setting my niece down who ran off the instant her feet touched the ground. "They're dating Drake, the character, while she's dating Travis, the man."

Jada thought about that for a moment. "So, when Drake played by Travis leaves her after the ceremony and goes back to his life on the set of *Secret Shadows*, who's going to pick up the pieces?"

I tried to tell her I'd never hurt Daphne, but she was having none of it.

"And don't tell me she won't remember any of this when she

leaves. That's cruel." A pit formed in my gut at the thought of causing Daphne any pain, and my sister continued. "Do you have any idea how she and her fiancé broke up?"

I didn't.

"He left her at the altar, Travis. She trusted a man, and he let her down in a very spectacular way. So, don't you dare do that to her too."

CHAPTER TWENTY-SEVEN

Daphne

I sat on the sofa in the drawing room of the hotel with the remaining contestants, camera crew on the periphery. I was trying not to act too depressed, but Sarah didn't get a charm last night and I missed her already.

Mia jumped to her feet and ran to the mail slot in the door. "It's a date card. My bet is that someone has a one-on-one tonight."

There were only four of us left now: Mia, Lauren, Alice and me. Although I wasn't as friendly with them as I had been with Sarah, they all were nice enough. Mia, however, did have her moments. But if any of them caught wind of what had happened with Travis and me in the cabin, things probably wouldn't be as cordial. I bit my lip to keep from thinking about how things had ended.

Mia waited until she got the nod from Jada, who stood just off camera. Then she ripped the envelope, like a child opening a big shiny present on Christmas morning. As she held the card up and read it, all the joy and excitement drained from her face.

"What does it say?" asked Lauren.

Mia's voice was like the edge of a knife. "Roses are red, violets are blue, grab your hiking boots, Daphne. I'll see you in two." She tossed the card on the table in front of us. "Good. I hate to hike."

Travis was taking me hiking? *Again?* A shot of excitement coursed through me that we were going on our first actual one-on-one. The other night didn't exactly count. At least, not as far as the contest was concerned.

Alice reached forward and picked up the card. "Whew. 'Hours' is in parentheses. I was afraid it was two minutes and I was gonna be like, Girl, you gotta go now!"

Two hours later, Travis and I were strolling through downtown Darkaway, camera crew in tow. As it turned out, I didn't actually need the hiking boots. That was just for the poem. Comfy walking shoes were all that was required.

I wore tennis shoes, a denim jacket and a handmade dress from a cute store in town that I found during one of my morning pilgrimages to Unholy Grounds. I also brought with me my determination to keep things casual and easy-breezy with Travis. *Yeah, good luck with that.*

Okay, so he was a pretty great guy in many respects, but that didn't mean I should fuel my growing feelings for him. I had to keep reminding myself that, sure, this was fun, but it was also temporary.

I could do easy-breezy, no problem. I could do casual.

With a slow exhale, I wondered if he'd been intimate with any of the other contestants. And because I enjoy torturing myself, I forced myself to picture him with each of the remaining women. It wasn't pretty, but this was a dating contest, and those things happened. The safest thing for my heart was to assume the obvious, and not believe in some ridiculous fairy tale.

"You didn't need to take me on another one-on-one, Travis."

I gave him a platonic hip bump. "We already had ours." I knew the subject would eventually come up. Might as well rip off the bandaid on my terms.

"Not officially, we haven't." He brushed a flyaway strand of hair from my cheek and tucked it behind my ear. His touch burned my skin, sending electricity skittering everywhere and my thoughts instantly turned feral. I wanted more of him. All of him. The other night, he'd been so gentle, so focused on what turned me on, that a tiny part of me wondered if I'd been delirious and dreamed the whole thing. I'd never experienced such raw intimacy like that before, where my partner's pleasure seemed so dependent on my own.

What had happened in the cabin was really *something else*, though. At the thought of how it all ended, I couldn't help but giggle.

"What's so funny?" he asked, looking around to see what I was laughing at.

I made sure the camera crew was out of earshot for this. They were taking b-roll and we weren't miked up. "I'm just thinking about the eyeful you gave those hikers when they came in."

His lip quirked. "Damn hikers' cabins with no locks on the doors. I can't believe my wolf didn't hear or scent them first."

"In all fairness, you were a bit occupied at the time." *And boy, could that man focus.*

Now it was his turn to chuckle.

Travis had given me several of the best orgasms I'd ever had —I mean really, they were *incredible*—and just when he went to retrieve the condom and put it on, four hikers had burst through the door. I screamed and pulled the sheets up to my chin. But poor Travis was standing there at the bedside in all his naked glory. The hikers—two men and two women, with backpacks the size of compact cars—stood there in the doorway, staring at him, mouths agape.

And what a sight he was too. The man was...very blessed. Both in skill and in physical attributes. But then, given the size of his dire wolf, it shouldn't come as a surprise that everything else about him was impressive too. As a human woman, I had to admit I'd been a little concerned about the logistics had things continued in the direction they were headed. In retrospect, maybe it was a good thing we'd been interrupted.

He draped an arm around my shoulder now, leaned in close, his lips brushing the shell of my ear. "We need to finish what you started..."

"Me? I didn't start anything." Remembering he was ticklish, I poked him in the ribs and he jumped, screeching like a six-year-old on a playground, which made me laugh so hard my stomach hurt.

Damn it. I could see the cameras zooming in.

Travis straightened. He'd seen them too.

"Does someone need a memory stone?" His thumb stroked over mine, sending little jolts of electricity up my arm. "Because I seem to recall a different chain of events. I was just innocently trying to keep you warm, minding my own business, when you went feral on me."

"Oh my God, you are— That's not..." When I went to shove him, he moved fast, grabbing my wrists and pulling me to his broad chest. I made a little *umph* as I collided with all those hard muscles. I craned my neck up and saw a glint of his wolfish yellow eyes.

"We've got company, darlin', so keep it G-rated, will you?" *Me?* He was the one with the dirty mouth. "Have I told you I really hate leaving things unfinished?"

I cocked an eyebrow at him. "Sounds like a you-problem, not a me-problem." And then, before I could stop myself, I added, "But if you'll have your people call my people, maybe we can arrange something."

He tipped his head back and laughed.

However, the instant the words tumbled out, I wanted to take them back. For me, physical intimacy led to attachment, and the last thing I needed was to get any more attached to this man than I already was. Even though I'd have no memories of my time on Darkaway when I left, the emptiness in my heart would remain.

I just wouldn't know why it was there.

CHAPTER TWENTY-EIGHT

Travis

As we strolled through downtown Darkaway, I thought about this morning's conversation with Jada. Although Daphne *seemed* pretty fucking into me, she hadn't asked anything about the contest outcome or the final charm ceremony, when all the others had. Was she afraid of being let down again? Or maybe she didn't think she truly fit into my world—beneath the bright lights of stardom *and* here on Darkaway. It was...a lot.

Recalling what she'd shared about her ex-fiancé back at the cabin and what Jada had told me, a fresh surge of anger boiled up inside of me. No one who disrespected this woman should be allowed to breathe the same air.

Or maybe she was preoccupied with everything waiting for her back home, and the contest and island vacation were just interesting distractions. *I* was an interesting distraction.

I ran a hand through my hair. Was it possible she wasn't as into me as much as I was into her? After all, I couldn't forget she'd called me bad boyfriend material. Maybe she still felt that way.

I pondered that as we watched several large, black raven shifters putting up Monsterval banners that spanned across Nightshade Avenue. The festival wasn't until the end of next month, but the preparations were starting early.

"Are those bird-whisperers?" Daphne asked as we walked under one of the signs.

She looked especially beautiful tonight—brown eyes sparkling as she took in all the sights, cheeks slightly flushed, a tiny smile on her lips. My inner wolf filled with pride that my outing was bringing her obvious joy.

"Who?" I wrenched my gaze away and glanced past her. "The city workers?" She nodded, and I shook my head. "The ravens are actually bird-shifters, and the ones directing them are, well, human."

"Are there any animals that *aren't* shifters?"

I thought about it for a moment. "I was about to say reptiles, but there are a few. Dragons being one of them. There's a small clan of gator-shifters down in the Louisiana bayous. But they mostly keep to themselves."

She chewed on her lower lip making me want to bite it. "Dragons I can handle, but alligators? Ugh. I mean, I'm sure they're friendly enough—"

"No, they're not," I interjected, not wanting her to have any misconceptions. Darkaway Island may be cozy and safe for the most part, but the rest of the world was not. "The gator clan made it onto the CNN last year when—"

"CNN? Are you serious?" Her eyes went wide and she gripped my forearm.

Anticipating that she was going to poke me in the ribs again, I clamped my hand over hers. "*The* Creature News Network."

"Oh," she said. "I missed that you said *the*."

I relaxed my hold on her and she intertwined her fingers with mine, the sudden intimacy making my cock swell.

"Articles of speech may be tiny, but they're mighty." She snorted at my grammar joke, and I continued my story. "A group of gator-shifters pulled several fishermen off a riverboat in broad daylight and ate them. From what I understand, it was fairly gruesome. The Patrol had a terrible time covering up that one."

She cocked her head to the side. "Sorry for all the questions but the...*Patrol?*"

"Monster Patrol. The MP. Supernatural fixers who help keep our existence secret from humans when a paranormal creature goes rogue in the human world. And I love all your questions." Truth was, I loved the curiosity she had for my world and I enjoyed giving her the answers. Maybe if things made more sense to her, she could picture herself staying in it—with me.

She raised her brows. "Like the Ministry of Magic? Or the Volturi?"

I laughed. "Yeah, something like that."

We stopped in front of a shop, and I told the camera crew they had to wait outside. They tried to argue, saying my sister gave them strict instructions to follow us everywhere, but I pointed to a sign in the window that said *No Cameras Allowed*, and they relented.

I opened the door for Daphne and followed her inside.

Cozy banquets lined the walls studded with wine bottles and dimly lit display cases, while thin fabric hung in swoops from the ceiling. On a dais at the far end, my friend Cassie was hunched over a lighted work table, a jeweler's loupe in one hand and a pair of tweezers in the other. Several couples were sipping wine and casually watching her, like sushi eaters watching the sushi chef.

"Where are we?" Daphne slowly spun a 360, taking in

everything. "I didn't see what the sign said. I mean, I can tell they sell wine but it smells like donuts in here."

"This is Baubles and Barrels, a wine shop that sells magical handcrafted jewelry. They host wine tasting and jewelry-making events that are very popular with the tourists."

Cassie evidently heard us and looked up. She set down her project, stepped off the dais and hurried toward us, but then she stopped, patted her apron pocket and returned to her worktable.

I lowered my voice. "Don't mention to her that it smells like donuts."

Daphne frowned. "Why not?"

"Trust me." I pressed my lips together. "It's a sensitive topic."

Cassie grabbed something from a drawer and came back, introducing herself warmly to Daphne. "Portia's told me all about you."

"You're her friend from the coven who made these, right?" Daphne jangled her bracelet and returned the smile. "I just adore her, but did she tell you what a hot mess I am?"

Cassie laughed. "She said you're lovely and has enjoyed doing your hair and makeup for the contest. Hey, Trav."

"Thanks for putting up that sign." I jutted my chin at the door. Normally, the B&B had no such policy.

"Of course," she replied then led us over to a table.

CHAPTER TWENTY-NINE

Daphne

I instantly liked Portia's friend, who was also Travis's friend. What was it with the island and its residents? Except for Dr. Eisenhorn the Third and that jerk in Nightmare Alley, though technically that guy didn't live here, they were all so nice. It felt as if I'd found my people even though I wasn't actually *one* of them.

Travis took a sip from his wineglass and set it down next to mine, brushing my pinkie finger in the process. "I have a confession to make."

"Do I look like a priest to you?"

He lifted a dark brow. "Very funny. But first I want to talk about Date-A-Wolf."

His face was all hard lines and angles, and I steeled myself for what he was about to say. Was tonight all about gently breaking the news that I wouldn't be getting a charm at the next ceremony? It was against the rules of the contest for him to share his intentions, so was that why he didn't let the cameras film any of this? He hadn't told Sarah ahead of time, but maybe

189

because of what happened in the cabin, he felt he owed me something more?

Despite telling myself not to, I had developed real feelings for this man. I was actually falling for him. Not only was he incredibly patient, even when people didn't deserve it, he was sweet and thoughtful. He made me laugh, and he gave me strength without taking away my agency to handle things on my own terms.

"Okay," I said slowly.

He took my hands in his, and my body stiffened. It was better to find out now than to be blindsided at the very public charm ceremony, I told myself, recalling a similar unpleasant memory when Gavin left me high and dry in Hawaii. Having had that happen once in my life was one time too many.

His expression darkened. "Daphne, you look like you're about to get an enema."

I'd rather get an enema than this, I thought, biting back the stupid tears that were threatening to fall. I warned myself not to get attached to this man and what did I do? I stupidly got attached to him!

Fine. I'm just going to say it. "Aren't you about to tell me this is the end of the line for me?"

He lifted my chin with a finger, forcing me to look him straight in the eye. The hurt I saw in them mirrored what I was feeling, like he couldn't believe I'd just said that. "Quite the opposite, my little skeptic."

I frowned, not sure what he meant.

"This contest was my sister's idea," he continued. "And I thought it was a ridiculous waste of time." His broad hand came down to possessively cover my throat, and he caressed the side of my neck with his thumb. "Until I met you."

I blinked a few times, not trusting myself to hope. "So, you're not sending me packing?"

His hand slid to my nape, pulling me close to him, and he

kissed the tiny, sensitive spot under my ear, making my entire body quiver. "Not unless you want me to."

A tidal wave of relief rushed over me that he wasn't letting me down gently, that things weren't ending tonight. "Heaven's, no."

"Good. Because I'm choosing you at the end."

His words slid through me, spearing the center of my pounding heart.

I pulled away from him and looked him square in the eye to see if he was shitting me. The man was really breaking all the rules now. Normally I wasn't a rule-breaker, but not all rules were meant to be followed. "You mean I'm going all the way?" When a naughty smile tugged at the corner of his lips, I realized I could've phrased that differently.

"Yes." He twirled a lock of my hair around his finger. "With me. But only if you want to. After all, someone once told me I'm bad boyfriend material."

I had the sudden urge to climb this man like a tree and kiss the hell out of him, but the sound of someone clearing their throat next to our little booth stopped me from making a fool of myself in public. What was with this man that made me want to do naughty things?

"Would you like me to come back later?" Cassie asked, brows raised, sleek black hair skimming her shoulders.

Travis's eyes were more wolfish yellow than brown as he stared at me, not bothering to look over at her. "No."

My gaze bounced between them. "What's going on?"

Travis inclined his head to Cassie, and she set a small wooden box on the table. I couldn't help but notice that it had an ornate clasp not unlike the one on the evil spell book back in my hotel room.

His hand slid from my neck to rest on my knee, shooting warmth straight to my core. "My confession is that I took something from you, Daphne. And I want to give it back—with a few modifications, thanks to Cassie."

He reached for the box, but Cassie reprimanded him. "*No*, Travis! Keep your mitts off. *She* must be the one to touch it first."

He pulled back, folded his hands and waited.

With a nod of encouragement from her, I took the small box and opened it. Inside, on a bed of black silk, was an iridescent pink moonstone with delicate veins of purple and blue in a simple bezel setting. I took it out and held it in my hand. "Oh my God, it's beautiful."

"Do you recognize it?" Travis asked, his lips brushing the shell of my ear.

"Wait! Is this one of the ones I found? But how—?"

"When your clothes were drying in the cabin, the stone fell from your pocket. I took it and gave it to Cassie for her to work her magic."

Cassie was a witch, so I knew what this meant, but I wanted to hear her say it. "Magic?" I asked, holding my breath. "What kind of magic?"

"You found the moonstone, so I was able to imbue it with your memories." She gave a little shrug, like it was no big deal. But it was a *very* big deal! A huge fucking deal!

With his warm hand on my knee, Travis looked at me as if I were the only one in the room. "If you give her your bracelet, she'll solder it on while we wait. That way, you'll be able to cross the island's charmed barrier without losing your memories of your time here."

I tried to undo the clasp myself, but my fingers were shaking so hard my hands wouldn't cooperate. Travis had to do it for me and handed the bracelet to Cassie.

Of your time here, he'd said. Not *of me*. Did that mean when the contest was over I'd be leaving the island...alone?

Travis and I enjoyed a candlelight dinner on the rooftop terrace of Cucina Vincenzo overlooking Darkaway Bay. Soft Italian music played on hidden speakers while boats bobbed out in the harbor, their lights flickering on the dark water. It would've been romantic if not for the camera crew and several tables of gawkers, but we did our best to ignore them. He had the spaghetti bolognaise, and I had the chicken piccata, both of which were delicious.

Before tonight, I'd have thought that when he fed me a bite from his plate, it was simply for the cameras. After all, the romantic gesture by a talented actor played right into the dating show theme. But given what he'd had to orchestrate to get me a memory stone, and the possessive way he'd touched me at Baubles and Barrels with no cameras around, I didn't think it was just for show anymore.

I cut him a piece of my chicken piccata, making sure to get plenty of capers. With a hand underneath to catch any sauce, it was my turn to feed him. His lips closed over the tines of my fork, and I slowly pulled it out. He groaned softly as he chewed, and I couldn't help but think of that night in the cabin when he'd made a similar sound.

When I reached for the bottle of Chianti to refill our glasses, I heard his phone vibrating with an incoming call. It wasn't the first time either, but he was choosing to ignore it.

"Do you need to get that?" I asked, filling our glasses back up.

"It's fine," he said. "It's not an emergency."

How did he know? He hadn't even looked at it. His phone buzzed again. "Are you sure?"

"Positive." He leaned in close and cupped a hand to my ear. "I can't let the cameras hear this," he whispered. "It's one of my little nieces. Matthew, my brother-in-law, sometimes lets the little one play games on his phone in the evening. Jada would lose her shit if she knew because she has a strict no-screens policy at night. I was there this morning, and my niece asked if she could call me tonight. I told her no, but—" He gave a little shrug. "She's four."

It was my turn to cup his ear. I tried to ignore how amazing he smelled. "We could video-call her."

He pulled back from me slightly. "Really?"

"Sure. I'd love to meet her."

He looked at me with an expression I couldn't quite read, and over a shared dessert of tiramisu, we concocted an elaborate lie so as not to get Matthew in trouble. He sent the camera crew away, saying we needed a few minutes alone, and then he video-called his niece.

"Uncle, I've been trying to call you. I want to show you a picture I colored." His niece was utterly adorable with her big brown eyes, space buns and dimple. A family trait, I wondered? I was pretty sure Jada had a dimple too, but honestly, I had paid little attention to hers. The girl held up a page with random scribbles that were vaguely wolf-shaped. You could tell her father was holding the phone because it was very steady.

"Wow, Ginnea, that's really good."

Ginnea frowned. "Is that your gull-fend?"

Travis bit his lip to keep from laughing and glanced over at me, his gaze searching my face. "Yes, this is my girlfriend, Daphne."

Why did an introduction to a four-year-old make me all melty inside? My ovaries were obviously very much in charge here.

"Hi, Ginnea, it's really nice to meet you. You're such a talented artist. Is that a mama wolf and her puppies?"

"No," the girl said, sighing dramatically. "It's a daddy wolf and his puppies. The mama is over there, telling those people what to do."

Travis and I exchanged amused glances. Sounded just like his sister.

"She's really pretty, Uncle," Ginnea whispered, as if she didn't think I could hear her. "I like her hair."

"I know, right? I like her hair too." A little smirk turned up one corner of his mouth.

When I was on top of him at the cabin, my damp hair had fallen in curtains around his face. A flicker of heat curled low in my belly at the memory, my breath hitching a little. The way he was looking at me now made me wonder if he was remembering the same thing.

Later, after a horse-drawn carriage ride past a bunch of beautiful old mansions, Travis walked me back to my villa. He stopped on the walkway to speak to the camera crew, telling them they didn't need to follow us to my door, and instructed them to film us walking down the path and disappearing around the corner. But unlike last time, they pushed back.

"No, I'm not staying with her," I heard Travis argue. Which made me a little disappointed, to be honest. "But if you film that footage and leave it a mystery, the audience will wonder whether I stayed or not. It'll be good for ratings. Trust me."

So that was how it came to be just Travis and me at the arched door of my villa, as I fished the key from my small handbag. "Thank you for tonight. I had—"

He pushed my back to the door, pinned my wrists above my head, and kissed me so hard that my soul left my body for a moment. Then he thrust a thigh between mine, and I felt the hard ridge of him through the fabric of my dress. His free hand cupped my breast, and he gave a soft growl. Need rushed through me—unstoppable, all-consuming—wiping out every thought except *him* and *more*.

"Would you...like to...come inside?" I somehow managed to say against his lips. Although my little villa was tucked into a quiet part of the resort, we were still out in public here. Anyone could walk by.

"I thought you'd never ask."

He released his hold on me just long enough so I could shove the key into the lock and open the door, and then he was on me again. We didn't even make it through the alcove. My heart pounded, and molten heat pooled between my legs as he reached under my dress and shoved my thong aside. I was thankful I hadn't worn the flowy pants I'd been considering; otherwise, I was certain he'd have torn them off. Easy access *did* have its benefits. My hands speared through his hair, and I rose on my toes to kiss him again. He tasted of herbs, red wine and something this side of feral.

But just as he slid two fingers inside me and his thumb pressed against my clit, he stilled, his whole body going rigid.

"What's wrong?" I said, panting against his lips as my inner muscles clenched around him.

"Shhh. Something isn't right."

CHAPTER THIRTY

Travis

I shoved Daphne behind me as I stepped from the entryway into her room. Although she didn't seem like a neat freak, I doubted she routinely draped her bras over the TV and hung jeans from the overhead fan, either.

Empty drawers were overturned on the bed. A chair on its side. Cabinet and closet doors open. Toiletries strewn over the floor of her bathroom.

And amidst it all, the faint smell of werewolves hung in the air.

White-hot rage boiled up inside me, threatening to overflow. *When* I found out who did this, not *if*, I would rip their insides out.

"What happened in here?" Daphne gasped, clutching the back of my shirt. "Oh my God, George! Here, kitty-kitty." She rushed past me, fell to the floor and lifted the bed skirt. Then she turned back to me, tears rolling down her cheeks, and my heart nearly broke. "He's not here, Travis. My kitty isn't here."

I summoned my inner wolf and sniffed the air. Besides

Daphne's sweet scent, an older scent of one, possibly two, werewolves lingered in the room, as did a newer, stronger scent of cat. "He's still here, my love. He's just hiding out somewhere."

I pulled her to her feet, and she collapsed into my arms. "Are you sure?"

The pain in her voice ripped through me. "I'm positive. I could shift and easily find him, but I'm afraid that would traumatize him further."

"Yeah, he hates dogs." She sniffed against my chest. "Who would do something like this?"

"I don't know," I said, grinding my teeth. "But I swear I'm going to find out who—and they'll regret ever fucking with you like this."

She stood taller in my arms at my vow of revenge.

The French doors to her courtyard were slightly ajar. "Let's start out there." I took the lead, keeping her safely behind me. The perpetrators were long gone, but I wasn't taking any chances.

I followed the scent to the far side of the patio and spotted the cat instantly. "There he is!" I said, pointing at two glowing eyes staring down at us from the branches of a dogwood tree.

"George!" Daphne rushed to the base of the tree and reached up to him. "My poor, scared little kitty. Are you okay?"

I stayed a few paces back so as not to scare him further and called the sheriff's department. As I quickly explained what had happened, I watched Daphne unsuccessfully try to coax George down from the tree. The cat was just out of her reach...but not mine.

I hung up and went to her side. "Want me to give it a try?"

She grimaced, but I could see the gratitude in her eyes. This was traumatic for her too, and she needed to hold her cat to know that he was fine. "But he'll scratch the hell out of you, Travis."

I shrugged. "You're worried about him and that's all that matters."

Sheriff Alverse Aldrich arrived a short time later as Daphne was massaging some healing lotion into the scratches on my forearms. Getting George down from the tree had turned out to be tricky as hell. I probably should've used gloves or something, but love is blind and hindsight is twenty-twenty.

The sheriff was a bald, broad-shouldered bear shifter with a bushy mustache, and colorful sleeve tattoos.

"Causing trouble again, son?" he asked, referring to the altercation I'd had with the vampire tourist in Nightmare Alley as he clapped me good-naturedly on the shoulder.

"Trying the fuck not to."

A low, menacing growl emanated from George's cat carrier as the sheriff walked past. *Must not like bears either.*

As the sheriff sniffed around the suite, Daphne snatched her undergarments from the TV and shoved them into her open suitcase.

"Do you have any valuables?" he asked her. "Is there anything missing?"

After rescuing George, we'd found the evil spell book still safely stashed in her beach bag on the closet shelf.

Daphne gave me a pointed look that said, *Should we tell him about it?* And I gave her a look back that I hoped said, *Your call.*

She flashed me a quick, tight-lipped smile. Good. It seemed as if she understood me.

"I was worried about George, so I haven't really checked. But I don't think so. I don't own much jewelry or keep any cash around."

Without warning, the sheriff shifted into his bear form. Daphne jumped and made a sound of surprise. I set a hand on the small of her back and guided her out of the way as the large brown bear lumbered around her villa and out into the courtyard. At some point, she slipped an arm around my waist, making my wolf very happy. He loved to protect her and puffed with pride that she turned to me to feel safe.

I kissed the top of her head. "Doing okay?" I whispered.

She nodded and nestled closer.

After the sheriff sniffed in every nook and cranny, he morphed back into his human form and stood in the middle of the room, chewing on a toothpick. "So, tell me about this Date-A-Wolf contest?"

"What do you want to know?" I asked, my tone suddenly guarded. Some folks on the island thought the contest was nonsense. And I had too. I only agreed in order to keep the ranch out of my half-brother's greedy hands. But if not for Date-A-Wolf, I'd have never met Daphne, so my opinion had done a 180.

He tapped his nose and looked around the room. "Clearly, another werewolf has been here."

I tensed. "Yes, and..."

"Could this have been carried out by a disgruntled former contestant? From my understanding, you sent home a werewolf the other night."

"That's ridiculous," Daphne sputtered, looking stricken.

Alverse gave a little shrug. "It's just a question."

"You're referring to Sarah, and no, she would never do something like this." She put her hands on her hips. "She's a good friend of mine."

"Are you sure? How well do you *really* know her?" The sheriff was relentless. Like a barbed hook, he wouldn't let go of this line of questioning.

"Well, for one thing," Daphne said, "she didn't even want to be in the contest, but her family made her."

"Or so she says." The sheriff lifted a bushy brow.

"Oh, for Pete's sake, Alverse," I said, pulling Daphne closer and rubbing the curve of her hip. "If Daphne said her friend

Sarah didn't do this, she didn't do it. Plus, I know her scent and this wasn't her."

His eyes narrowed, not missing the possessive way I was touching Daphne. "Or maybe it's a current contestant, with a werewolf friend, trying to sabotage her competition?"

I hesitated. I'd completely forgotten about the mole. "I know their scents, Sheriff. These two are unfamiliar."

Alverse pointed with his toothpick around the room. "One is definitely canine, but the other is...human. What's curious is that they used a masking elixir to hide their scent."

My jaw nearly hit the floor. "You're good, Sheriff. I didn't pick up on those nuances."

He clamped a meaty hand on my shoulder and gave it a rough shake. "That's okay, son. We bears have a much better sense of smell than you dogs."

"Very funny," I said, shrugging his hand away.

"It's not funny." He guffawed. "It's the truth."

I clenched my jaw, feeling the muscles tense as my irritation flared. Bears did have a more acute sense of smell than wolves, but he didn't have to be a dick about it.

While Daphne was in the bathroom, picking her toiletries off the tile floor, I pulled the sheriff aside and told him about the possible mole.

He nodded thoughtfully. "You're picking Daphne at the end of the contest, aren't you?" When I nodded, he tapped his nose. "I thought so. Both of you are giving off some strong mating pheromones."

It would suck to be a love-struck teenager in that man's house. He'd catch you sneaking out during the planning phase.

"It's likely that the mole was responsible for this." The sheriff jutted his chin in Daphne's direction. "Who does she think it is?"

I rubbed my neck. "I haven't exactly told her about the mole yet."

"Why not?" he asked, a confused expression on his face, then he lowered his voice. "Do you think she's involved somehow?"

"Hell no," I growled.

The sheriff cocked his head and narrowed his eyes. "So, you have feelings for this girl and yet you're not being honest with her?"

I cursed under my breath. I didn't need this asshole poking his nose into my personal business, questioning what I did and didn't do. The truth was, I should've told Daphne about the mole and wasn't sure why I hadn't.

Elbowing past the sheriff, I headed to the bathroom, leaned around the doorframe and saw that Daphne was lining up all her bottles into neat little rows on the counter. "What the hell are you doing?"

Her head snapped up. "Just tidying up after my room was ransacked," she said in a sing-song, don't-be-such-a-douchebag tone. "What's it look like I'm doing?"

"Don't bother. Just throw it all into a bag."

She gave me a withering look that would intimidate a lesser man. "I'm not going to *just throw* my nice skincare and potions into a bag."

I'd had enough of this. "Yes, you are. And when you're done, you're going to throw your other shit into a bag too. Or I can do it for you."

"I'm...ah...going to let you two lovebirds sort things out," the sheriff called from the hallway behind me. "Daphne, I'll need you to visit the station to fill out some paperwork." And then he was gone.

Daphne turned to fully face me. If her eyes were laser guns, she'd have changed the setting from stun to kill. "In case you didn't know, Travis," she said through clenched teeth, "the resort is full. Whoever's working the front desk isn't going to be able to find me another room at this time of night, especially not one that is cat-charmed."

I gave a cold laugh. "You're not staying here. You and George are coming home with me."

"But—"

And then I was all up in her personal space, pushing her against the wall and cupping her neck, forcing her to look up at me—really look at me. "Darlin' you can either walk out of here on your own WITH your shit or I carry you out with NONE of it. What'll it be?"

When she didn't answer me straight away, I began counting backwards, starting at ten.

CHAPTER THIRTY-ONE

Daphne

"I can't believe you Drake Valentino'd me to get me to come home with you," I said with a mouthful of toothpaste to Travis's reflection in the bathroom mirror.

"Whatever works," he replied. Or at least that was what I think he said because he was currently flossing.

It was well after 2 a.m. by the time we got to Darkaway Ranch, so it was nice to see that he was as committed to dental hygiene as I was, regardless of the late hour.

Although I would never admit it, when Travis took charge at the villa after the break-in, it was kind of hot. I knew he would stop at nothing to protect me and keep me safe, but hell if I'd ever tell *him* that. The man was cocky enough as it was. Would he have actually carried me out of there if I hadn't quote/unquote thrown my shit together on time?

I shivered deliciously at the thought.

When we got to the ranch, we'd had to tiptoe through the main part of the Big House with all of my things, including George's carrier, so as not to awaken any of his family. His suite of rooms was at the far end, down an elevated breezeway. The alpha wing of the house had been his father's, which was why it was currently under renovation, he'd explained. Plastic from the new mattress was still balled up in one corner, but the massive bed itself had been in his family for generations. The various paint samples stuck to one wall reminded me of the ones I had on my apartment wall, and I realized I hadn't thought about that place in ages. I shivered—and not in a good way—at the danger that could be awaiting me there.

I spit out my toothpaste and rinsed out the sink. "Although I haven't finished watching all the seasons, it's clear that Drake Valentino is a grumpy alpha-hole."

"Yeah, well, I modeled him after my inner wolf."

I raised an eyebrow. "He's a grumpy alpha-hole too?"

He shrugged. "Pretty much. He's extremely protective of those he lo—cares about—and he *always* gets his way."

I kept my eyes down and rummaged through one of my bags, not wanting to address the fact that he almost said *loves*. Had to be a slip of the tongue. We hadn't known each other long enough for that. I was fairly certain he'd called me *my love* back at the villa too, but it was probably just his way of comforting me during a very stressful time.

But what if he meant it, though? I certainly was developing feelings for him. Was a relationship between us even possible? I mean, he'd given me a memory stone. Was I a fool for even thinking about it? After all, we were from two very different worlds. I had my own life back in Atlanta—well, at one time I had.

I found one of my homemade herbal tea packets. Now, where was I going get a mug and hot water? I padded into the bedroom dominated by that giant bed. Did Travis have a kitchenette somewhere in his suite? I hoped I wouldn't have to go back to the main part of the house. This place was huge, and I'd most likely get lost in the dark.

Travis came up behind me and slid his hands up my arms. "What do you need?" he murmured, moving my hair aside and kissing the back of my neck. Was he feeling guilty for being an incorrigible jerk a while ago?

Heat rushed through me at his touch. "I like to make myself a cup of tea before bed."

He reached under my silky pajama top for my breast, gently twisting my nipple between his thumb and forefinger. "You do?"

I arched into him, feeling that huge erection of his pressing hard against me. "Yes." And because I couldn't just cave to the whims of this man any time he touched me, I forced myself to say, "If I wake up in the middle of the night, I like to sip on cold tea."

"Is that so?" He slipped his other hand under the waistband of my pajama bottoms and growled when he discovered how wet I was. "I'll make you a deal."

Did this man *ever* stop playing games?

"Get into that bed and wait for me."

"And?"

"And I'll go make your damn tea."

So much for not caving, I thought, licking my lips with anticipation. "Fine. You've got yourself a deal."

"Good girl." He released me and gave me a pat on the ass. "Oh, and my wolf says you'd better not be wearing those pajamas when I return. You need to be naked in that bed, ready for me."

I crossed my arms and made a sound of protest. "Is he always this demanding?"

"Only with you, little prey."

"And what happens if I don't?" I wanted to know what the consequences were so I could decide whether or not to do what he wanted. Sometimes the punishment was more fun than the crime.

Travis reached for the door then turned back, his wolf-yellow gaze locked onto mine. "I'll just tear them off and they'll be ruined."

It wasn't lost on me that he said *he* would, not his wolf.

I waited for him naked under his high thread-count sheets. I really liked my silky pajamas with the smiling cactuses, so it was worth it—this time—to do his bidding.

The massive headboard was a deep, rich mahogany and incredibly detailed. The thing had to weigh a ton. In addition to various scenes depicting wolves and moons—*shocking, I know*—you couldn't miss several well-worn handles carved into the wood. But for the life of me, I couldn't figure out what the carved parts in the footboard were for.

I found out soon enough.

CHAPTER THIRTY-TWO

Travis

When I re-entered the suite, the first thing I saw was a flurry of fur as George bounded from the bed and disappeared into the adjoining sitting room. But the second thing I saw took my breath away. I actually had to pause in the doorway to compose myself.

Generations of my family grew up in this house and these rooms had always belonged to the pack's Alpha and his mate. Given my strained relationship with my father, I didn't want anything that was his or that reminded me of him after his death. Jada had insisted I take these rooms, even though I was happy enough staying out in the apartments over the garage or in one of the guest houses when I was here. After officially signing the ranch over to her, I planned to be Alpha in name only and didn't expect to come to the island much, anyway. No use having a huge part of the house go unused, I'd told her. She should just move her family in here.

But Jada didn't listen and immediately began renovations to change things up for me. While I was on set, we talked about color palettes over the phone, and she sent me a shit ton of aesthetic pictures. She had walls knocked out, ordered new rugs, paint, décor, gutted the bathroom, and more. She'd even had movers come and transport the bed to a different location. Even though it looked very different from when my father was alive, I kept imagining *him* in these rooms, and they never felt like mine.

That is, until I walked back in and saw Daphne waiting for me in that big bed—*my* bed—and suddenly I was home.

Not trusting myself to speak, I quietly placed her cup of tea on the nightstand, then carried the tray to the adjoining room where I set down a water dish and a plate of tuna for George. His blue eyes glared at me from under the sofa, but at least he didn't hiss at me.

When I returned to the bedroom, Daphne was holding the sheets open for me with a look I couldn't quite read.

"Those need to come off," she said softly, indicating my pajama pants.

"Et tu, Brute?" I said it in a French accent even though I don't speak French.

Her serious expression vanished, and she doubled over with laughter. "Oh my God, Travis! That is so *not* the correct use of that phrase."

Lifting a brow, I shucked off my pajamas and joined her under the covers. She was gloriously naked, and my inner wolf preened that she'd obeyed me. This time. "Why? Doesn't it mean *same as you* or *also like you?*"

She was still laughing. "Not exactly! Julius Caesar says that to Brutus after Brutus stabbed him." She reached for me, cool fingers closing possessively around my thick cock. "I don't plan to assassinate you, Travis. Well, maybe just a little."

I cupped the nape of her neck and kissed her deeply, pressing my tongue past the seam of her lips and into her mouth. After everything that had happened today, I thought this would never come, but all that fell away as I focused on this gorgeous woman in my arms. She moaned softly as I kissed her, and the sound went straight to my cock as she stroked me.

I wanted nothing more than to bury myself in her right now, but I had to take things slowly. The full moon was still a few days away, but I couldn't rush this. The last thing I wanted was to hurt her. And given my size, I knew it was a real possibility unless I was careful and took my time.

The animal inside me was surprisingly quiet as I spent time playing with Daphne's breasts, lightly twisting the peaked nipple of one between my finger and thumb and suckling on the other. He didn't want to rush and hurt her either.

"Travis, please." Her entire body trembled as she ground her hips against my thigh separating her legs.

"Please what, my love?"

"Please, I need to feel you inside me. I'm sick of this stupid edging."

I chuckled. "Such a greedy little thing. I plan to thoroughly fuck you but only when you're ready."

She huffed. "Are all Alphas as bossy as you?"

"Only the hot ones."

I slipped two fingers inside her, then added a third, moving them in and out, while pressing her clit with my thumb. My mouth came down over hers as she cried out and soon her inner muscles were clenching around my fingers in the first of several orgasms. The soft breathy sounds she made as she came, nearly had me coming as well. Heaven's Moon, I was hard enough.

Withdrawing my hand, I nuzzled her neck and held her close as she came back to earth.

She ran her hands over my back. "Where are your condoms?"

"Mmmm," I said, kissing her collarbone. "I'm afraid, you're still not ready for that yet, but let's see what this bed can do."

I pushed the covers aside and dropped the center panel of

the footboard. Then I gave each of her ankles a little kiss before positioning her heels on the carved indentations, conveniently located just beyond the width of my shoulders. Although I'd never bedded a woman in an Alpha's bed before, it was surprisingly intuitive and all males knew how they worked.

"What are you doing, Travis?" she asked, breathlessly, sitting up on her elbows to watch.

I slowly ran my hands up her shapely legs to her inner thighs. Spread out before me, she was a delicious, but delicate dessert to be devoured with the utmost care. "Just giving you some leverage for what I'm about to do to you."

When I lowered my mouth to her, I was suddenly grateful that the Alpha's quarters were set off far from the rest of the house. Anyone closer would've heard her beautiful cries of pleasure.

CHAPTER THIRTY-THREE

Daphne

I f this man didn't fuck me soon, I was going to get violent. My need for him was that desperate, that primal.

When I said as much to Travis, he laughed, so I sunk my teeth into his muscular shoulder—not enough to break the skin, but hard enough for him to know I meant business. I wanted to mark him as my own. "How can one man be so incredibly hot yet astonishingly frustrating at the same time?"

"It's a gift, my love."

There. He'd said it again. I exhaled slowly, tabling that knowledge for now, because I had more pressing issues to deal with at the moment.

I was done waiting. When I pushed him back on the mattress and reached for a condom, I was struck by a sudden déjà vu. He'd done this exact thing back at the cabin when he'd let me take charge. Just like before, he wanted this to be completely on my terms. And I...I *loved* that about him.

"Is the door locked?" I asked.

"There are no hikers here," he said, the corner of his mouth turning up in a smirk. "And yes, the door is locked."

Good. Because I planned to ride this man like a stallion and I didn't want any interruptions.

He propped his hands behind his head and watched me as I rolled the condom down over his large cock. I could almost get my hand around it, but not quite. "Think it'll fit, darlin'?"

Not this again.

"Shut up, Drake, and let me handle this."

"Whatever you say. You're the boss. I'm just along for the ride."

I soon wiped that cocky smirk off his lips when I straddled his hips, grabbed his cock to position it between my thighs and eased myself onto him.

He let out a half groan/half growl. His hands gripped the bedsheets and the muscles in his neck strained. "Fuuuck. You're so damn tight." I could tell he wanted to grab my hips and use them to drive into me, but he was fighting against his nature to let me stay in control.

I closed my eyes and concentrated on the incredible sensation of him inside of me. The thickness. The pressure. The delectable stretch. And as I took him deeper, I was thankful now for all the foreplay. I'd have never been able to accommodate him had he not prepared me well beforehand.

With him caged beneath me, our hips moved in a fluid rhythm. Like the tide, advancing then retreating, over and over and over. His lips parted, his dark brows furrowed. His expression was one of pure lust...and something much darker. He stared at my breasts as they swayed before him, then he lifted his head and drew a nipple in his mouth. I arched into him, softened a little more, and he slid even deeper.

"You're....so...fucking...wet," he said, the words coming with each thrust.

I sank a little lower then hissed. Something strange and

wonderful pressed against my hypersensitive clit, sending jolts of electricity careening everywhere. My toes curled and I gripped fistfuls of his hair. "Travis, what is...?"

He gave a soft, masculine chuckle that echoed through my core. "Shhh, little prey. Just enjoy it. I'll explain later." This beautiful man beneath me sounded so fucking proud of himself.

I'd have known if he'd slipped on a sex toy. No, this was all him.

And then I felt a gentle, yet unmistakable vibration against my clit and my world shifted on its axis.

I cried out his name as wave after wave of intense pleasure slammed through me, both relentless and exquisite. And just when I thought I might break in half, he groaned and shuddered with his release.

Utterly boneless, I collapsed on top of him. He was still very hard inside me as he pulled up the sheets to cover our naked bodies. With my ear to his muscled chest, his arms tightly around me, I felt his racing heart as if it were my own.

A few moments later, he pulled out of me. I wanted to ask him how, what, when and where, but rational thought escaped me. He slipped from the covers, disposed of the condom and brought me back a warm washcloth.

Never had a man taken care of me and my needs like this before. He took his pleasure only after seeing to it that I'd had mine first—several times. And not just tonight in this amazing bed. From the first moment I met him, when he gave up his privacy on the ferry deck to guide me out of the fog, Travis had been putting my needs above his.

"What. Was. That?" I asked, still hardly able to speak. If I wasn't already hopelessly addicted to him, I was now.

He caressed my cheek with the back of his fingers. "It's a wolf thing, but we can talk about it later. You need to sleep."

Tears of emotion leaked from the corner of my eyes as he spooned me. Damn it. I was falling madly in love with this man.

CHAPTER THIRTY-FOUR

Daphne

Travis nuzzled my neck as we walked across the breezeway to the main part of the house where his family was gathering for a late brunch. We were supposed to be down there fifteen minutes ago, but we got a little sidetracked.

"Are you sure your sister won't be mad at me? You know, the contest rules and everything."

He slipped a hand around my waist. "First of all, it's me she would be mad at, but she's not. And as for you, she's had your back from the beginning. Annoyingly so. Besides, I already told her I was picking you at the end."

Heart stuttering in my chest, his words stopped me in my tracks. "You told her before you told me?"

"I *had* to. She's been hassling me for not spending much time with the other contestants, and I told her it was because..." He studied my face like he was searching for what to say, and something dark passed behind his eyes. "...I was falling for you."

The physical chemistry was definitely there, but to hear that he was feeling something deeper too, made my knees a little weak.

He ran a hand through his hair, still damp from the shower. "I tried hard not to pursue you. Heaven's Moon, I tried. You were thrown into a contest in a world you only just learned about, and it was so unfair to you. I kept telling myself to send you home, but I couldn't go through with it. Every. Damn. Time. You're just so—" He sighed heavily and made a grumbly sound of frustration. "I like every fucking thing about you, okay?"

I laughed. "And I like every fucking thing about you too. Plus, some of the non-fucking things."

With a low groan that sounded suspiciously like a growl, he hoisted me up so that my legs bracketed his waist. "Only *some* of them?"

"Okay, most of them." I cupped his jaw with both hands and pressed my lips to his. But before things got even more heated, little footsteps sounded on the breezeway, and Travis quickly set me down.

"Look what I have, Uncle!"

I turned to see Ginnea and gasped. She was holding George in her arms like a rag doll. If he scratched or bit her...

"Wow, honey," I said as gently as I could, bending down to her level. I didn't want to make any sudden moves or say something to scare or startle George. That could be disastrous. "Where did you find him?" I looked up at Travis. He seemed to be as confused as I was. Our bedroom door had been locked all night. Was there another way into his suite? Had we left a window open and George escaped?

The little girl laughed. "I didn't. I woke up this morning and he was on my bed purring. He loves me."

George was on her bed? I shot Travis another glance and he shrugged.

"Guess I left the door open when I went to the kitchen for

that water." Both of us had been parched. My little cup of tea didn't quite cut it after all the... *activity*. "I'm not used to having a cat around. He must've run out then."

"His name is George," I told her. "I think maybe he wants to walk now. Do you think you can put him down?"

She plopped him on his feet and turned back toward the main house. "Come on, George. Let's go play in my room."

And wouldn't you know it? George padded dutifully after her, tail stuck in the air, without a backwards glance at me.

Travis's family was sitting around a huge table in the sun-drenched kitchen when we walked in, silverware and glasses clinking, and he introduced me to each of them. There was Matthew, his sweet brother-in-law, who asked if I'd like a vanilla latte with a sprinkle of nutmeg, to which I replied that I'd love one. Travis had obviously remembered my preferred coffee drink and had told him at some point. There were his two other nieces—Anna was the oldest at seven years and then Helena who was five, his twin brothers Rhylan and Reece, who were in college here on the island, and of course, Jada.

She gave me a broad smile, held out a chair for me, and pushed a plate of pancakes in my direction. Guess Travis was right—she wasn't upset about us.

"Travis told us about the break-in," she said. "That's terrible!"

Matthew leaned over and chimed in. "That must've been so scary for you."

My hand paused, pancake speared on my fork. Travis was looking at me from across the table, concern knitting his forehead. *You okay*, he mouthed. I gave him a quick nod.

"Thankfully, your brother was with me," I told her, realizing that my hand was shaking. "I'm not sure what I'd have done if he wasn't."

Jada reached over and gave my back a little pat. "I'm so glad he brought you here, Daphne."

Emotion welled up inside me at her genuine concern. I

didn't trust myself not to cry, so I just nodded again and swallowed at the brick in my throat.

"If Rhy and I find out who did it, we'll take him out behind the woodpile and—"

"Reece, please," Jada said, giving him a stern look and then glancing at the girls.

After everyone went back to eating and talking, she turned to me again. "So, how did you sleep last night? And how was that mattress? It only arrived a few days ago. Poor Travis has been sleeping in the apartment out in the garage. Not exactly appropriate quarters for the pack's new Alpha."

I bit my lip. "Um good. It's really... comfortable."

As Jada reached for the syrup, I saw a knowing spark of amusement in her eyes.

I ate my blueberry pancakes slathered in whipped butter and maple syrup, while Travis sat opposite me and ate his. He was having a somewhat passionate discussion with one of his little brothers about some sports team I'd never heard of, but every so often, he'd glance over to check on me and I'd see a flash of that dimple again.

"I hope this," I said to Jada and twirling my finger to indicate Travis and me, "doesn't mess up the contest."

"Not at all." She consulted a small notepad on the table next to her plate. "We only have two days of filming left, anyway. The group dinner and then the final charm ceremony. Although it's probably best if you don't share this," she mimicked my twirling finger gesture, "with any of them."

I thought about Mia and the others. "Definitely not." I was glad I wouldn't have to lie to Sarah. She was on a weeklong guided rockhounding trip, courtesy of Date-A-Wolf, and was currently on the other side of the island.

After we finished eating, Travis and I cleared the table while Jada and Matthew loaded the dishwasher. We had just finished tidying up when the front door opened at the other end of the house. We could hear someone rustling around in the entryway, probably taking off their shoes.

Travis looked at Jada. "You expecting anyone?"

She shook her head. "It can't be Mom. She's still on the East Coast. And the kids are outside on the sport court."

He called out, "Hey, Rubes, is that you?"

"Trav-ey?" A moment later, a woman about my age came bounding into the room. She threw herself into his arms and he spun her around. "I didn't know you were going to be here."

"Yeah, well, there's this crazy dating contest our older sister cooked up," he told her, finally setting her back on her feet.

"Of course, I know about that, silly." She pulled off her beanie and shook out her long, auburn hair.

So this was his little sister, Ruby. Not his fiancé like I once thought. I bit back a smile at the wrong conclusions I'd jumped to in the emergency room.

"I just wasn't expecting you to be here on the ranch and not —" She spotted me and stopped mid-sentence. "Oh my gods, are you Daphne?"

I stood there, feet rooted to the floor. How did Travis's little sister know about me too? Had Jada told her? Had Travis? "Depends on what you know and who said it."

She grinned. "All I know is that Jada messed up and accidentally invited a human that Travis then fell for."

As she came over and hugged me, I thought about how astonishing it was that yet another member of his family knew how he felt about me.

Travis shrugged. "That's pretty much it."

I needed to set the record straight for Jada's sake. While Ruby made herself a latte, I told her about my former addiction to online quizzes and how I'd used my secretly supernatural friend's wi-fi.

She took a sip of her oat milk latte. "Jada is Miss Perfect all the time, so it's fun to point out when she's not. Imagine if she were your big sister and you had to live up to that in school." She set down her mug and put her hands to her mouth like a bullhorn. "It was torturous."

"Don't listen to her, Daphne," Jada said from the table. Helena was on her lap and she was braiding her hair. "She's the dramatic one in the family."

And as I thought about Travis's beautiful, boisterous family, who seemed to know everything about each other, I couldn't help remembering how Gavin hadn't told any of his relatives that we were even engaged until a few weeks before the wedding. It was a surprise to all of them.

I put my hand to my chest, expecting to feel that familiar pang of not being enough for someone else to love me, but surprisingly it wasn't there.

When Ruby found out that no one had shown me around the place yet, she took it upon herself to be my tour guide while the boys planned to shoot hoops.

The Big House was an impressive old lodge with lots of wood and high beamed ceilings. Worn leather chairs and sofas adorned many of the rooms as did several deer heads and mounted antlers. I wasn't a fan of dead animals, but it worked with the decor. They were a family of werewolves so I guess that meant they killed things.

Ruby pointed to a wall of old photos. "That's a picture of the old ferry docks before the boardwalk was built. And that one's when the Governor came and stayed at the ranch."

"The Governor of Washington is a supernatural creature?"

"Not the current one," she replied. "No, this was several governors ago. I can't remember his magical ability, but several of his daughters were very talented spellcasters." She pointed to another photo. "And that's the old ski resort."

"On the backside of Mystic Mountain?"

Ruby's eyes lit up. "You're a skier? You've been there?"

I laughed. "No, no. I just read about it in one of the guidebooks. I heard that it's haunted."

She gripped my arm enthusiastically. "I can teach you, if you want."

Travis's voice boomed from the other room. "You're not teaching Daphne how to ski, Ruby!"

Ruby frowned. "Why not? I'm an excellent skier."

"Because the last person you tried to teach got hauled off the mountain by the ski patrol."

She chuffed and rolled her eyes. "How was I to know he was going to break his leg?"

We headed down a long hallway, and she paused at the doorway to a cluttered office piled high with packing boxes. "I'm glad to see my sister is clearing this out."

"Your father's?"

"Yep," she said tightly. "I should probably offer to help, but..." She walked in and as she looked around, her shoulders visibly relaxed. "I can't tell you how different this place feels without him. I'm not sure what Travis has told you about our dad."

"He's told me a little."

Ruby grabbed a stack of magazines, including Paranormal Paradise, pushed aside a few boxes on the leather sofa and motioned for me to sit with her. "He wasn't an easy man to be around, and that's being generous. But he *loooved* the fact that his eldest son was a famous actor and collected every article he could find about him. I'm sure he showed them to all of his barely legal mistresses. He'd have his hunting buddies over and casually have one of these magazines open. It was comical, really. If you weren't one of his other children."

It couldn't have been easy for Travis, either, to have his father so obsessed with his outward fame yet care so little about the person he was inside.

As I paged through a few of the magazines, I couldn't help but notice that Travis had been photographed in many glamorous places—movie premieres, private jets—and was often accompanied by very attractive supernatural women. While I knew theoretically that comparison was the thief of joy, a tiny part of me wondered what he saw in a human girl from the Midwest who thrifted most of her clothes and whose idea of a good time was going to a bookstore that served cocktails.

"So, you live on the mainland?" I asked Ruby.

She nodded. "In West Seattle, near the water. It's quirky, like Darkaway, but without the magic or emotional baggage."

Seemed as though their father had done a number on her as well.

"But I'm not there much," she continued. "I'm an investigative journalist and travel around a lot."

"Sounds exciting." I pointed to the stacks of magazines. "Did your father save any of your articles too? I'd love to read your work."

She scoffed. "Are you kidding? He cared only about my brother's glamorous life." I was glad she didn't seem to harbor any ill feelings toward Travis and put the blame solely on their father where it belonged.

We talked about some of the favorite places she'd traveled to and about a few of the scandals she'd uncovered. We thought it was funny that both of our mothers were having solo adventures later in life—although mine was with her girlfriends and hers was with a 'gentleman friend.' When I told her about being a lab tech and what had happened with Pharma-Douche, she got just as pissed as Travis and wanted to rip the guy's liver out. God, I loved this family.

"How about you?" I asked. "Anyone special in your life?"

Ruby shrugged. "No, not really. I've been seeing this one guy for a while, but I'm kind of getting bored with him."

"Why don't you break up then?"

She gave a little laugh. "Because he knows where the clit is."

I snorted. Her brother did too.

CHAPTER THIRTY-FIVE

Travis

"You haven't told her?" Matthew asked, dribbling the basketball like the professional he used to be, deciding when to make his move to get around me.

"No." I lunged, but he dodged left and easily made the lay-up.

Damn. I should've seen that one. Rhylan whooped like an idiot and Matthew flicked the ball to me. I stepped out of bounds and passed it across the court to Reece.

"Why not?" he asked as we watched the twins battle it out. It was an innocent enough question but without an easy answer. "She deserves to know what may be behind that break-in. I mean, it's her personal space and her things that were violated."

"I don't know." I ran a hand through my sweaty hair. "Maybe I'm just an asshole."

"Well, you're certainly acting like one."

When I'd followed Daphne to Wickedville, I was sure she was the mole. And when I found out she wasn't, I didn't have the balls to admit I hadn't trusted her.

Trust, or rather, the lack of it, had been an issue in my last relationship, if you could call it that. Since the network fabricated the one I was having with my co-star Pamela, I couldn't exactly date other women out in the open. To call Meredith my girlfriend was being generous, though we hooked up fairly regularly when I was down in LA and I needed a decent lay. I hadn't thought she considered it more than that, but then she started accusing me of shit—blowing up my phone, believing everything the supernatural tabloids wrote about me —I eventually tired of it and stopped the booty calls.

Distracted now, I missed a pass from Reece, the ball bouncing off the tip of my fingers. Rhylan quickly snatched it up and passed to Matthew, who easily dunked it again.

I held up a hand. "That's game for me, guys. My knee's still bothering me." *Liar.* "Sorry, dude," I told Reece.

"That's okay, old man."

I gave him the finger, grabbed my water bottle and took a long swig.

Matthew was right. Daphne did deserve better.

I found them in the girls' room, Daphne and Ruby on the floor with Ginnea, and George stretched out on the bed like he owned the place.

At the sound of my voice, George lifted his head and hissed at me. *Cute little motherfucker.* But at least he didn't run and hide. Yay, progress.

Daphne was biting the tip of her tongue, trying to get doll clothes on a doll, while Ginnea was giving her orders.

She glanced over at me and did a double-take, her eyes instantly darkening. I realized I was still shirtless and sweaty from the game. And I probably smelled. She handed the doll to Ruby and came over.

"What's up?" She ran the back of her fingers over one of my biceps, and I could feel myself getting hard.

"We need to talk."

I grabbed her hand and we high-tailed it out of there. My little sister and niece didn't need to see what was happening to the front of my sweatpants right now.

I led her outside to the covered wrap-around porch. From here, we could see the outdoor riding area where some of the dude ranch guests were learning how to rope.

"Listen, Daphne, I... There's something I need to tell you."

She sat next to me on the porch swing, smelling like maple syrup, with a purple pen mark on her cheek and a piece of glittery confetti stuck in her loose ponytail. The woman was such a hot mess and so fucking gorgeous that I had a hard time collecting my thoughts.

She took my hand and stroked the back of it with cool fingers.

I cleared my throat and started over. "I should have told you last night. No—I should have told you this a while ago. But the fact that I'm a complete asshole and said nothing shouldn't really surprise you."

She frowned, looking confused. "What do you mean? I take it this is going to piss me off."

"Probably." I recounted to her what my attorney, a psychic, had said about a mole thwarting the contest. "And when you seemed so secretive after our hospital visit—"

"You assumed it was me and then followed me later in Wickedville to catch me doing mole-things," she finished.

"Not exactly." She narrowed her eyes, and then I quickly amended myself. "Well, maybe."

Damn. I was fucking this all up.

"Okay, let me see if I have this straight." She hadn't dropped my hand yet, so at least there was that. "Because I declined your offer to have lunch, you thought it was suss. I mean, who says no to *the* Travis Monroe, right?"

Just like my father, I had assumed it was all about me. The

truth hit me like a punch to the gut as I looked away and nodded.

"And then you learned about the mole and it all made sense. Because of course I should've fallen all over myself when Drake Valentino asked me to lunch."

We were bringing Drake into this now too? I gritted my teeth, but I suppose I deserved it.

"So, my question is," she continued, the hurt evident in her tone, "why didn't you tell me when you realized it was the spell book I was hiding? And if not then, why not when my villa was ransacked? I know you may have been developing feelings for some of the other women but—"

Desperation clawing at me, I lifted my head to meet her gaze and grabbed her hands. "No. I didn't have feelings for any of them." I searched her eyes, looking for the right words to say, and decided just to blurt it all out. "I didn't want to fuck things up with you, okay? At first, I thought you'd be pissed I hadn't trusted you. And then, when I realized I was falling for you, I wanted so desperately for you to feel comfortable in my world. To feel safe among monsters. Especially when it wasn't safe for you back home. I thought if you learned something negative or scary about the contest or things here, you'd never consider staying. You'd leave at the end and forget all about me." I released a ragged breath, then blurted out the rest. "And I know this sounds crazy, because I haven't considered Darkaway Island my home for a long time—that is, not until I saw it through your eyes—but I really wanted you to love it here. And want you to consider staying in this world. With me."

I dropped my gaze. There. I'd said it. I admitted it was all about me and what I wanted. Not about her. I was just like my fucking father after all.

Cool fingers brushed my chin and turned my head to face hers. Moisture glittered in the corners of her eyes.

"I never thought your world was perfect, Travis. Remember

when you almost killed me on the ferry dock? That was literally right when I got here. So, no, I'm not scared of you or your world—what I know of it, that is. But you have pissed me off a time or two."

Then she leaned over and pressed that beautiful mouth to mine.

CHAPTER THIRTY-SIX

Daphne

O ur last group date was at Mama Luigi's restaurant, located just off Nightshade Avenue and down a quaint cobblestone alleyway. Twinkle lights—actual lights, not fairy sprites—hung from potted crab apple trees and draped across the walkway.

I was surprised to learn that the island had two Italian restaurants. Apparently, the owners used to be married, but they got divorced and now competed for business. But who was I to complain? It was one of my favorite cuisines.

Once inside, we were led to a private room in the back with a large round table. Mia grabbed the spot next to Travis, and Lauren picked the other side. I took a seat directly opposite him. I enjoyed looking at him from a slight distance anyway. Gave me a nice perspective. He shot a heated glance at me as if he knew exactly what I was thinking.

My *primo piatto* was a vegetarian minestrone soup and was delicious. Mia had chosen the risotto, and I was surprised she was actually eating it. Either she wasn't trying to impress Travis anymore or it was just too delicious to resist.

After the main course—my lasagna was chef's-kiss amazing—Travis nodded to our server, who brought out tall flutes of champagne on a very tiny platter.

He tapped on his glass with a fork to get everyone's attention. "With things wrapping up, I wanted to take this opportunity to say a few words. First of all, it's been my pleasure getting to know all of you, and to the camera crew, *bravo!*"

Everyone clapped and he continued.

"Mia, I've checked out your social media profiles, and I love your vibe. Brands would be crazy not to partner with you. Lauren, your fitness videos are incredible. I think my personal trainer can get some tips from you. Alice, your music is amazing. I've already mentioned you to the *Secret Shadows* producers, who are committed to showcasing indie artists next season. And Daphne," he said, turning to fully face me, "Your lotions and potions are remarkable. You seem to know exactly what someone needs, even if they don't know it at first. No doubt you're a wonderful lab tech and very accurate with your measurements."

The room buzzed with laughter. Mia bounced in her seat with delight, Lauren did a silly biceps 'which way to the beach' pose, and Alice fanned herself with a napkin.

Travis tapped his glass again. "Which is why I'm going to break dating show protocol tonight. I've got a tremendous amount of respect for all of you and don't want you to be blindsided at the final charm ceremony." He gave a dramatic pause and looked around the table at each of us. He was really good at this. Everyone hovered on his every word. "But I'm choosing Daphne. Or rather, Daphne let *me* choose *her*."

My heart jumped to my throat, and chills skittered down my

arms at his public proclamation. Part of me, the part that had been left at the altar once, wondered if he would really go through with it.

The room erupted and all the women looked at me. I expected to see at least a little malice, but all I saw were smiles.

Mia was the first to rush to me. For a half-vampire, she gave great bear-hugs. Then the others joined her in a group hug around me. We laughed and exchanged stories, with Mia saying she knew from the start that he was going to pick me. She said it with the confidence of a content creator who went viral and now sells a course.

From the other side of the table, Travis was grinning. It was crazy to think that I'd met this incredible man in a supernatural dating contest, and my rivals were happy for me. It reminded me of one of my favorite island slogans: *I found myself, and my people, on Darkaway Island.*

When it came time for dessert, we made our way back to our seats. It was a house-made ricotta with lemon/raspberry sauce, and I couldn't wait to dig in.

But as soon as the crystal dish was set in front of me, I caught a whiff that made the hairs on the back of my neck stand up. I could eat it, but something told me Travis shouldn't, and a vision flashed before my eyes of him clutching at his throat, trying to breathe.

He was talking to Lauren and had already dipped his spoon into the dessert.

"*Travis, stop!*"

He looked over at me, the spoon inches from his mouth. Had he already taken a bite?

Without thinking, I leaped across the table, scattering plates and cutlery, and batted the spoon from his hand.

Mia gaped at me and someone screamed.

Travis looked disconcerted. "Daphne, what—?"

"The dessert. It's got..." I didn't know exactly what substance was in it. All I knew was that it could kill Travis if he ate it. As I climbed off the table, it came to me. A *lycanthrope weakness*. Of course.

"Wolfsbane," I blurted. "The dessert has wolfsbane in it."

"Wolfsbane!" he exclaimed, taking a step backwards. "That's poisonous to werewolves."

At some point, Jada had told the crew to stop filming. "What's wolfsbane doing in the dessert?" she demanded to the waitstaff, who stood bewildered near the door.

Then the chef came out of the kitchen. A rotund man, he twisted his hands in front of him like he was kneading a ball of dough. "What is the problem here?"

"The problem is," Jada said through clenched teeth, carefully enunciating each word as if she might shift and do some real harm, "is that Daphne says there's wolfsbane in the dessert. Why would that substance be in the dessert? One small taste makes our kind very sick. More than that is deadly."

The chef sputtered in disbelief. "*Impossible.* I've never cooked with wolfsbane in my life. I don't keep it in my kitchen."

I appreciated Jada's belief in me, but a terrifying thought occurred to me. What if I were wrong? What if I'd made a complete fool of myself and—

No, I wasn't wrong. I was sure of it.

I went back to my side of the table and grabbed my dessert, since I'd splattered Travis's all over the floor. It was still artfully plated in a crystal goblet with layers of raspberry sauce between the dollops of sweet ricotta and a sprinkle of lemon zest on top. It really looked delicious. I held it to my nose and sniffed. There was definitely something in this that would make Travis sick. I felt it in my bones.

"Here," I said to the chef. "Try mine."

The chef huffed over, examined my dish and then his whole demeanor changed. "Who garnished these desserts?" Then he pulled a spoon from his apron and took a bite. Although I didn't know what kind of magical creature he was, I'm guessing he wasn't a werewolf.

His eyes widened. "It's wolfsbane all right." His face went ashen as he turned to Travis. "I'm terribly sorry, Mr. Monroe. I...I...don't know how this could have happened."

CHAPTER THIRTY-SEVEN

Travis

"Y ou can't be serious!" Daphne glared at Jada, hands on her hips. I was glad not to be on the receiving end of her ire. "Travis could've been killed!"

We stood in the kitchen of the Big House as I made Daphne's sleepy tea. It had been a long night and everyone was on edge. Jada held her planner to her chest like a shield. I had a feeling she was going to need it.

"I know, Daphne," Jada said, "but he didn't, and the network needs to see the final charm ceremony before they consider green-lighting it. You can't have a show like this without a proper ending."

Daphne did that thing with her eyes that made you think they were lasers. "There is no *but* when it comes to Travis's life."

A thrill shot through me that this feisty human with no supernatural abilities was standing up to my werewolf sister on my behalf. My wolf beamed with pride at how brave our mate was.

Maybe I could broker a deal between the two warring parties.

I waded in cautiously. "What if the ceremony were held here at the ranch, instead of at the resort?" Jada started to protest, but I stopped her. "With some creative editing, the change in venue shouldn't be a problem. Besides, it would be more publicity for the ranch to be featured at the end." That shut my sister up.

Daphne, however, wasn't as easy.

"You heard the sheriff, Travis." As she turned all of her attention to me, I resisted the urge to step backwards. "They don't know who tried to poison you. The perpetrator—who is still out there, by the way—used a scent-masking elixir. When they didn't scare me off when they ransacked my room, they went right for their actual target. You. It could be anyone. I will not..." Her voice caught, and she started over. "I will not stand by while the man I love is in danger. Until we find out who's responsible, all filming should stop."

I wasn't sure I could love this woman more than I already did. Her fierceness. Her loyalty. "It's most likely a rival pack— these things happen sometimes. They can't set foot on our land without us knowing about it."

She crossed her arms. "No."

I tried to ignore how incredibly hot she was right now and tried a different tactic. "What if I ask a friend—a dragon shifter friend, who is a former MP and sometimes works for a private agency—to coordinate security? The sheriff said he'd ruled out the remaining contestants. Mia, Lauren and Alice had nothing to do with it. Even though I picked you, they'll still benefit from the publicity if the show sells to one of the networks. But that won't happen without an ending."

Daphne pressed her lips together into a thin line. I could tell she was considering it.

"Does your friend breathe fire?"

"Of course."

She exhaled loudly and paced around the center island. Then she stopped in front of me and poked a finger at my chest. "If you die, Travis, I will come into the afterlife and kill you again."

I pulled her into my arms and kissed that beautiful mouth. "Such a vicious little Alpha."

She fisted her hands in my hair. "Only when provoked."

My inner wolf was right. She abso-fucking-lutely was my fated mate. I was smitten the moment I laid eyes on her on the ferry; I just didn't know it then.

But that got me thinking about the White Wolf Moon, and a fresh wave of uneasiness settled over me.

CHAPTER THIRTY-EIGHT

Daphne

The final charm ceremony went off without a hitch a few days later. Portia was thrilled to do my hair, makeup and nails again. I even let her put on short tips in Midnight Garage and Nails' signature color combination. The blush pink gossamer dress I wore, which matched my moonstone charm perfectly, billowed out behind me when I walked. The girly-girl in me, which wasn't a huge part of my personality, really wanted to look pretty for Travis. I didn't give a shit how I'd look for the cameras. Well, maybe just *a little*.

Mia, Lauren and Alice looked amazing as well. Mia took a few group selfies and promised not to post them until she got the okay from Jada.

Travis brought in that private security firm with his dragon friend, Xavier, who locked the place down tight. I truly felt safer with fire-breathing dragons circling the perimeter. If I were a baddie, I wouldn't want to risk doing something nefarious and getting scorched by one of them.

The ceremony itself was held in the garden gazebo used for weddings at the ranch. Fairy sprites lined the walkway, and I admired their beautiful colors as I made my way over the cobblestones to where Travis waited for me. He'd already spoken to the three other women to get their "reactions" on camera. Mia was classic-Mia and actually cried. But afterwards, she quickly wiped her tears and gave Travis a hug, then introduced herself to one of Xavier's men, and they made plans to hook up later.

Jada had insisted on using Drake/*Secret Shadows* branding. After her meltdown about the final charm ceremony's cancellation, she quickly got on board with it being moved to the ranch and went all in on the cowboy theme. She even found me white cowboy boots to wear, which was why the cobblestones weren't giving me too many problems tonight.

Travis held out his hand and guided me up to stand in the center of the gazebo with him, a soft smile playing on his lips. He wore a pair of fancy cowboy boots and a western-style suit, open at the collar, with a yoke and whip-stitched lapels.

"Heaven's Moon, you take my breath away," he whispered for my ears only, but the boom mics probably picked it up anyway.

"Thanks. You do too." I took in every detail of his handsome face. The strong nose, dark brows, chiseled jaw, and those beautiful, wolfish eyes. Was that a hint of worry in his expression or just my lingering insecurities about public displays of affection that promised the moon and ended in tears?

He waited for the nod from Jada to start his monologue. While it was heartfelt and lovely, it was definitely scripted for the camera, and more than once, he called me 'darlin'.

But then, who was I to talk, because mine had been scripted for the cameras as well. I put my foot down, though, when Jada wanted me to refer to him as my Big, Bad Alpha.

"Daphne, will you allow me to put this final charm on your bracelet and become my fated mate?"

It was only after I held out my wrist and told him yes that I realized he'd added the word *fated*. At no time when we'd rehearsed our lines had he used that word. Was it a slip of the tongue? Had Jada told him to add it to boost the Date-A-Wolf narrative like she tried to do with me? Were fated mates even a thing?

Just as my arms slid around his neck and he bent his head to kiss me, I noticed those faint lines of worry between his brows again.

CHAPTER THIRTY-NINE

Travis

"Do you want me to have a woman to woman talk with her?" Jada asked, setting down her planner.

It had been several weeks since the final charm ceremony, but she still carried it everywhere. You'd think there was an affinity spell between her and her calendar.

I paced around my sister's newly designed office in the Big House and looked for something to smash. I couldn't believe Matthew had shared with her what I'd told him in confidence. Although Jada knew through the pack bond that something had been bothering me, she just didn't know what it was until Matthew opened his big fat mouth.

"No!"

She leaned back in her white office chair. "Well, it's not something you can exactly keep hidden from her forever, Travis."

"Why not? At the last full moon, I made sure I was up in Vancouver. It's not a big deal. It's just one night every moon cycle."

"Okay, but what about the White Wolf Moon when the entire pack will gather to see you officially named the pack Alpha? And since it's the same weekend as Monsterval, you can expect that many of our mainland cousins will be here as well. They'll all want to meet your new mate. You can't exactly send *her* away. Or should I say your *fated mate?*"

I glared at her, hoping she realized how close I was to committing capital murder.

"Don't give me that look, little brother. We can smell your Alpha scent all over her."

I chuffed. "All wolf males scent their females."

She tapped her nose. "Not like that, they don't. I've met a few of your girlfriends over the years. With Daphne, it's very different. If you don't believe me, ask Sheriff Aldrich. With that bear shifter nose of his, I'm sure he noticed."

I ground my teeth together, recalling what the man had said about pheromones. "I am not going to ask the sheriff for advice about my love life."

A sound stirred in the doorway. I turned and there was Daphne. *Fuuuck.*

She wore a Darkaway Island apron and was crushing herbs in a mortar and pestle. With Monsterval coming up, she'd been busy making potions and lotions for her pop-up shop at Unholy Grounds.

"What about your love life? Is this something that concerns me or...are you talking about someone else?" Although her tone was meant to be lighthearted, I could sense a slight edge to it.

Jada jumped to her feet and took the mortar and pestle from Daphne. "After you finish talking to my brother, if you want to hear a woman's perspective and get some ideas, come see me."

"*Perspective?* About what?"

I spun Daphne around and frog-marched her out of the office. "Come on. Let's go. The people who live in this house are too damn nosy for this conversation to take place under this roof."

CHAPTER FORTY

Daphne

Small branches snapped under our feet as Travis led me deep into the forest, the path barely more than a game trail. The sound of nearby crickets stopped as we passed them, then started up again behind us. His bold, even strides told me he knew exactly where he was taking me. This wasn't just a random evening stroll through the trees.

"I hope that was a joke back there," Travis said, his voice rough. "Because there is no one else. There will *never* be anyone else."

"Travis, I know. You don't need to—"

He put a hand to my sternum, pushed me against a tree trunk and leaned in close, his brows two dark slashes above his eyes. "Yes, I do. If you have even a trace of doubt about the depth of my feelings for you, then I've failed as your mate. There is no one but you." Closing his wolf-yellow eyes, he took a deep breath and let it out slowly. "I am not my father's son."

I stood on my tiptoes and pressed my mouth to his full lips. "I know you're not."

"And I am not *him*, either," he growled, pulling me into his arms with a jerk, and burying his nose in my hair. He meant my ex-fiancé, so I was glad he didn't say his name aloud in this moment. "I would never disrespect the woman I loved like that."

Tears stung the back of my eyes and I melted into him. I loved the man that he was. "Are you going to tell me what you and Jada were talking about then?"

He mumbled something incoherent under his breath, then grabbed my hand and tugged me along the path again.

"Don't tell me you're going to take me somewhere to shift into your wolf and chase me down. If so, I should've worn running shoes."

He cast me a sidelong glance, one brow lifted, and I swear, I saw a wolfish gleam in his eye. "Would you be into that sort of thing?"

I wasn't really serious, but the way he asked made my heart race just a little. Some women had a masked man kink. Maybe I had a werewolf-chasing-me-through-the-woods kink.

I shrugged. "Depends on what would happen when you caught me. If murder is involved—namely mine—then probably not."

The corner of his lip quirked. "Definitely *not* murder, but I can't promise there wouldn't be a little death or two."

The terrain got a little rockier, the slope a little steeper, and soon we were standing on a bluff overlooking half the island. Way down and to the right twinkled the lights of downtown Darkaway, while slightly behind us and to the left, you could see the lights of the ski resort. Straight ahead, beyond the misty foothills barely visible in the darkness, was the Pacific Ocean.

"This view is incredible," I breathed, stretching my arms out and taking it all in. "It's like I'm on top of the world."

When Travis said nothing, I turned. He had a faraway look in his eyes. "I used to come up here after I had it out with my father, when I needed the clarity to think. Sometimes I even brought a sleeping bag when I couldn't stand to sleep under the same roof as him, and unrolled it right over there." He indicated a flat spot near a large boulder.

"Alone?"

He nodded. "I've never brought anyone else up here until now."

Warmth bloomed in my chest that he wanted to share this special place with me.

He spread out a small blanket he'd grabbed from the porch, and we laid down on the tall grass. I snuggled into him and together, we watched the night sky. Turned out, he knew the names of all the constellations without having to resort to a phone app. Not surprising given his obsession with the moon.

A shooting star blazed into view and my breath hitched. I'd lived in the city for so long that I couldn't remember the last time I'd seen one. I tracked it until it fizzled out, while his hand lightly stroked the back of my arm.

"I realized something recently, but I didn't think it was possible, so I told myself I was imagining things. Which is why I hadn't said anything."

I waited patiently for him to continue, my ear pressed to his chest.

"I confided in Matthew to get his opinion, and the bastard told Jada."

A terrifying thought occurred to me and my stomach bottomed out. "Are you ill, Travis?"

A chuckle rumbled through his chest, and he gave my arm a reassuring squeeze. "No, nothing like that, my love. Quite the opposite, in fact."

What was the *opposite* of sick? Being ultra-healthy? I couldn't see how that was a problem.

"I don't know how much you know about werewolf lore, and there's a lot of horseshit out there, but some of it says that when the Alpha meets his fated mate, his inner wolf becomes absolutely feral for her. The rutting urge dominates his thoughts."

He'd called me his *fated mate* at the final charm ceremony, and yes, we were having a lot of sex, but what did that even mean? Irritation snaked up my spine at how male-centric it was. "And what does werewolf lore say about the female in this scenario? Or is she just a vessel for the Alpha's potent seed?"

Travis snorted. "I told you it was horseshit."

"So why bring it up?"

He took a deep breath and blew it out slowly. "Lore says that during a full moon, the Alpha not only wants to mate with her, but the goal is to impregnate her."

I stiffened. Was he bringing this up to broach the subject of wanting to keep me barefoot and pregnant so I could birth his ten children? A litter of pups that carried his DNA?

No, I told myself. He wasn't like that. He gave off none of those vibes.

"If that's what you're concerned about, Travis, you know I'm on birth control."

While the thought of having a mini-Travis or two running around the island was pretty appealing to my overactive ovaries, I certainly wasn't in any hurry.

"No, that's not it," he blurted. "I'm not sure I even want to be a father. I didn't exactly have the best example."

I relaxed. We seemed to be on the same page after all.

He propped himself on his elbows and stared into the valley. "The only reason I'm bringing this up is that I've...noticed some things. Things that make me think that some of the lore may be legit."

I frowned. "Like what?"

He sat all the way up and ran a hand through his hair. "So those ridges you feel when we have sex?"

A laugh burst from my throat. How could I forget them? "Travis, it's one of your best features." Just the thought of it rubbing against my clit made all my girly parts tingle now. "So how is that lore? I thought you told me that all male werewolves had them."

"Lore says that during a full moon, once the Alpha is deep inside her, those ridges flare out, forming what's essentially a knot. It locks them in place when they climax, thus giving him the best chance of getting her pregnant."

To be honest, it sounded kind of hot. Damn. I didn't have a breeding kink now too, did I?

"Since I've been on the island, hasn't there been a full moon or two?" Being mated to a werewolf, I really needed to pay better attention to the moon cycles. "Or were we not fated at that point?" I didn't understand how any of this worked, but I vowed to do better.

"My trips to Vancouver? Those were timed so I wasn't around you then."

"Let me see if I have this straight—you're worried that no amount of birth control is enough to stop that potent Alpha seed of yours, so you had to leave the country?" I poked him playfully in the ribs, trying not to laugh at how ridiculous that sounded.

Instantly, he was on me, pushing me back on the blanket with a hand to my throat. Not enough to hurt, but enough that I gasped in surprise. Lips slightly parted, he gave a low, masculine growl, letting me know he did not find any of this remotely funny.

Okay, message received. A thrill chased through me at this unexpected show of dominance. "Fine. Sorry. I'm listening."

He loosened his hold a little, but his eyes were dark, and he still looked mad as hell. "According to the lore, it can be painful for the female but impossible for the male to pull out. Even if he wants to."

"*Painful?*"

"Extremely."

My mind raced with what that meant. Like going through childbirth once a month? Losing your virginity every full moon? *Yeah, good times.*

I blew my breath out slowly. My man was deeply concerned about how this fated mates thing might affect me, that he would be the cause of my pain but would have no way to stop it. And here I was, making a joke of it. With the White Wolf Moon right around the corner, he couldn't just leave like he had before to keep me safe from him. It would be impossible for us to be apart. *This* was what had been bothering him these past few weeks.

He caged me between his muscular forearms and kissed me. Long and slow and deep. His tongue delving into my mouth, claiming me, as an aching heat pooled between my legs. I rolled my hips against the steel length of him pressed to my thigh, cursing the layers of clothing that separated us.

He drew back slightly, his breath hot against my skin. "And all of this is assuming the Alpha's fated mate is a wolf. Who knows what it will be like for a human."

My heart swelled as if it might burst from my chest. I loved his version of masculinity with every fiber of my being. The feral protectiveness. The intense desire to place my safety and comfort above all else.

I unbuckled his belt as he stripped off my jeans. Then he made love to me under the stars.

CHAPTER FORTY-ONE

Daphne

The weeks before Monsterval passed like a fever dream.

Not only was Travis busy with *Secret Shadows* business, mostly video-conferencing with an occasional trip to Vancouver, but he was also helping out around the ranch. Imagine the surprise when guests discovered Drake Valentino was the one taking them on a trail ride through the backcountry. One even fell off her horse. Thankfully, there were no broken bones this time.

As for me, my raw materials order was very late in arriving, so I had to work like a madwoman to get all my lotions and elixirs made and packaged in time.

Cassie introduced me to Kaori, a middle-aged member of her coven who sold the best local herbs at the farmer's market. I was able to source a lot of my ingredients from her. Rumor had it she'd poisoned her cruel husband years ago then moved to the island to escape the authorities. I liked her immediately.

Somehow, Jada was able to find the time to redesign a really cute logo for me in between the huge influx of guests and everything she had to do to prepare for the White Wolf Moon.

But I couldn't have done any of it without Sarah's help.

I stood in the center of the Daphne's Apothecary and Botanicals vendor booth and looked around. Artfully arranged displays of my lotions and elixirs sat on several tables with beautiful hand-lettered signs in soothing earth-tones explaining the benefits of each one. From the tablecloths to the crystals and colorful stones scattered about, to the little mason jars of fresh flowers, no detail had been overlooked. Same with my pop-up shop at Unholy Grounds.

Tears threatened to overflow. I tried to sniff them away but wasn't having much luck. "Sarah, this looks absolutely amazing." I gave her the biggest hug I knew how to give, which made her laugh.

She looked around, eyes sparkling with a real sense of accomplishment. "It really does, doesn't it?"

"I still feel like crap that I won't be able to help run the booth with you." She was also going to monitor my stock at my Unholy Grounds pop-up shop.

She waved me off. "This was my idea, remember? You were just going to have the pop-up shop, which doesn't require you to be there. I knew you'd be too busy. As the mate of the new pack Alpha, you'll be meeting people and attending events. I'm just grateful to be sharing in the profits. It'll help me get on my feet."

Turned out that Sarah's rockhounding trip had been a vision quest of sorts. She came back a changed woman with a clear plan for her future. She wanted to live her life the way she wanted and not what her parents expected from her. I was there for moral support when she called them and told them she was going to follow her dreams with a goal of starting her own adventure travel business. Needless to say, they weren't pleased and promptly disowned her. But she'd already secured employment with the rockhounding company, rented a small apartment in town, and had a wonderful group of new, supportive friends (cough, cough).

Monsterval officially kicked off at sunset on Friday with the Tiny Monsters Parade through town. All children, whether they lived on Darkaway or were just visiting, were welcome to participate. They could march in their animal forms—if they were old enough to shift—wear costumes, or simply come as they were, while their parents waved from the crowds lining Nightshade Avenue.

There was one notable exception to the under the age of eighteen participation rule, however.

At a recent town council meeting, residents had voted overwhelmingly to name Travis the Parade Marshall. Which was how the island's favorite son, who hadn't been to a Monsterval in years, ended up driving a pink cartoon car, knees up to his ears, leading a flotilla of his nieces and their friends behind him.

"That man is a god among men," said Sister Mary Francis, her hand to her chest.

Sister Elenor nodded. "A saint."

I gave them the side-eye. Nuns weren't supposed to talk like that, were they? I knew they had two sets of eyes and ovaries, but it sounded marginally blasphemous. Hopefully, they were referring to how cute Travis looked and not how incredibly hot he was. I wasn't sure how I'd feel if it was the latter.

I tried not to recall in vivid, motion-picture detail just how thoroughly I'd worshipped his body last night. It didn't seem appropriate.

At that moment, Travis saw me in the crowd and waved, giving me the biggest, goofiest grin. I waved back just as enthusiastically. My insides melted at all the fun he was having and that I was a part of it.

"You're so adorkable!" I yelled.

He blew me a kiss. "I know."

God, could I love this man any more?

When Portia's son Austin marched past, I waved my miniature Darkaway Island flag and wolf-whistled at him. He was dressed as a very serious superhero, who evidently thought smiling wasn't appropriate. Angus's daughter, whom I met on my first visit to Midnight Garage and Nails, was... I wasn't sure. A colorful Viking shield-maiden decked out in hearts and knives? Viktor waved at me as he and Angus trailed behind the kids on the sidelines, letting them bask in their glory.

"Portia wants to have you guys over for dinner soon," he said, cupping his hand to his mouth.

I gave him a thumb's up. "We'd love that," I called back.

Tears suddenly welled up again, and I quickly brushed them away. I loved everything about this quirky small town and the people who lived here. I'd never felt such a feeling of belonging before. My gushy feelings quickly changed to amusement when the Sisters started arguing rather loudly about something stupid.

Travis and I planned to meet up at the roasted corn-on-the-cob booth after the parade ended, so when the last group of children passed—an electric scooter gang of teenagers in their bear forms—I said my goodbyes to the Sisters and made my way over there.

As I strolled down Nightshade Avenue, I made a mental note to go into the cute yarn store I had just passed as soon as I had time. I hadn't knitted or crocheted in ages, but I'd been feeling all sorts of creative energy since coming here. In fact, I'd even been considering taking a painting class at the community center that I'd seen advertised at Unholy Grounds. Apparently, the instructor was a very talented ghoul who'd apprenticed under Picasso.

Just as I arrived at the corn stand, I felt a hand on my arm. Thinking it was Travis, I smiled and turned, planning to plant a zillion kisses on his handsome face. But it wasn't him. It turned out to be a very thin woman with sharp angular features, and my smile instantly faded. I didn't get a good vibe from her at all.

"Daphne, right?"

I nodded tentatively. Although I'd met many people recently, she didn't look remotely familiar.

"I have some information that I think you'll be very interested in hearing."

I narrowed my eyes. Who *was* this woman? And how did she know me?

Sensing my skepticism, she smiled back, but it didn't reach her eyes. They remained cold. "I'm coming to you as a friend."

"I'm sorry...have we met?" I knew, however, that we hadn't.

The woman flicked her hand, dismissing my question. "If I were in your shoes, I'd want to know the truth about Travis and the Date-a-Wolf contest."

I took a step away, not trusting this stranger. While most of his fans were nice, he was bound to attract a few loons. "I'm sorry. I've got to—"

She closed the distance between us, her Cheshire cat smile gone. "Didn't you ever wonder why someone like Travis— famous, handsome, a good catch by anyone's definition—was taking part in a dating contest? I mean, come on. The man doesn't have problems getting dates, if you know what I mean."

I didn't know what she was getting at, and frankly, I didn't care. I looked around for Travis but didn't see his familiar dark head above the crowd of people and various monsters. Where *was* he?

The woman was talking fast now. She could tell I wasn't interested in what she was peddling and was just about to bolt. "Did you know he and his sister cooked up that little contest as a way for them to save the ranch? That his father's will stated if his eldest son, Travis, wasn't mated by the next White Wolf Moon after his death, that he would lose the ranch."

She was telling me nothing I didn't already know, so what was her point? Did this deranged fan think she could drive a wedge between Travis and me, making him available to her?

"There's the mating ceremony tomorrow night, right? After which he'll be officially named as the pack's Alpha. Did he actually tell you he loved you in order for you to agree to go through *that?*"

This woman was clearly mental, but I didn't want to completely reject her in case she was dangerous. "Go through what?"

She plastered on a fake look of concern. "Oh, he didn't tell you?" Then her expression turned almost gleeful. "The ceremony involves what you could call a very public display of his affection with his new mate. After which, he'll be named the Alpha, thus saving the ranch."

Public display of affection?

"I'm just saying that if I were you, I'd be prepared to be humiliated and left at the altar as soon as the Alpha ceremony has concluded."

My stomach clenched at the memory of that actually happening to me.

"He would never—"

"Are you sure?" the woman hissed, waving a stack of papers at my head. "Here's a copy of his father's will and notarized signature. Go ahead. Read it."

I put a hand up to protect my face, and the papers scattered all over the sidewalk, but not before I caught a glimpse of the letterhead. It was the address of an attorney on Darkaway Island. Blazoned across the top, it said: *Last Will and Testament of Franklin Monroe.*

I narrowed my eyes. "Who are you anyway? And why do you have his father's will? If it's even the real thing."

"Oh, it's the real deal, all right. Pardon me for not introducing myself." The woman's tone went from sugary sweet to acidic. "I'm Lavinia Monroe. I'm married to Merrick Monroe, Franklin's next eldest son. Per the terms in the will, if Travis isn't mated by the next White Wolf Moon after his father's death, my husband inherits the ranch. Travis had no marriage prospects, so he and his sister concocted the Date-A-Wolf contest to find him a temporary mate. He's just using you, Daphne. And once he's done, he'll throw you away."

I tried to swallow, but my throat muscles had suddenly tightened. That was how I'd felt when Gavin left me. He'd tossed me away like a piece of trash, and I had to pick up the pieces myself.

Sensing she'd found a chink in the armor, she went in for the kill. "After the ceremony is over and he's named the pack Alpha, he'll go back to his jet-setting life as a famous actor dating glamorous models, and you'll return to your boring lab tech job in Atlanta."

I stared at my cuticles, suddenly wanting to pick at them. Travis wasn't like that—he would never do something like that. But a tiny niggle of doubt gnawed at my stomach, reminding me that my intuition had been wrong once before. Maybe it was wrong again.

I recalled the photos of him in the magazines his father had—

Wait. How did she know I was a lab tech in Atlanta? My head snapped up, and I looked around. But Lavinia had disappeared into the crowd.

I wasn't sure how I got to the apothecary booth, but I needed to hear from Sarah that my fears were unfounded. That these were old wounds of mine and had nothing to do with Travis. So I poured my guts out to her.

"What did she mean by a *public display of affection* anyway?" I asked. "Does it mean what I think it means?"

Sarah looked uncomfortable. "Most packs have done away with those old rituals. But yes, it means what you think it does."

At my raised brows, she continued. "After the ceremony, the Alpha has sex with his new mate, sometimes in the Alpha's bed or in a wooded clearing, while pack elders watch to give witness. She meant to scare you off, Daphne, because I know for a fact that the Darkaway Island pack doesn't practice those old ways. They haven't for generations."

Seeing my shocked expression, Sarah added, "It was one of the first questions I asked Travis." She looked down at the ground between her feet. "Because the pack I come from does."

A huge surge of protectiveness had me reaching for her shoulder. Now I was the one comforting her. "I'm glad you got out of there. I mean, it's one thing if you're into that sort of kink, but to have it thrust upon you, pardon my pun, that isn't right."

Sarah laughed and wiped at her nose.

A new thought occurred to me. "Sarah, did you know Travis thought there was a mole in the contest? That my room break-in and his almost-poisoning were the work of that person?"

Sarah rubbed her forehead as if she had a headache. "Could my family have tried to sabotage the front-runner—*you*—in order to increase my chances? And when that didn't work, and I didn't get a charm, they tried to go after him?"

Spelled out like that, it sounded even more sinister. "They would do that?"

Sarah gave a mirthless laugh. "With my family, anything is possible." She paused, looked around, and lowered her voice. "Did you know we're distantly related to the Crutchfields?"

My jaw dropped. Travis *despised* them. "The ones who own a few sketchy businesses in Wickedville?"

"The one and only. I didn't know until I ran into one of them downtown and recognized his scent as part of my pack." Sarah chewed thoughtfully on her lower lip. "So what else did that woman tell you?"

"Her name is Lavinia, and she claims she's married to Travis's half-brother, Merrick."

A tiny muscle in her jaw pulsed. "Lavinia?" Sarah cursed under her breath, so I knew she was really pissed.

My eyes widened. "You know her?"

"Bony lady with fake eyelashes and a permanent, judgmental scowl?" I didn't remember the eyelashes, but yes to the scowl. "She's the daughter of my father's second-cousin. Her maiden name is Crutchfield."

My hands flew to my mouth. So, the Crutchfields were definitely behind all of this. When their legal wrangling didn't work to gain control of a rival pack, they tried to rig the contest to install one of their own as the Alpha's mate, and when that failed, they went for the jugular and tried to poison Travis.

I jumped to my feet and looked toward the corn-roasting booth. Where the hell was Travis? I needed to warn him immediately. He wasn't safe.

"Can I borrow your phone?" I asked Sarah.

She gave me an apologetic look. "I didn't think of bringing it. I get terrible coverage on the island."

Damn the island and its spotty cellular service. "I'll call him from Unholy Grounds. If he shows up, tell him I'm over there."

CHAPTER FORTY-TWO

Travis

My agent called right as I got to the end of the parade, delaying my meet up with Daphne. I probably shouldn't have answered it, but she was negotiating a new contract for me, and I was eager to hear the updates.

Now, as I made my way through the crowd to the roasted corn stand, I politely declined to sign autographs because I knew that once I started, it wouldn't stop.

With the White Wolf Moon less than a day away, my wolf was easily agitated being apart from Daphne for even short periods of time. She'd have ridden in the parade with me if there'd been room in that tiny car.

By the time I got to the corn stand, however, she wasn't there. I debated standing in line, but maybe she'd already bought two ears and was waiting for me at her booth. I knew she felt guilty about having Sarah run it all weekend.

But when I got to her booth, I didn't see her there either, just Sarah helping an elderly couple sample *Daphne's Miracle Balm*.

I started to ask her if she'd seen my mate when my phone vibrated. The call was from Unholy Grounds. Why would one of the Sisters be calling me?

I kept my head on a swivel, scanning the crowd for Daphne, and answered the phone.

"Travis!" It was Daphne. "Thank goodness you're there."

My shoulders relaxed at the sound of her voice. "I've been looking all over for you."

"I could say the same about you. Listen, I ran into your sister-in-law, Lavinia."

The hackles on the back of my neck stood up. "And what did she have to say?"

Daphne gave a humorless laugh. "She's definitely not a pleasant woman. She tried to tell me about the will, thinking she was dropping a bombshell that would—"

"That would instill doubt in your mind about me?" I white-knuckled my phone so hard I almost crushed it.

"How did you know?"

"I hope you didn't believe anything she said." I leaned against a nearby light pole and dropped my voice. "Because White Wolf Moon or no White Wolf Moon, Alpha or no Alpha, I love you with every fucking fiber of my being."

She gave a low chuckle, and I continued, looking around for inspiration.

"You're the butter to my roasted corn, Daphne. The cotton to my candy. The wind to my kite. The sauerkraut to my sausage dog."

"Oh my god, Travis!" She snorted with laughter so loudly that I imagined the people around her were staring at her with eyebrows raised. "But just so we're clear, I'm not really a fan of sauerkraut."

I sniffed. "No one's perfect. But the point is, I'm not me without you, Daphne."

"Okay, I love you too, she said hastily. "And we can discuss everything in much more detail later, but I need you to be careful because—"

Then she gasped, and then the line went dead.

CHAPTER FORTY-THREE

Daphne

I should've known that something was wrong when the coffee shop sounds around me became muted. But it didn't register at first because I was in deep conversation with Travis.

Realizing how unusually quiet it was around me, I looked up. The place was bustling as normal, but it seemed as if everything was on the other side of a warbled piece of glass. People's features were slightly blurred, and the signs on the walls were hard to read. I couldn't even tell if the cat-shifter in line was a tiger or a leopard.

It was as if I were inside a bubble looking out. Or in a dream. Even stranger was that everyone seemed to be going about their business as if they couldn't see me.

And that was when I saw *him*.

With his legs crossed and coffee cup in hand, Mr. Griffin sat at the table next to me, his features crystal clear. He was on my side of the bubble-thingie. Pharma-Douche in the flesh.

He'd found me.

"Hello, Daphne," he said with that smooth, every-woman-wants-me-because-I'm-a-rich-ass-son-of-a-bitch smile on his lips.

The phone slipped from my hands and clattered to the floor.

CHAPTER FORTY-FOUR

Travis

Blood pounded in my ears as I ran down Nightshade Avenue, dodging the huge Monsterval crowds as best I could while not mowing down tiny children. Every few steps, a fan recognized me, but I ignored them and kept going.

I thought I'd heard a man's voice before the call with Daphne suddenly ended. I'd tried calling her back, but I kept getting the coffee shop's voicemail.

The bell above the door at Unholy Grounds jangled noisily as I burst through, banging it against the opposite wall. Several people jumped, startled at my loud entrance. Stomping inside, I spun around but didn't see my mate anywhere.

"Where's Daphne?" I barked.

Sister Mary-Francis blinked at me, bewildered. "Daphne... was here?" she asked slowly, glancing around.

"Yes! I was talking to her on the phone. Your phone. She was just here."

Brow furrowed, Sister Mary-Francis tapped her forehead

with the tips of her fingers as if to clear her head. Apparently, it worked. I could see the realization in her eyes.

"Of course, Daphne was here," she said, more to herself than to me. "I don't know what just happened to me. She was sitting right over there."

The nun pointed to an empty table where a cup and saucer sat next to several crumpled napkins. I scowled. Something was very off. The nuns ran a tight ship and rarely left a table looking like this.

"Well, that's odd," she said, echoing my thoughts as we made our way through the line of magical creatures waiting to place their orders. "She didn't bus her table. She always busses her table."

"And you're sure she was sitting right here?" Daphne's scent wasn't particularly strong, so it could've been from another day.

"You bet your tail she was. I brought her the phone to call you. What in heaven's name?" She bent and picked up the coffee shop's phone from the floor.

My rising panic had me seeing red. "Did you notice her talking to anyone? Did someone come over to her table?"

"I...I honestly don't know," she said apologetically. "My last recollection is of Daphne sitting here, talking on the phone. I didn't see anybody approach her. And I didn't see her leave." She pursed her lips and scrunched up her nose as if she had caught a whiff of something bad. "Some strange magic has been used here."

I took a deep breath and sniffed the air. I smelled nothing rancid, but I did detect a scent-masking agent. The same one used when Daphne's villa was ransacked.

Rushing outside, I scanned both sides of the street. Where could she have gone? There were people, so many people. And magical creatures. *Everywhere.*

I was about to shift into my wolf form to better pick up her scent when I caught sight of Merrick and his wife standing outside Dark Tarts. They appeared to be having a heated argument. She pushed him hard in the chest, then her claws came out. She tried to take a swipe at his face, but he grabbed her wrists before she could scratch him. Catching my eye, he said something to her and shoved her away. Then he jogged over to me.

"You're looking for Daphne," he said, eyes dark with anger. It was a statement, not a question.

I could barely contain my wolf from coming out and tearing him to pieces. "What have you done with her?"

Merrick looked me straight in the eye, a ballsy thing for one male wolf to do to another. Then he cast his gaze downward, a sign of respect from a pack member to the Alpha. "Nothing. I would not hurt your mate, Travis. But I think I know who has her. Does the name Griffin Pharmaceuticals ring a bell?"

The blood in my veins went ice cold. The CEO who had killed Daphne's co-worker. He was here? On Darkaway? Which meant that he now had Daphne.

"Come on," he said. "I think she's at the marina on his private yacht."

As we dashed through the streets down to the waterfront, Merrick explained what he knew.

"Lavinia has been acting strangely lately. Stranger than normal, so I followed her to her cousin's place in Wickedville, where she met up with Griffin."

Her cousin? Wickedville? Then it dawned on me, and I nearly tripped on an uneven cobblestone. "Your wife is a Crutchfield?"

Merrick looked like he had just bitten into a lemon. "Unfortunately, yes. I'm not sure if our...our father knew. He wasn't exactly of sound mind this last year. I certainly didn't know until after the wedding a few months ago."

"How does Griffin fit into all this? Daphne worked for him."

"From what I've been able to piece together, Lavinia cyber-stalked all the Date-A-Wolf contestants, and she contacted Daphne's employer." At the confused look on my face, he added, "She wanted to rig the contest so you'd choose Sarah, a distant cousin of hers. Who, by the way, does not know she was a pawn in all this. From what I can tell, she's completely innocent."

I flexed my fists, wanting desperately to punch something. As if sensing my ire, Merrick moved further away from me as we ran. "So that's how Griffin knew Daphne was here. He must be a magical creature to have found his way to the island."

Merrick gave me a grim nod. "He's a dark wizard."

"Who wanted his spell book back." At Merrick's confused look, I added, "I'll fill you in later." It must've been his scent and Lavinia's at Daphne's villa after the break-in. And when Griffin either couldn't find the spell book or it wouldn't go with him, he had to kidnap Daphne to get it.

When we got to the marina, Merrick pointed to where the yacht *should* be, but the slip was empty. And it was nowhere in the harbor either.

I nearly fell to my knees.

Daphne was gone.

CHAPTER FORTY-FIVE

Daphne

The ocean air had a real bite to it as the boat headed toward the magical fog bank shielding the island from the outside world. Wind whipped through my hair, down the neck of my t-shirt, and swirled around my bare legs. But unlike when I first arrived on the island, I didn't care to go inside the main cabin to get warm. I knew where we were going.

We were headed to the mainland.

Away from Travis.

Away from Darkaway.

Away from everything else I'd come to love.

If I weren't wearing this bracelet with my moonstone charm, all my memories of Travis would be gone once we went through the island's magical barrier, and I didn't want to lose a single one. I hoped with all my heart that Cassie's spell worked. If it did and I made it through this, Travis wouldn't be the only one I'd be kissing.

I swore under my breath and wrapped my arms around myself. I had no business being hopeful right now.

And what about George? Last I saw him, he was lounging on a triangular piece of sun coming through the window at the Big House. If my memories failed, at least he was happy since he totally adored Ginnea.

Movement through the window drew my attention. Pharma-Douche was motioning for me to come inside. He was trying to pilot the boat with one hand and open the latch of the evil spell book with a butter knife. I gave him the bird.

As soon as he'd shoved me aboard and motored out of the harbor, the book had appeared in my hands, even though it was squirreled away at the Big House. Just like it had when it reappeared in my book bag after I thought I'd given it to Deanne. And what it tried to do at Dismal Devices. The thing *knew* I was being taken away.

Pharma-Douche had been elated. "It has an affinity for you, just as I suspected. Otherwise, it never would have left me."

As the island grew smaller on the horizon behind us, so did my hopes of Travis coming after me before it was too late. The wall of mist loomed before us, rising from the sea and stretching to the sky. As soon as we crossed through, that would be it. I grabbed my wrist with the charm bracelet and held it to my chest.

"This is it." I closed my eyes as we sailed through the cinnamon-scented mist.

CHAPTER FORTY-SIX

Travis

As soon as we touched down at the marina on the mainland, I jumped off the massive dragon's back. In all the years I'd known Xavier, I'd never seen him with a rider. Two other dragons landed next to us. One with Sheriff Aldrich and the other with Merrick.

We'd spotted Griffin's yacht cutting through the gray water and debated swooping low so I could jump onto the deck, but we didn't know if Griffin was armed. We had to assume he was. Thing is, dragons have a real aversion to pain. And when they're hurt, they often strike back with fire without thinking. It's a natural reflex for them. I didn't want one of them to inadvertently torch the yacht with Daphne on board.

"Thanks for your help with this," I told Xavier as he shifted into his human form.

He waved away the dragon magic that kept us hidden from human eyes. "No problem, Travis." He smoothed out the sleeves of his jacket. Wrinkled clothes were a universal problem for shifters.

I'd thought about flying my plane here, but I wasn't sure I'd find a good place to land wherever Griffin was heading. Plus, it would've been hard to fit six adult male shifters in the cockpit. As I tried to calculate the total payload, Xavier had said, "Fuck it. I'll give you a ride." He turned to his men. "Boys, you okay with that?" They nodded and he turned back to me. "Just this one time, Monroe, and that's it. So, don't be getting any ideas."

Griffin's yacht was motoring past the jetty now. We stayed out of sight near the harbormaster's office. I didn't want the asshole to suspect that the authorities were waiting for him. Who knew what he would do to Daphne if he were cornered?

"That's strange," the harbormaster said, looking through the lens of his binoculars.

I stiffened. "What is?"

"It's coming in at a really hard angle. It's never going to dock properly. He'll have to turn around and come at it again. I thought you said this guy was an experienced seaman."

Sheriff Aldrich spoke up. "According to our intel, he is."

The harbormaster nodded. He didn't know Sheriff Aldrich was with the Monster Patrol, just that they were members of law enforcement. He peered through his binoculars. "And I thought you said the captain was a man."

I stiffened. Something was wrong. "He is."

He handed me the binoculars. "Here. Look."

But when I peered through them, it wasn't Griffin in the captain's seat at all, but *Daphne*! And from here, she looked perfectly fine. Griffin hadn't hurt her after all. A staggering surge of heat rushed through me, then pride. What the hell had she done to him?

And then the reality of the immediate situation hit me. I didn't know everything about this woman, but I had my doubts she knew how to dock a sixty-foot yacht.

Also, there was a genuine possibility she might not know who I was, in case that memory charm didn't work the way it was supposed to. Cassie was good, but I didn't know if she was *that* good.

If Daphne loved me once, would she love me again if she didn't remember me?

I shoved those thoughts from my head as I ran onto the dock ahead of the harbormaster. The yacht was approaching slowly—and at such an angle that made mooring it nearly impossible.

Daphne stood behind the wheel and was gesturing wildly.

At me? Did she recognize who I was?

Or was she just waving for help from the random men she saw?

She slid the window open beside her and cupped her hands. "Travis, do you know how to dock this fucking thing?"

The relief hit me so hard, it felt like a ton of bricks had lifted from my shoulders.

She knew me. Daphne knew me!

My worst fears—that Daphne would be hurt, that she wouldn't remember me—remember us—hadn't come true.

I didn't feel the chill as I dove into the water.

CHAPTER FORTY-SEVEN

Daphne

Travis cut through the water like an Olympic gold medal swimmer after the final turn. *My* man. And he was coming for me.

He made it to the boat, hopped aboard and pulled me into his arms. He kissed my face, my lips, my hands. I didn't care that he was dripping wet. The only thing that mattered was that he was here with me and I knew who he was.

"Are you all right, Daphne?" His voice was raspy with emotion.

"I'm fine," I said, laughing through his kisses.

"I thought—" Travis's words caught in his throat "—I thought you might not remember me."

I lifted my wrist and the charms tinkled. "Cassie's magic held."

He looked around the yacht, evidently deciding we should finish this conversation later. "Where's Griffin?" he growled.

I pointed below deck. "In there. I tied him up."

The look on Travis's face was priceless, making me laugh. I loved surprising people with unexpected badassery.

"How?" he asked.

I gave a nonchalant shrug, but to be honest, I was pretty proud of myself. "He wanted me to make him some tea. So, I scoured the galley kitchen and came up with a concoction of herbs and spices that I knew would make him sleepy. As soon as his eyes got heavy, I conked him over the head with a wine bottle and tied him up."

Travis's deep baritone laugh thrummed through my body like a tuning fork. "You and your herbal skills never cease to amaze me, Daphne."

After a quick check to make sure Pharma-Douche was still firmly secured, Travis went to the bridge and took over the controls. Besides piloting planes, it was clear he'd driven a boat or two. It was a marvel to watch him dock it. He circled expertly around the marina and came at the pier from a different angle. Then he activated some thruster thingies that made the vessel go sideways. I'd never have known to do that on my own. I'd have crashed into the dock, damaging it and countless other boats.

Sheriff Aldrich, Xavier and several of his men jumped aboard the vessel. They wasted no time escorting a furious, though somewhat sleepy, Pharma-Douche out of the cabin. A fifth man stood waiting on the dock, a melancholy but pleased expression on his face. He looked a little like Travis. Was this his half-brother Merrick?

As Pharma-Douche was being led off the boat, he sneered at me with contempt. "I can't understand why the book chose you. You're nothing but a stupid human girl."

The hackles on the back of my neck raised. "Guess it's better than a lying sack of shit who only gets someone to blow him if he threatens to fire them." A lame comeback, for sure. No doubt I'd come up with a snappier one in an hour or so.

"The choice was simple," Travis told him. "It's obvious the magical spell book prefers the light to the dark."

Griffin made a low growl. If I hadn't known he was into dark magic, I'd have thought he was a shifter.

He was fast. *Lightning fast.* I hardly saw him move when he lunged at me. Even the sheriff was caught off guard.

Griffin's hand closed around my wrist like a vise. "This wasn't the revenge I had planned on taking. But it will have to do." He hooked a finger under my charm bracelet. "Thanks for the memories."

The next few seconds played out in slow motion.

Travis's hands on my shoulders, pulling me backwards.

Pharma-Douche flailing.

The sheriff activating a pair of glowing handcuffs.

The delicate links of the bracelet cutting into my skin.

"Nooooo!" I screamed.

Then the bracelet broke, scattering the charms—and my memories—everywhere.

CHAPTER FORTY-EIGHT

Daphne

The almost-full moon sat high in the night sky as I stepped into the alley behind the coffee shop. A man strode toward me, his face masked in shadow, so I quickly threw the trash bag into the dumpster, keeping an eye on him the whole time. A girl could never be too careful when it came to strange men in dark alleyways.

When he stepped into the moonlight, my breath hitched at how beautiful he was. Tall and broad-shouldered, with dark hair and slashes of brows above whiskey-colored eyes, he wore cowboy boots and well-worn but well-fitting jeans. Handsome, yes, but beauty could also be dangerous.

Then he smiled at me.

I forced my face to stay expressionless, even though my heart was about to pound out of my chest, and I took a step backward at his familiarity. "Do I...do I know you?"

Before I could take another breath, he lunged at me, his powerful body looming over mine. He grabbed me, pulled me in close, and slapped my ass. "Very funny, Daphne."

I yelped and struggled to get away from him, but he held me tight against him. "Who are you?"

"Don't you recognize Daddy?" His voice was dangerously low in my ear.

Okay. That was it. I officially lost it, laughing so hard that my knees went boneless and I nearly peed my pants.

He'd never pulled that daddy-talk before. It wasn't really my thing, but coming from him—it was kind of hot. Still laughing, I snaked my arms around his neck and... Yep, he was *very* happy to see me. Teasing him like this, pretending I didn't know him, would never get old. It had been an ongoing joke since I'd rescued myself from Pharma-Douche last month with Travis's help.

When the bracelet broke and charms scattered on the deck of the yacht, it didn't take my memories like I had feared. Turned out, I was a latent magical creature, and my memories had remained where they belonged.

In my head.

I didn't know I had magical abilities living amongst the non-magical. The time I'd spent on the island had ignited my dormant powers, as it did for some humans. Being a magical alchemist explained how I was able to derive the perfect BBQ sauce for Travis, make an effective arthritis salve for the Sisters and their friends, detect the poison in his dessert, and make that sleeping tea for Pharma-Douche. It also explained why I'd been drawn to working in a pharmaceutical lab and starting an online apothecary shop before I'd ever stepped foot here. When my mother had referred to my father as a monster, she must have meant that *literally*. We were going to have a serious talk the next time I saw her.

At the White Wolf Moon ceremony last month, Travis—being the incredibly stubborn male that he was—had insisted on staying apart from me. Not only was he still very concerned about hurting me, but he didn't think it was right to subject me to anything potentially traumatic after being kidnapped the day before. Okay, maybe he had a point about the trauma part, but I wasn't happy to be missing out on his big day when I wanted to be by his side as his mate.

So instead, I'd holed up with Ruby and Travis's friend Alexander. The vampire doctor possibly had a thing for Ruby, but I didn't know for sure. When I asked her about it, she laughed and said he was like a brother to her. If Travis became uncontrollable and came looking for me during the White Wolf Moon, we were certain his vampire best friend and packmate little sister could thwart him. We'd eaten pizza and Ruby's ginormous cupcakes while watching movies in Alexander's brownstone apartment with the Monsterval fireworks visible through his windows.

In the end, the ceremony had been pretty low-key, as evidenced by his own little sister not in attendance and his mother being on the east coast with her gentleman friend. For the most part, Jada told us later, Travis held his shit together, only snapping at a few distant relatives when he was officially named Alpha.

His broad hands warmed the backs of my thighs now, and he lifted me up, my legs wrapping automatically around his waist. He made a deep, masculine sound that shot straight to my core as he pressed my back to the brick wall and kissed me. He smelled of laundry soap and earthy shampoo, and tasted like he'd just eaten something minty. I changed my angle to accommodate him better, and his tongue pushed into my mouth like he owned me and could do whatever the hell he wanted. Which was perfectly fine with me.

"Heaven's Moon, I missed you," he growled against my lips, no doubt sensing how feral my thoughts were.

"Same."

He'd flown up to Vancouver yesterday for a *Secret Shadows*

thing, and I'd been half expecting him to call and say he'd decided to stay over. But nope. Here he was...kissing the hell out of me in the dark alley behind Unholy Grounds on the day before the full moon. The Sisters had been so kind to let me use their commercial kitchen after hours for my experiments. I hadn't shared with them what I was working on, but they probably had an inkling.

These past few weeks, I'd been perfecting a salve that lessened the pain and heightened the pleasure of an Alpha's knot during the full moon, and I was really looking forward to the clinical trials tomorrow night.

It meant a lot to me that Travis had enough faith in my abilities not to stay away this time, so I planned to make it worth his while.

Travis drew away from me slightly. "Before you thoroughly ravage me in this alley, there's something I want to show you."

I snorted. "Says the man who has *me* pressed to the wall, his hands up *my* skirt."

He lifted a shoulder and rolled his eyes. "Semantics." Then he set me back on my feet, took my hand in his, and led me out of the alley.

Thankfully, the large crowds here for Monsterval were gone, and just the normal number of tourists were milling around downtown Darkaway. No one noticed the famous actor walking down the sidewalk, holding my hand.

We passed Midnight Garage and Nails, Baubles and Barrels, and the Midnight Cinemas.

"Where are we going?" I'd already eaten, so I hoped he wasn't taking me out for dinner number two. Snacks, maybe? "Just don't tell me we're going to Dismal Devices. I was there a few days ago and don't feel like seeing Eisenhorn the Third again so soon."

On the last day of Monsterval, after the White Wolf Moon

was over, the wizard and his friends had broken the affinity spell, but only if I promised to visit the book regularly. It was such a relief not to have it hanging around anymore. And although the spell book really wasn't good juju, it was the catalyst that brought me to Travis, so I couldn't be too upset with it.

"You'll see."

We walked another block, and just before we got to Island Candy, he stopped and dangled a set of keys in front of my face.

I furrowed my brow. "What's that?"

He gripped my shoulders and spun me around. "The keys to your new place."

"What?" The shop windows were dark, but the signage on the door said J&J's Bookkeeping and DIY Taxidermy.

"When I heard Joe was closing up shop and moving to Costa Rica, I leased the space for you before anyone else could snap it up."

My jaw dropped and I tried to blink away my blurring vision. "You leased this place? For me?"

"If you don't like the location, we can look someplace else, but I know how much you like watching the saltwater taffy being pulled and thought you might enjoy it here."

My heart felt as if it might burst out of my chest. I'd always dreamed of opening my very own apothecary shop, where people could walk in and try my lotions and potions, and I could make personalized recommendations. Online is great, but brick and mortar is better. And now, Travis was making those dreams come true.

When I didn't speak right away, he took my silence to mean I had concerns. "If the taxidermy thing bothers you, just know that Joe's wife, Jo, was the taxidermist, and she died a long time ago. Joe never got around to changing the sign."

"No, I love it." I spun in his arms, lifted on my tiptoes and kissed the hell out of him.

He laughed against my lips. "How do you know? You haven't even seen the inside yet."

"Because everything my man does is perfect."

CHAPTER FORTY-NINE

Travis

"I doubt this is necessary, Travis," Daphne said, checking my restraints. "I trust you completely."

"I'm done having this conversation." We'd discussed this countless times before, and I was over it.

She frowned at me in her blue skincare mask, hair piled high on her head except for one long curl that had escaped its confines. I wanted to reach up and tuck it behind her ear, but I couldn't exactly move right now.

"Easy, fella," she said, sensing my dark mood.

I gave a low growl.

The full moon was less than thirty minutes away, so I wasn't taking any chances. But I wasn't happy about it either. Lying on the Alpha bed like this, my wrists bound by thick leather cuffs and chained to the rings on the bedposts, I could feel the moon's pull heating my blood.

The need to impregnate my female through whatever means necessary was getting stronger with every passing minute. And my patience was already tightrope thin. Soon it would be unbearable.

Several weeks ago, Viktor had fashioned the restraints in his workshop and came out to the house, blow torch in hand, to install them correctly. When I asked him if he thought they'd hold, he'd rolled his eyes and said they were used by bears during mating season, so restraining a wolf was a no-brainer. It was widely known that bear shifters liked it rough, so this information was somewhat encouraging.

Daphne was humming as she headed back to the bathroom and then the water turned on. I couldn't decide if I liked that she didn't seem worried or pissed off that she wasn't. Although I couldn't see her from this angle, I knew she was finishing up her elaborate skincare routine. She'd even started me on a simple one. On more than one occasion, we'd sat in the adjoining sitting room, face masks on, reading our books. But I had no tolerance for that bullshit tonight.

This was the sixth full moon I'd experienced since meeting my mate, but the first one we were going to spend together. This human woman was my heart and soul, and I'd just as soon gnaw off a limb than cause her any pain when my knot flared inside her. She was also a brilliant alchemist and believed that her special concoction had more than a snowball's chance in hell of working.

I hoped to the moon she was right.

I tracked her like prey as she came back into the bedroom, dark hair cascading past her shoulders. She'd loosened it for me, knowing how much I loved it splayed on my pillow when she was beneath me and how it gave me something to grab when I took her from behind. Neither of which I'd be doing tonight. Was she purposely trying to set me off?

Wearing a long, sheer robe, she lowered the pulley holding up the wrought-iron chandelier and began lighting six of the thirteen wax candles. Each one represented how many full moons would occur during our first year together. She'd had Viktor's friend Angus craft it for her at the shop. I swelled with pride that my human mate respected and adopted some customs of my kind.

That wasn't the only thing swelling, I thought wryly, noting the thin sheet tenting over my lower torso.

Daphne tugged on the chain to raise the chandelier back up, and it cast a warm glow around the room. Her robe gaped open, and I saw those gorgeous tits and the luscious curve of one hip. Fuuuck. This was torture.

Daphne approached the bed, her gaze landing on my sheet. "Are you ready to get started?"

"I've *been* ready," I rasped.

She laughed softly, then shrugged out of her robe, letting it slip to the ground, revealing every inch of her naked body to me. My mate was astonishingly beautiful, perfect in every way. It fucking choked me up every time. I blinked to make sure this wasn't some fever dream. I did the same thing the first night of the contest, when she'd rounded the corner in the Moonlight Lounge. I'd stared in awe then as well, wondering if this creature was a figment of my imagination or if she were actually real.

I pulled at my restraints, wanting desperately to touch her. "Heaven's Moon, little prey. What are you doing to me?"

She gave another little laugh but this one had an edge to it. "Who's the prey tonight?"

I narrowed my eyes. What was she up to?

She moved to the foot of the bed and slowly tugged off my sheet. My cock lay thick and heavy on my abdomen, a drop of pre-cum already glistening on the tip. The soft feminine sound she made got me even harder as she dropped the middle section of the footboard. Because I was so mesmerized watching her breasts move in the candlelight, she'd set each of my heels into the wooden divots before I realized what she was doing.

Hold on! She was using the Alpha's bed on me? But *I'm* the Alpha.

I started to protest, but she shushed me. "I thought we'd start first by giving you a chance to let off a little steam." She looked at the pillows behind my head. "Are you comfortable, my love?"

Tied to a bed with heavy iron shackles making it hard to move? But how could I argue with this woman? "Yes," I grumbled.

"Good."

She produced a purple glass jar and scooped out a small amount of the salve onto her palm.

The missing part of the footboard made it easy for her to settle between my legs. As she rubbed her hands together, the smell was similar to eucalyptus with a touch of something musky.

She gripped the base of my cock and cupped my balls. I hissed in a ragged breath. The salve was warm and silky as she coated my shaft, moving her hand up and down the length of me.

I fisted the sheet beneath me as my inner wolf strained. I was going to come like a geyser if she didn't stop. Or a teenager getting his first hand job behind the school bleachers. Not exactly the pinnacle of alpha-ness.

The tip of her tongue darted out. My beautiful little alchemist was deep in concentration. And I was her test subject.

She shifted position and loosened her hold. I relaxed, the pressure subsiding just a little. Then the purple jar came out again and I saw a flash of metal.

She gripped me again, dipped her head and took me into her mouth. I groaned and thrust involuntarily into her. She opened wider and took me even deeper.

Heaven's Moon, I was going to come. She should move off of me. Now.

"Daphne!" I grunted. I didn't want her to choke.

Then something slid lower. Something metallic. On the tip of her finger.

I sucked in a breath. Was that—? Was she—?

We agreed beforehand that nothing was off the table tonight, but she hadn't specifically mentioned *that*.

As if sensing my hesitation, she lifted her head, and my dick dropped from her mouth with a *plop*.

No, no, no! Don't stop!

"Are you okay with this, my love?" she asked, her eyes sparkling in the candlelight. "Would you like me to stop?"

I'd done anal play a few times, sure, but it wasn't something I was into. With Daphne, though, I was game for anything. "Keep. Going."

She smiled. "Good boy." Then she took me back into her mouth.

The pressure in my balls increased, and I was right there again. Heaven's Moon, did I have a praise kink along with a full-moon breeding drive? Yes. Yes, I did.

I was such a goner for this woman.

My knot was thickening at the base of my cock. She rubbed it with some of her salve, and my body went rigid with pleasure. Then the dam broke and I was coming. I pulled at my restraints, wanting desperately to fist my hands in her hair to regain some control.

There was that metal tip again. Oh fuck, were those ridges? Stars popped behind my eyelids, and I was coming even harder.

When I was finally done, I collapsed back on the mattress, chest heaving from the exertion. I wished I could mop the sweat from my forehead, but all I could do was lie there, completely spent. For the moment, that is. The moon's pull on my wolf was still strong.

Daphne cleaned us up with a warm washcloth, a wicked smile dancing on her lips.

"What *was* that?" I asked, sounding as if I'd gargled a handful of rocks.

"You liked my salve?" She was rummaging around in her nightstand drawer, that perfect bare ass inches away yet completely out of reach.

Frustrated, I yanked at the chains. "I'm not talking about your damn salve."

Her head snapped around. "You didn't like it?"

My wrists were chafed, so I stopped struggling for now. "I fucking loved your salve. That's not what I meant."

She grinned, looking like a cat with a bird in its mouth. "Ah, my surprise. I had a feeling you'd like it. Mind if I tell the girls later?"

I froze. "The girls? What girls?"

"Okay, *women.*"

"What are you talking about, Daphne?"

"We went to this little shop in Wickedville that—"

Wickedville? My veins heated to a million degrees. "Why the hell did you go there?"

Any other time, Daphne going into Wickedville wouldn't be that big a deal. I didn't exactly like it, but she had to go there weekly to visit the spell book, and I wasn't always around to go with her. Tonight, however, wasn't a normal night.

"Ruby, Sarah and one of Ruby's friends, Hattie, were with me. We went to this cute sex toy shop and we all bought a little something. Well, Sarah didn't. I think she's still a virgin. We tried to talk her into—"

"You went to a sex toy shop with my little sister?" I said, my voice going up an octave on the word *sister.* "Never mind. I don't want to know anything about my little sister's sex life, okay? As far as I'm concerned, she's never been kissed and plans to join the convent." I couldn't *believe* we were talking about this right now.

Daphne laughed. "Oh my god, Travis, you are such a tool."

"Yes, we've established that already," I growled. "Now get over here and sit on my face."

CHAPTER FIFTY

Daphne

Before the moon had reached its fullest point, Travis had had two orgasms and I'd had one. A pretty spectacular one, if I was being honest. Having my man go down on me would never get old. Though I ached to feel his hands on me too, I wasn't complaining.

I opened my pretty purple jar of salve again and scooped out a little more. Pleased with its performance so far, I knew the real test was yet to come.

Travis looked absolutely feral tied to the bed, dark hair curling at the ends from his sweat, his wolfish yellow eyes following my every move. He was holding his shit together, but just barely.

His wrists were worn raw from where the thick leather rubbed his skin, so I applied a little salve there first. He told me to forget about it. I told him to zip it. I didn't know if it would ease his pain, I had other tinctures for that, but I knew it wouldn't hurt.

A quick glance at the clock revealed it was time.

I'd be lying if I said I wasn't nervous. But I was also excited. Travis was my fated mate and I was his. I wanted to experience the entirety of what that meant. The exquisiteness *and* the pain.

He groaned as he watched me spread a little of the salve on myself.

"I should be doing that for you," he snapped. Even after two orgasms, he was still very much on edge.

"You will, my love. Just not tonight."

I reached for his thick cock and coated it as well, concentrating on the area at the base where I thought the knot would flare from. This part vibrated against my clit during sex the closer we got to the full moon, but it was just a guess. None of my research had been conclusive.

I glanced at my nightstand. Everything was still within reach.

Slanting my mouth over his, I kissed him deeply.

"Whatever happens, Travis, I want you to know how much I love you. And that I trust you with all my heart."

"Daphne," he said, voice thick with emotion. "You've become my entire world, but my wolf is very powerful. If I hurt you—"

I cut him off with another kiss. "This is simply the physical expression of our mating bond. It's powerful, yes, but so is the love we have for each other."

I straddled his hips, then reached back and grabbed him. As I slid down the length of him, I tried not to notice that the tips of his fingers had turned into claws.

My head fell back and I concentrated on relaxing and taking him all in. It was difficult, but I could do hard things. After all, I went to an island filled with monsters and fell in love with a werewolf. He felt bigger tonight, like he might just touch my backbone.

"Heaven's Moon, Daphne," he rasped. "You're so. Fucking. Tight."

I leaned forward and suckled on his earlobe. "Because you're so fucking huge."

His masculine chuckle rumbled through me.

The stretch was exquisite. Almost to the point of pain, but not quite. The fullness I felt was all him. He wouldn't need to do much more than this to get me screaming his name.

His lids were hooded with lust, gaze hungry as he stared at my breasts. I knew what he wanted, so I adjusted myself to give him better access. He pulled a nipple into his mouth and I moaned.

Fully seated on his cock now, my clit pressed against him, we began moving together in a perfectly synchronized rhythm. The sounds our bodies made were borderline criminal.

If that wasn't enough, the vibration started, amping up every glorious, toe-curling sensation. Much stronger than before the full moon. My vision tunneled, I saw stars behind my eyelids, and then we were both coming. I clung to him as wave after wave crashed over us.

I felt it then. Inside of me.

Smooth barbs along his entire shaft. When I tried to lift off of him just a little, they dug in, and sharp, agonizing pain shot everywhere, locking me in place.

"Daphne," he choked. "Are you okay?"

I must've cried out. I slid back down and the pain thankfully subsided. His wolf clearly rewarded good behavior, so I planned to stay obedient.

"I'm fine, my love."

Worry lines creased his beautiful face, and tears pooled in the corners of his eyes. "I knew I would hurt you," he hissed, not believing me.

The venom in his voice was directed at himself, and I needed to set him straight.

I cupped his cheeks and touched my forehead to his, looking him square in the eye. "I'm fine," I repeated. "I wouldn't lie to you, Travis. Yeah, it hurts when I try to move off of you, so I sure as hell am not doing that again. Guess you're stuck with me for a while."

His hard gaze searched my face, looking for signs that I wasn't telling him the truth. Then his expression softened with relief when he realized I was. He nipped my shoulder. "I can think of worse things."

I agreed. "Being intimately attached to the man I love isn't a half-bad way to spend the evening."

He snorted with laughter, which caused me to bounce slightly and I felt those barbs again.

"Ouch! No laughing."

"Then stop making me laugh."

I reached under his pillow, pulled out a key, and unlocked the cuffs around his wrists. I knew this had been overkill, but Travis hadn't wanted to take chances this first time, and I loved him for that.

"Thank the moon!" he groaned as his arms went around me. I could tell he was being careful not to move too much as he held me tight and stroked my back with his fingers. "For how long do you think we need to stay like this? Not that I'm complaining."

With my ear pressed to his chest, wrapped in his warm embrace, I could feel the beating of his heart as if it were my own. This right here was my definition of heaven. "Until your wolf thinks he's given his little swimmers enough time, I guess."

We'd talked about starting a family someday, but Travis wasn't convinced he'd be a good dad. He hadn't had the best role model. I knew he'd make a wonderful father, and if it was meant to be, he'd come around. But regardless of what the future held for us, he would always be enough for me.

He glanced over at my nightstand. "Good thing you brought snacks."

I hope you loved Darkaway Island and Travis and Daphne's story as much as I loved writing it! I spent many nights at my keyboard, giggling manically to myself, so I hope it brought you similar joy.

BONUS: Remember when Daphne wonders if she has a werewolf-chasing-her-through-the-dark-woods kink? Sign up for my VIP reader newsletter, and I'll send you that **spicy bonus epilogue**. The fun on Darkaway Island is just getting started, and I want you there!

https://laurielondonbooks.com/rwtw-nl/

Keep scrolling to get the recipe for Unholy Grounds Peanut Butter Cookies AND for some slightly unhinged book club discussion questions.

As an indie author, I'd be forever grateful if you left an online review at the retailer and/or wherever you talk about books. Reviews, even short ones, help other readers decide if they'd like my books too. Without a big publisher behind me, word-of-mouth really helps. Thank you!!!

Unholy Grounds Peanut Butter Cookies

Adapted from a recipe I've used for years from my friend
Kandis. This was her mom Joanne's recipe.

1 c. butter (Joanne used shortening)
1 c. granulated sugar
1 c. brown sugar
1 t. vanilla
2 beaten eggs
1 c. peanut butter (If you use crunchy, just forget what was
mentioned in the book.)
3 c. all-purpose flour
2 t. baking soda
Dash of salt

Cream butter and sugars together. Add vanilla, eggs and peanut
butter. Sift dry ingredients together then mix in. Roll into balls,
press them criss-cross with a fork to flatten. Bake 375 degrees
for 7-8 minutes. Enjoy!

You can also freeze the dough balls, then pop them out 3-4 at a
time. Just defrost for a few minutes so you can press with a fork
and bake in a toaster oven for warm, fresh cookies anytime. I
did this many times while writing this book!

SLIGHTLY UNHINGED BOOK
CLUB DISCUSSION QUESTIONS

1. Have you ever been a fish-out-of-water like Daphne? (Perhaps not as a human trapped on an island of monsters.) If so, can you describe what happened and how it made you feel?

2. Have you ever had a first impression of someone that turned out to be wrong? Or right?

3. Hopefully, you've never been in a situation where your boss wanted to kill you, but have you ever been asked (at home, school, work) to do something you felt was wrong? If so, how did you handle it?

4. If you owned Dark Tarts, what tart would you make and what would you name it?

5. If you owned a business on Darkaway Island, what is it and what is it called? Would it be in downtown Darkaway or in Wickedville?

6. If you could be any supernatural creature, what would you be and why?

7. If you could have any supernatural power, what would it be and why? Describe a scenario where you'd use your power and what would happen.

8. If you had to run for your life like Daphne, what are three things you'd take with you?
9. Which character on Darkaway Island did you identify with the most and why? Who did you hate the most and why? Who annoyed you the most and why?
10. Did the town you grew up in have any quirky traditions? If so, did you participate? (Nosy bitches need all the details.)

ALSO BY LAURIE LONDON

Sweetblood Vampire Romance Series

Bonded By Blood

Embraced By Blood

Tempted By Blood

Seduced By Blood

Enticed By Blood

Unraveled By Blood

Hidden By Blood

Enchanted By Blood

Iron Portal Series

Dark Assassin

Midnight Rogue

Hidden Warrior

Heartless Rebel

ABOUT THE AUTHOR

Laurie London is a bestselling author of paranormal romance, set primarily in the Pacific Northwest. Publisher's Weekly has called her work "sexy" and "sizzling."

Laurie lives in a small town outside of Seattle with her family.

After getting a business degree from Western Washington University, she got married to a guy from her dorm, then worked for a Fortune 500 company in IT. She had some children a while ago and then she got a horse. Now she's a part-time licensed optician and a full-time author.

Find Laurie online:
www.LaurieLondonBooks.com